THE LEGEND OF

ZERO

FLEA, AGENT OF CHAOS

WORDS BY SARA KING
IMAGES BY LANCE MACCARTY

ISBN: 1942929102
ISBN-13: 9781942929109

AUTHOR'S NOTE
(IMPORTANT)

BEFORE WE START: *THIS IS NOT BOOK 4 OF THE ZERO SERIES.* While it does have hints (*lots* of hints, if you're paying attention) as to what is coming in Book 4, this is a side-story about Flea from Book 2. It is best read either after Book 2 or Book 3 of the ZERO series—either one will work—but BEFORE book 4.

Second: Fans of the ZERO series, you are amazing. Thank you for your support for this project. If it works, you have my solemn word that I will publish *Outer Bounds 2: Fortune's Folly* the moment I've regained rights to the world. (It's been complete since February 2015!!)

A little history: About two years ago, I sold one of my favorite babies (The *Outer Bounds* universe) to a big corporation. It was dumb. It was stupid. And I was recently given the chance to buy it back—if I can collect the money in time.

So to that end, Lance and I spent the last 14 days utterly working our *asses* off to create something fun for fans of the *The Legend of ZERO* series who want to support their favorite author in her last-ditch effort to regain a world she created. We utterly exhausted ourselves for your pleasure. (Yeah, I totally meant to say that.)

Make no mistake: This is essentially a rush, slapdash charity case, because the clock is ticking, and people wanted to help, and neither Lance nor I wanted to take free money. We wanted to give you guys something fun in return for your outpouring of support (which totally blew us away). We know it's not our best. We fully expect there to be errors because we are both brain-dead jenfurglings at this point. We also think it's pretty damn good, considering our time constraints. (She says at 7:00am having not yet slept tonight.) And as they say, some people's crap is, well…

Also, because we're REALLY grateful for the support, and we know that $6.99 is a lot of money, Lance is offering up the best of these images in high-res for download as desktop wallpapers via a super-secret link in the back of this book.

To Recap: This is a special project for ZERO fans to help me get my rights to *Outer Bounds* back before they are lost to a big corporation forever. If you somehow picked up Flea's story and you have never read *The Legend of ZERO*, you're going to be totally out of your depth. READ THE OTHER BOOKS FIRST. Start with *Forging Zero* and go from there. Flea's story is crazy, convoluted, and utterly *different*. It's going to bend your mind around a Pepsi can and then slap it around a bit. But, if you're a fan, it's going to be a lot of fun.

Keeping in mind our deadline—14 days!!—a lot of the detail we normally put into our work is missing, especially regarding the aliens. Therefore, for both newcomers and people who want a refresher, we're going to give you a brief rundown on what is…

WHAT IS A BAGA?

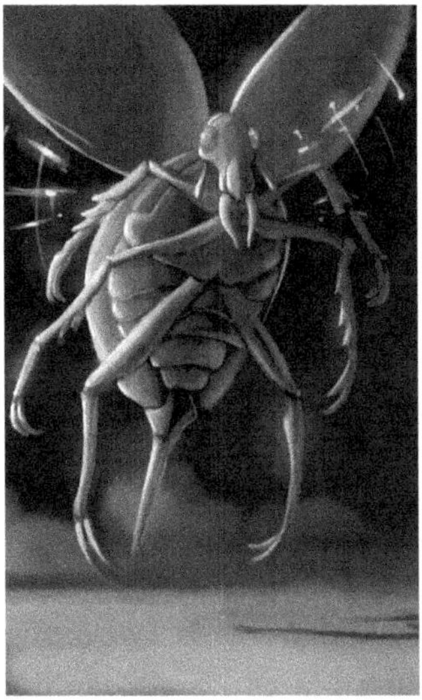

Flea, the champion of our story, is a Baga. They generally look like a cockroach with wings. Because that's what they are—a flying alien cockroach the size of your head that can essentially survive a nuclear detonation, that has a superiority complex, a numbers problem, an irrational desire to do stupid things, and can spit a substance from a tube in its ass that immediately *becomes* whatever it lands on. He looks like the critter on the cover.

WHAT IS AN OOREIKI?

Ooreiki are generally peace-loving, boneless, lumpy, hairless brown gorillas with tentacle arms. They weigh about 500 pounds and make up a good portion of the sheer numbers of Congress.

WHAT IS A JAHUL?

Jahul are, to put it simply, disgusting. They are six-legged walking stink-bombs that evolved as herd/prey animals. Their defense mechanism, like a skunk, is to spew toxic, indelible fluids over their skin on the off-chance that whatever chasing them won't want to take a bite out of them. Unfortunately, that means every time they get anxious, stressed, upset, or afraid, they shit themselves. All over their skin. They also have extreme empathic sensory organs that allow them to sense the moods of other species, making them great ambassadors. Or crime lords. Especially crime lords.

WHAT IS A TRITH?

Trith see the future. Imagine the 'grays' of UFO lore. There ye go. They like to try to meddle with certain people that give them headaches by changing the future. They are also the only species in the known universe that has not been absorbed by Congress. The three times Congress tried to induct them, it got its ass handed to it. Because they see the future.

WHAT IS A HEBBUT?

If you don't remember this one, I don't blame you. It only got a passing mention in the ZERO books. It's basically a space-ogre that likes big guns and death-matches. They also aren't very bright. The cannon-fodder of Congress.

WHAT IS A HUOUYT?

These are nasty. Sociopathic—they stick together as a species only for the common goals of wealth and power over other species—and they can use the genetic material of other creatures to transform into that creature. They are a boneless, semi-aquatic species with three legs and three fingers on each arm, entirely covered in a downy white cilia that wriggles. The best assassins are Huouyt, and they can produce poisons and drugs within their own bodies from many years of training. They're nasty. Don't screw with Huouyt. Jer'ait Ze'laa and the former Representative Rri'jan are Huouyt.

WHAT IS A JREET?

Big earthworms. Very, very big earthworms. With arms, scales, and predator teeth. The hardcore warriors of Congress (think Spartans), shunning both battlefield and medical technology because anyone who needs that crap is a weakling. They also have the ability to energize their scales and disappear from the visible (and heat) spectrums. Oh, and they carry a gross fang in their chests that they both mate with and kill people with. Unfortunately, due to the habits mentioned above, they're also considered an endangered species in Congress.

WHAT IS CONGRESS, KOLIINAAT, THE REGENCY, AND THE TRIBUNAL?

Congress is the conglomerate alien super-state pieced together over the last two and a half million years. Earth is just another newly-acquired planet in its never-ending march to expand its borders throughout the galaxy. It contains 3244 sentient species. Koliinaat is the artificial planet it created to house its hub of government, which is called the Regency. Each species in Congress has one Representative that is sent to the Regency to look after its interests. The Tribunal is an elected three-Representative panel that wields the most power of the Regency (think three presidents who have to vote before something can get done).

Hopefully that was enough to get you back into the ZERO universe groove. Good luck!

(And yes, we really did put this together in two weeks…)

TABLE OF CONTENTS

PART 1

AGENT OF CHAOS

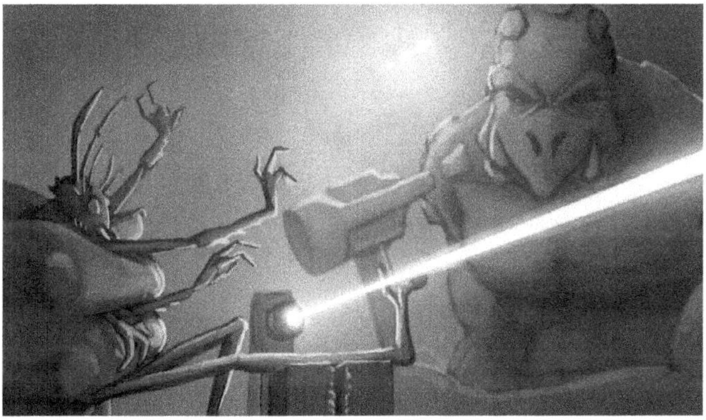

"Oh come *on*," Flea whimpered, as they pulled his front foot across the laser block. "I told you I'll get you your money."

"You had money," the big Hebbut holding him grunted. "Now you don't. Now we take your money with feet." It nodded to the other Hebbut holding the switch.

"Wait!" Flea cried, desperately wriggling under the gigantic oily paw holding him down on their boss's desk. He would have glued Moxi and his two Hebbut henchmen given even half a chance, but one of them had set a ruvmestin-gilded paperweight on his klett, shutting off any excretions from his abbas and locking them inside his body. Which would suck. The whole situation sucked. They obviously didn't understand he was a war hero, or that he had very important friends in Congress who would bail him out of a few credits in a heartbeat. "I am friends with Commander Zero and the Voran Jreet Representative! I can get you your money! I just need to contact them!"

The two Hebbut glanced at each other, then behind them at their putrid criminal overlord. Even for a Jahul, Moxi stank. He assaulted every pore of Flea's skin with his powerful stench, even from where he reclined on his rancid couch nine digs away.

The sticky green Jahul sighed, plucking another wriggling black bug—a bug that looked uncomfortably like Flea himself—from his plate. He popped it into his big toothless mouth almost thoughtfully. Then Moxi said, "You have friends that can repay twenty million credits?"

Flea wasn't exactly sure how much twenty million was, but if it was much more than the cost of a shuttle ride, he was pretty sure Daviin would squish him again. "Yes!" Flea cried quickly. "Important friends! They *owe* me. They would do *anything* for me!"

Moxi and his bulky Hebbut thugs looked at each other, the two goons still waiting for the signal to make the cut.

"I'm more interested in the Peacemaster," Moxi said. "I'm told you have spoken to Jer'ait Ze'laa in person?"

"We're *friends*!" Flea cried, desperate, now. He wouldn't exactly say that he and Jer'ait were best of buddies—the last time he'd seen him, Jer'ait had shot at Flea for eavesdropping on one of his powwows with high-ranking Representatives and Peacemaker leadership—but he might still be able to call in a favor. Maybe.

Well, no, probably not, but all the tugging Moxi's thick-handed thug was doing on his extended leg was bringing him close to dislocating the joint, and Flea was pretty much willing to say anything at this point to keep his leg. He *hated* growing back legs. They were so *clumsy* and made it so much harder to cling to the ceiling.

Besides, Daviin—the stingy greasebag—summarily halved Flea's experience points if Flea lost legs during his adventures, because the Jreet claimed that a *Human* monk couldn't lose legs, so it was cheating.

Stupid Jreet. Flea couldn't wait to be Dungeonmaster. He'd take off points every time the huge, scaly warrior told someone to 'dance on his tek' or threatened them with his tek, or especially if he actually skewered someone with his tek. Daviin liked to play dwarves, and dwarves didn't have huge poisonous spears sticking out of their chests, and therefore making people dance on them would be cheating.

Though telling Daviin he got half the experience for an adventure because he cheated would probably result in whatever edifice in which the Jreet was in when he received the news becoming reduced to a pile of rubble and the Peacemakers getting called in to pacify him before the prince could hurt himself. Because apparently, by becoming a Tribunal member, they were now more worried about Daviin hurting himself than they were about him bringing down hotel casinos by yanking out support posts. Which he'd done. Because Flea had gambled away the contents of their Joint Adventure Account on one of Daviin's rare vacations a few turns back instead of going to the café to get their lunch.

Still reclined on his greasy couch, Moxi plucked another wriggling creature off the platter, this time eying it thoughtfully. "The Peacemaster and I…" The slick-skinned Jahul twisted the disgusting black bug this way and that, allowing it to glisten in the light. "…need to have an understanding." He squished the bug between his thick forefingers, making its little black legs twitch and go still. "He's been confiscating my peysh and karwiq lately—haven't managed to get a single shipment through the Old Territory in six rotations. That needs to stop."

"I can stop him," Flea agreed quickly. "Just let me go. I can get close enough to get a message to him."

"I'll let you go after he agrees," Moxi said.

That made Flea a little more uncomfortable. "Okay, yeah…"

"First," Moxi said, "you're going to get him on the vidcom."

Flea felt his doom rapidly approaching. "I don't have his direct channel," he managed.

"Yes, but you know someone who does." Moxi cocked his head, waiting.

Flea grimaced. Trying to convince a Jreet to do something illegal was like trying to convince a Jahul to bathe. "Okay, but let *me* speak to him. If he thinks I'm in a drug den…Well. You know. Jreet and their honor…"

Moxi grunted, then gestured for the two Hebbut to release him. "Give him a comm. Stay out of the shot." Then, to Flea, he said, "And you obviously understand that I use encrypted waves, and if you call for help, I will have Roog, there, smack you with his hammer and we will end the transmission before it can be traced."

Roog—which happened to be the most common Hebbut name after Loog—grunted and hefted a crude sledgehammer with a head several times bigger than Flea's entire body, giving Flea a menacing leer.

Flea swallowed, because any way he sliced it, Daviin was going to take off points for the way their latest Dungeons & Dragons adventure had derailed. His new, long-distance dungeonmaster—a replacement for Rat, since Rat hated using comm—got ridiculously fussy about things like honor and glory and time limits. And he'd specifically said the most glory would be found by Flea completing his quest and acquiring the loot in seven tics, with added points for gore and humiliation of the enemy. That had been four days ago, back when Flea had been gambling in the casino overhead and Daviin had been monologuing at length about how to best vanquish the evil hobgoblin lair for the most glory.

Daviin gone on at length as to why the evil, wandering hobgoblin tribe of K'lath, who had stolen at least eight million in platinum coins from the innocent citizens of Akest in their rampaging and looting, had to be brought low, why their ancestors' ancestors had to be brought to task for their part in creating such honorless abominations, but Flea had been more interested in the riches. His task—which he had miserably failed—had been to infiltrate the hobgoblins' cave deep underground in order to gain his next level. Instead, he'd been captured and he was *late*.

Though Flea didn't quite understand why four days was more than seven tics, he was pretty sure Daviin was going to dock him for getting captured, too. Which was, unfortunately, the greatest humiliation according to a Jreet. Flea would have gotten more experience for this catastrophe if he'd let the Hebbut kill him.

"Could someone get this thing off my spitter?" Flea demanded. "My abbas are starting to hurt."

Moxi threw back his head and laughed until his big, stupid goons started laughing with him, then he stopped suddenly. "No."

Damn. "What, you want me to talk to a Representative of Congress with a *paperweight* attached to my *ass*?"

"Prut will ensure that the camera angle leaves that out...won't you, Prut?"

The other Hebbut grunted and pulled forward the image receiver, propping it in front of and beneath Flea so it looked like Flea was standing on the lens itself. The speed with which they set up the communication link and the fact that they had all the equipment on hand made Flea realize they must have planned for this from the beginning.

"You never wanted twenty billion credits," Flea accused.

"It's twenty *million*, and no," Moxi said. "I make three times that on a good peysh shipment."

Flea decided right then he was going to stick the Jahul right between the eyes. He'd probably even be able to salvage some of his dungeonmaster's good will if he stuck Moxi between his gooey eyes…

"Now before we start," Moxi said, "We need to go over what you're going to say. You've located what you think is a drug den, and you need to talk to Jer'ait immediately. Spend as little time talking to the Jreet as necessary."

Flea nodded. The Jahul definitely understood Jreet psychology. They—Vorans, especially—simply did not understand a bald-faced lie, especially coming from a friend. "Okay."

"Once you get Jer'ait Ze'laa on the phone, you will tell him that I am going to lock you in a cage and drop you to the bottom of the ocean unless he 'forgets' about a small section of space for a few rotations. Here are the coordinates. I want all Peacemakers within twelve standard skymarches to leave the area immediately, and not to return for two rotations."

Flea wasn't stupid. He knew a setup when he heard one. "You're gonna drop a bomb on those coordinates."

"Maybe," Moxi said, spreading his smooth, wide lips in a Jahul smile. "We'll see."

Flea sighed. This was the third time this *week* that he'd been assaulted by drug-runners with similar demands. "Fine. Get him on."

The connection was almost instantaneous. "Flea," the big red-and-cream Voran Jreet growled, showing massive fangs in displeasure once his image came on screen, "If you interrupt my rest from a basement because some drug lord has you at gunpoint one more time, I will send an entire armada to annihilate that planet, care of the Regency itself." The Voran cocked his diamond-shaped head at the screen, so that the glittering yellow eye was given a close-up. "And if you think I can't trace this call, Moxi, you are obviously not taking enough nutrients. I have the power of the Tribunal at the tips of my claws. As we speak there are twenty Peacemaker shuttles on their way to your location. Release my friend, or I will release *you*."

In the background, Moxi choked. The two Hebbut grunted. Roog pointed questioningly at his hammer.

"Get the cash!" Moxi cried. "Not the hammer, the *cash*! Go! Leave the little prick—you couldn't kill him with that anyway! Now *go*! They're *coming*!"

Flea watched smugly as the three of them raced to start stuffing credit chips from the safe into a sack. He waited until all of their backs were turned, then strained to shove the ruvmestin statue off of his klett. He stretched the tubing, flexing it to make sure there was no permanent damage or ruptured muscles, then flitted to the wall and skittered up the ceiling.

As the druglords were stuffing money into a sack, he crawled across the top of the room until he was in the shadows above them. Then, carefully positioning himself, he said, "Hey Moxi."

The Jahul looked up, blinking startledly.

Flea spat, catching him right between the eyes, creating a little lump of flesh there as his glue fused with the material of Moxi's disgusting face, becoming it.

Moxi started to scream, which startled the two Hebbut into dropping the sack and running. When Moxi bent to try and scoop up the sack, Flea spat at him again, this time catching him on one of his big black eyeballs. The gob of glue solidified into extra eyeball almost instantaneously, bulging awkwardly out of his eye socket.

"You *disgusting creature*!" Moxi screamed, "That was my *eye*!"

"You make twenty credits a rotation," Flea said. "Hire a surgeon." He spat again, this time catching the Jahul on one of the sticky fingers he had pulled up to protect his face. The glue immediately fused two of his fingers into one.

At that, the Jahul crimelord gave up trying to collect his money and simply ran.

Once they were out of the room, Flea skittered across the ceiling, ensured that they had departed, then dropped back down in front of the camera. "So how much experience was that one? Like *billions*, right?"

"You were captured," Daviin said ominously.

Flea winced. "Yes, but I spent *days* on this quest. I followed the evil hobgoblin's every move and documented his every illegal deed."

"And you were captured. That's *negative* experience."

Flea, who had been looking forward to his next level, felt his mandibles fall open. "You can't do that!"

"I'm the dungeonmaster."

"What about *half* of billions?" Flea whined. "They stuffed me in a *terrarium* with a *vaghi*..."

"My point exactly," Daviin said. "There was no honor in your surrender. You quivered like a melaa the whole time. I have it on tape."

"You're such a *hardass*!" Flea cried. "I could have *died*!"

"People die in their sleep."

Rat was definitely the better dungeonmaster, but Rat had been too busy of late. "Fine," Flea said, "You don't wanna give me XP? Then all the loot is mine. I won't even bother adding it to the Joint Adventure Fund."

The Jreet flinched. "Perhaps..." Daviin cleared his throat. "Perhaps I was overlooking something."

Flea grinned to himself. Daviin had gone on for *hours* about how big the haul was potentially going to be. *Certainly* he would be willing to negotiate...

"Perhaps..." Daviin frowned. "Wait. I saw you *humiliate* the hobgoblin chieftain."

Flea felt warm and fuzzy inside. He puffed out, waiting for his just rewards. "Indeed."

"That's...*thirteen* experience points!"

"*Woohoo!*" Flea screamed, scuttling back and forth across the table, pumping his fists in the air. "Will that get me to level four?"

"No."

Flea deflated. "Aww. Damn." Level four was taking *forever*.

"So how much did we make this time?" Daviin asked, leaning towards his receiver curiously.

Flea glanced over his back at the pile of credits. He tried to count, but his mind started to twist as soon as he got past seven. He'd been practicing with a tutor, though. Several turns ago, he had been completely unable to count past three. He was now very proud of the fact that he'd more than quadrupled his counting ability, especially since even the best Baga could only count to eight hundred billion. It was a *big* pile of chips, though, so Flea assumed it was safe to say it had reached the hallowed level of 'trillions.' "*Billions* of trillions," he said, elaborating a little. He turned back. "How did you know how much it was going to be?"

"Jer'ait's had you on camera since you landed," Daviin said. He paused, offering the receiver a chance to focus on the Huouyt unassumedly standing off to one side. Jer'ait nodded at Flea.

Suddenly, Flea knew exactly who had been putting together such elaborate and detailed quests. He had *thought* it had been a bit too creative for Daviin, but then had written it off as the Tribunal member probably just purchasing a campaign from Earth and adapting it—or having his aides adapt it for him.

"You greasy miga, Jer'ait." Flea rubbed his wing casings in irritation. "You've been *using* me." He supposed he should feel insulted, but not only had the adventures been great fun, but he'd gained *billions* of credits for the Joint Adventure Account. Really, what hurt the most was that Jer'ait had used Daviin to do it—and Daviin had gone along with it.

Flea decided he would stick him later.

"He says you've led him straight to the criminal underbelly of every planet you land on," Daviin said. "Places no Peacemaker has managed to get into, ever. Usually within a couple hours."

"It's efficient," the Peacemaster said.

This time, Flea *did* feel insulted. "It's almost like you think I'm a criminal or something."

"You assisted in the escape of *the* greatest criminal mastermind Congress has ever seen," Jer'ait said. "Consider this penance."

They *still* brought that up, millions of turns later. It wasn't fair. "Fine. But eventually, I'm gonna get tired of—" Flea hesitated, catching a flash of black out of the corner of his eye. He turned to look. He saw nothing at first and had started to turn back when the wall moved. Then he saw a gun detach from the dirty stone and a Human's eerie green eyes flash from where the clothes of its body and mask had taken on the same color and patterns of the wall. The gun swung to take aim at Flea.

"Burn me!" Flea cried, spitting at the barrel in reflex. His glue immediately plugged the opening, becoming the same metal as the gun itself. "Jer'ait, tell your guys we're on the same side!"

Totally unfazed, the Human dropped the ruined gun immediately and pulled two pistols from sheathes on its hips. Realizing he didn't have time to spit, Flea rolled off the table, putting the desk between him and the Peacemaker. He heard a wet *thwap* as plasma went arcing through the air where he had been. "Jer'ait, they're *shooting* at me!"

Up on the table, the tinny comm device cried in Jer'ait's voice, "They're not mine! Flea, the Peacemakers won't be there for another ten tics!"

Flea heard the liquid *burps* as two more plasma rounds landed on the side of the desk between him and the Human in black, instantly melting a hole through the thin metal. Flea was startled by the grade of plasma—it worked almost instantly, something that only the military—or the deepest, darkest underbelly of the criminal world—had access to. Compared to the ones who could afford guns that threw that kind of plasma, Moxi was pond scum.

Flea used the opening to spit at the Human's boot, then scuttled backwards and up the wall behind the desk. "Jer'ait," he said, "they're using Grade 1 plasma and invisibility shields. What kind of wet-eyed criminal leafmunch uses Grade 1 plasma and invisibility?!"

"It's the Shard," Jer'ait's voice cried, sounding close to panic. And for the top Va'gan assassin to sound close to panic, it had to be bad. "Flea, get out of there right now!"

"But my loot!" Flea cried. "I *earned* that loot!"

"Leave it! Flea, they'll *kill* you!"

But now Flea was intrigued. Plenty of people had tried to kill him, and all had failed. With Baga, someone essentially had to cut him to pieces, feed him to a Dhasha, and then set fire to its droppings in order to kill him. He heard grunting as the Human struggled with his boot, which would now be fused to the floor. "It's all right," he called over the table, "I glued him! I'll just go grab my money now." He started scuttling sideways along the wall.

"Flea, they're *assassins*!" Jer'ait snapped. "There will be more than one! Get *out*!" He sounded like he wanted to come straight through the comm system to start shooting up the place.

Flea snorted. "Why would *assassins* care about *me*?"

"I'll tell you later—get *out of there*!"

"I'm not leaving my loot!" Flea called back, sensing an opportunity. "It's the only thing I'm getting out of this campaign," he whined. "Daviin took all my experience!" He peeked from behind the leg of the table, toward the safe and its trillions of pieces of hobgoblin bullion.

"*You can have your experience*," Daviin roared, predictably. "Listen to the Huouyt!"

Score.

Unfortunately, at that same moment, Flea discovered that the assassin's grunting had been a ruse, and his opponent had been in a crouch, guns raised, waiting for a good shot. Flea lost purchase, falling to the floor even as twin holes burned through the stone wall only inches above him.

"Flea, you need to—" Jer'ait's voice was ended by a wet *burp* as plasma disintegrated the comm unit.

Because, while it was ridiculous to think that a group of assassins had targeted him, Flea generally trusted the intelligence gathered by the Congressional spymaster when he was screaming like a Bagan hivelord that a miga was coming, Flea stopped trying to fight the Human and ducked through one of the fresh holes in the wall.

There was another one of them crouched in the hallway on the other side. Flea knew, because when he dropped from the hole in the wall, he landed on something invisible underneath him. Immediately, he started spitting, and whatever it was beneath him started screaming and flailing.

Flea clambered up the wall and fled through an air duct. Immediately, assassins started shooting at the entrance to the ventilation system, hoping a pot-shot would catch him off guard.

Flea was chuckling to himself, just a few lengths down the tunnel, when he turned a corner and suddenly came across a blinking bomb.

They funneled me in here, Flea thought, as he stared at the bomb.

Knowing he only had seconds until it went off, Flea started spitting at the bomb, fusing it with the metal on Flea's side of the duct. By the time his abbas ran out of glue, he had made a rough wall around the explosive, aiming it in the other direction. Still, when the bomb went off, Roog might as well have hit him with the sledgehammer. Flea rolled backwards into an adjoining duct, knocking legs and wing-casings against the metal in an uncontrollable tumble. He found himself on his back, staring at the duct above him, dazed and battered, his busted translator having dislodged from between his wing casing and shattered on the floor beside his head. Oh *ashes*.

Flea got up. Ashes and *slime*. He tried to pick up his translator thinking he could fit it back together, but it was in too many pieces.

That was not good.

Most Congressional species did not recognize him as a sentient species. In fact, most of them immediately assumed he was some sort of pest. Which was *hugely* insulting. Flea wasn't a pest. They were all just big, dumb predators. Hebbut, especially. Out of all the Hebbut he'd ever been around, there was really only one that Flea didn't want to spit at immediately, and Frog had been raised by humans, after a platoon in the Congie Ground Force had found him abandoned in one of the rebel camps as a worm.

Or was it? Flea concentrated, thinking. Yeah, Flea was pretty sure Hebbut started out as worms. Right? Or was that the Ooreiki? He cocked his head, having to keep track of so many different species starting to irritate him. No, he was pretty sure the Ooreiki started as little worm-filled eggs. That meant the Hebbut started as those little pod thingies that clung to branches…

Plasma rounds melted the floor of the duct a few digs from him, and Flea panicked and skittered away.

"Burn me to ashes!" one guy—Ooreiki, maybe?—shouted from the room below, sounding stunned. "He's still alive up there!"

"Of course he is!" a Human shouted back. "It takes an *ekhta* to kill those things!"

Flea laughed at them and told them their mothers were born in the wrong hatch if they thought they could kill him with a *bomb*. Then he waited for his translator to translate it. And kept waiting.

"I think it's wounded!" one of them shouted. "Is it flapping its wings and chittering!"

"Probably a last stand," the Human shouted. "It's not going anywhere fast! Send in the robot!"

Disgusted, Flea remembered that his translator was broken, and that he was considered on sight by most species to be a pest. That was going to cause issues, especially since he had to *approach* one of those species in order to get a new translator. He could steal one, but unless he grew a mouth and started croaking in, say, Whuoian Jahul, he wasn't going to be able use it.

Thus, he took to wing and shot down the duct to its terminus, then blasted out the other side, into the casino proper.

"Torrak!" one of the Ueshi gamblers called, its wet head-frills trembling in terror as it looked up at Flea. "There's a torrak in here!"

Flea frowned. A torrak was a highly poisonous *blue* flying creature with faceted red eyes, pincers, and a ribbed carapace about the size of a Human head.

Flea was definitely not blue. Besides, torrak couldn't fly, and only used their wings—which unfolded into huge sails—as mating banners. And they were stupid. *Incredibly* brick-stupid. Flea wasn't stupid. He was actually rated as one of the top three most intelligent species in Congress, if points weren't taken off for 'incapability to understand basic mathematics' and 'depressingly pervasive rash behavior.'

But, Flea had decided, 'rash' to one species was just normal conduct to another. It just meant that Bagans weren't as delicate as the big, fleshy predators that they had to share the universe with, and could therefore be more courageous when faced with danger. And the numbers thing, well, who gave a miga's wingtip about numbers, anyway? There were hundreds of them. It was ridiculous to think that any one creature could memorize them all.

Then the 'torrak' cry was taken up by more gamblers, and several of its patrons screamed upon seeing him. A moment later, there was a minor—and highly amusing—stampede as those closest to Flea tried to climb over themselves and the gaming machines to get away. Because he couldn't help himself, Flea dove in and swatted at their faces with his legs before returning to the ceiling to get his bearings. He was just starting to figure out which room he had landed in—and thus which direction was the exit—when a squad of casino goons in full combat gear came rushing in with a clatter of weaponry.

Weaponry aimed at the ceiling.

"Kill it, kill it!"

"Hey, come on, guys," Flea said. "It was only a joke."

And then they started shooting at him.

Crying out in dismay, Flea skittered across the carpeted ceiling—he *really* liked this particular casino because he could dig his claws in and didn't have to use the tiny abbas-glands in his feet to hold himself to the walls. The digestive juices that were required to destroy the glue connecting him to the walls sometimes ran out without warning, especially if Flea hadn't eaten anything in a while, and then he was left with the decision to either beg for help or to simply tug off a few legs. He usually tugged off legs, because he, like all Baga, had this paranoia about being stuck in one spot while there were predators around.

...or housekeepers with shovels.

Flea hid behind the chandelier, then launched himself out one of the big windows when there was a lull in the shooting. He twisted at the last minute to hit the glass with his carapace, intending a spectacular glass-breaking explosion out into the daylight.

He hit the glass and bounced, then fell to the floor behind a vase, wriggling on his back.

"It's down, it's down!" one of the casino guards was yelling. "Kill it, kill it!" Then the rug around him was erupting in poofs of hot laser smoke as they tried to shoot past the vase, and Flea was squirming, trying to right himself.

C'mon, he thought, flinging his legs as wildly as he could, trying to find purchase. *C'mon, c'mon!*

His back hind leg found the vase and instinctively latched to it with abbas glue—which was then was ripped from his body as one of the big Hebbut guards ran up and kicked him, full in the side.

But at least he wasn't on his back anymore. Flea took the launch in stride, spreading his wings and adding speed, flying straight at the group of thugs shooting at him. They screamed and scattered. Like pussies.

That was a good word he'd learned from Joe: Pussies.

Then, because one of the pussies had robbed him of a leg that would take *days* to grow back, Flea stopped and stuck himself to one of the guard's backs, effectively riding him as he shrieked and flailed, then jumping off before one of his buddies could swat at him with the butt of his rifle. *That* pussy got a faceful of Baga, as Flea launched himself at that most sensitive area that most species left delightfully exposed, then tapdanced on his cheeks, eyes, nose, and huge drooping forehead.

The group of Hebbut thundered in all directions as they ran. From Flea. Who was the size of their fists. Flea found that delightful. Take *that*, Daviin...

Then the two assassins were rushing in the entryway to the room, guns out, looking for him.

Flea released his victim's face and flew at the window again, harder, this time.

He hit it and bounced again, though this time he managed to keep from falling to his back. He clung to the window-pane and started scampering in a random zig-zag over the glass, daring the furgs behind him to shoot at him.

The Ooreiki must have taken the bait, because the Human made a dismayed, "No, don't shoo—"

Then *splat*, the glass dissolved only a couple ninths from Flea's carapace. Gleefully, Flea ducked through. "So long, suckers!" he called back at them, ducking to the side to make sure he didn't give anyone a clear shot. He'd gone perhaps two rods before he got hit by the biggest skimmer he'd ever seen, getting slammed to the windshield like an errant egg.

"Ugh, a torrak!" the tiny, gangly male Hebbut started screaming from the passenger seat. "Yiig, kill it!"

The big female in the driver's seat gave a long-enduring groan, then twisted the wheel suddenly, trying to fling Flea off.

But Flea hadn't eaten in a while, and two of his feet were stuck again. "Guys!" he called. "Everything is under control! I'm just having some technical difficulties..."

The big female Hebbut reached behind her into the backseat and, after a moment of groping, came back with the ever-present Hebbut club.

Flea groaned inwardly. "Oh, come *on*..."

The female stood up, still driving the skimmer with a big paw, and leaned over the windshield to swat him off her vehicle with the club.

Flea lost two more feet in the tumble that followed, and unfortunately, all three of them had been on the same side. He sat there on the ground, feebly groping at the paving stones with his three good legs, trying to clumsily drag his body forward towards the safety of a sewer entrance, when the female Hebbut stopped her skimmer and got out, club hefted in one hand.

Realizing he'd never make the sewer in time, Flea took to the air again. This was the last time, he decided, he would ever land on a Hebbut planet. They were so…Poundy.

He got up into the crude mud-and-stick Hebbut rooftops and started flying towards the airport, ready to get on a shuttle and go somewhere people actually recognized Baga. Maybe Kaleu or Tholiba. Sure, they were pleasure planets, but staff at pleasure planets were trained to treat even the most odd-looking sentient species with respect, and Flea could definitely use a little respect right now.

In fact, with only three working legs, he was ready to go hide under a rock until the others grew back. That was…humiliating. Thus, it was with complete confidence that he was about to leave this ash-strewn planet forever when he landed on the desk of the Hebbut shuttle attendant and said, "I need a ticket somewhere nice."

Her big brown eyes widened and she reached under the desk.

Flea actually thought for a moment that she was finding him a tissue to plug the three holes in his sides, but then she pulled out a club.

Flea sighed. "I'm sentient! We were entered into Congress. Have a Representative and everything!"

She hit him with the club.

Flea felt the unnerving sensation of his entire body deflating, then the weird bounce of his head against the table as she did it again and again. The last conscious thing Flea remembered was getting scraped off the counter with a dust-pan, then being dumped onto the dusty road outside.

• • •

Flea regained consciousness to the sound of music. It was a famous Ooreiki symphony, created by a collection of *yeeri* masters that had come together to create the perfect masterpiece over billions and billions of turns ago, a work of art that had still never been duplicated or surpassed in all the time following. It was, without a doubt, one of the loveliest, most soul-wrenching things that most people had ever heard.

For Flea, it was a constant grinding hum against his wing-casings, driving into his very carapace, vibrating his entire body like a drum. "For the love of the sky, turn it *off*!" Flea cried, putting his feet to his head in agony.

"I thought that might wake you," a cultured Jahul's—if there really was such a thing—voice said. The music, however, ended.

Then Flea realized he must be dreaming, because he had a translator again and his legs were back.

Then he *really* realized he must be dreaming, because the room around him was draped with Geuji.

Flea rubbed his feet together nervously as he glanced at the glistening black walls around him. "Uh. Hello."

"Do you realize," the enormous ebony slime-mold said, "that I have saved your life eight times in the last forty days?"

"Uh," Flea said. "Is that a lot?"

"Yes," the Geuji said. "But to be fair, it's not entirely your fault. You have a Trith by the name of Roq trying to kill you."

Flea immediately sucked in a breath. The Trith saw the future. The Trith knew exactly *how* to kill *anyone*, *anywhere*, *anytime*. Nobody even *saw* Trith because they knew exactly where they needed to be, when, to avoid the cameras. They were the only species in all of Congress—aside from maybe the Geuji draped across the room with him—that had completely avoided Congressional assimilation. Because they saw the future.

"Uh," Flea said. "Why would a Trith be trying to kill me?" He had had one *talk* to him, earlier, but that had been about Joe.

"It's about Joe," Forgotten said. "And it's about something that happens hundreds of turns from now, so it's not really relevant."

Flea stared. "They're gonna kill me because of something that happens millions of turns from now?"

"All you need to know is that your friend Joe Dobbs has the potential to change everything, and the Trith don't like change. They like to see a static picture, and because of what he is, he muddies the waters, gives them headaches. Kind of like I do."

Flea squinted up at the Geuji. "So…you're saying I'm dead meat?"

"No," Forgotten said. "I despise the Trith and their status-quo, so I made you a gift." He offered it to Flea via an unobtrusive robotic arm that seemed to come out of the floor itself...which immediately made Flea wonder if the whole room as a robot-arm-trap. He jumped to the ceiling, to avoid that possibility, and to get a better look at the object he was being offered.

"What is it?" Flea asked, frowning down at the object's tiny blue, oblong shape. It looked like a miniature version of what the Ooreiki were so excited about off of Earth, something he'd seen Joe drinking on multiple occasions. There was a blinking light at one end, right where the liquid usually came out.

"It's choices," Forgotten said. "Your three most likely choices in whatever scenario you happen to be in, to be specific, relayed to you with instantaneous comprehension and full recall, the moment you push the button." Forgotten paused. "I considered trying to hard-wire in your next two billion different choices and your best routes to freedom, but I was pretty sure that was too confusing, even for a Baga." The glistening black mold-body rolled with amusement. "Besides, I would have had to drag you back in here a few weeks from now, to do it all again. This is less invasive, but more permanent. Just don't lose it."

Flea flopped down in front of the robot arm and gingerly took the object in his front claws. It dangled from a string, a wire that Flea immediately recognized as having one of the strongest tensile-strengths in existence.

"I don't suggest you wear it around your neck," Forgotten said. "For obvious reasons."

"You gave me a *Pepsi* charm," Flea said, flabbergasted and a little amused. He had seen similar ones on Ooreiki necks and wrists, their beverage of choice since the discovery of Humans. "That gives me three wishes."

"No," Forgotten said, "I gave you a Pepsi charm that allows you to see your three most relevant choices into the future, the things you are most likely to do in any given situation, and gives you a detailed account of the three outcomes that would come of those choices."

Flea carefully suppressed his sudden, overwhelming excitement, realizing he could use it to gamble. He casually flipped the miniscule can over, to make a show of examining it, all the while thinking of the *hundreds* of credits he could make cheating the system.

"Do not use it to gamble."

Flea grimaced and lowered it from his fake inspection. "Oh come on."

"Further, because you have a weakness when it comes to numbers, and because numbers can often make the difference between keeping a respectable sum in your savings account and having nameless thugs shaking you down for money every three days, the device has a built-in method for reducing numbers to quantifiable sums you can better understand."

That perked him up. "Really?"

"Yes. The button on *top* of the can is the three-choices button. The button on the *bottom* of the can will immediately relate to you your most pressing numbers scenario using terms you can understand. For instance, my body weighs roughly eight hundred and eleven lobes, using standard measurements. Press the bottom button."

Flea did.

Immediately, his translator said, *"The Geuji's body is roughly the weight of a medium-sized Dhasha prince."*

Flea giggled with glee. It made so much *sense*!

"Or try this one. Flea's bank account was resting at negative four hundred eleven thousand, two hundred and thirteen credits before his credit agency realized he was frivolously spending money on blowing up spaceships and locked it."

Flea narrowed his eyes, but pressed the bottom button.

"Flea owes the price of a medium passenger shuttle to the bank."

Immediately, Flea's carapace began to crawl with the sensation of slicer lice. He'd had *no idea*...

"Want to try another?" Forgotten asked.

"Very funny," Flea muttered. "But no. How does the first one work, again?"

"Press the top button and find out."

Flea did.

Immediately, three choices slammed into the forefront of his mind, complete with the repercussions that would come with them, leaving Flea to pick amongst…

Option 1) Spit at Forgotten: **page 29**

Option 2) Toss the device aside and leave the room, content to try your luck without a smartass Geuji throwing you a bone: **page 32**

Option 3) Thank Forgotten for his help, for the Geuji is wise and benevolent, and this is exactly what you need to survive the flock of miga you've found yourself in: **page 35**

OPTION 1

FLEA SPITS, BECAUSE SPITTING IS FUN

Just to see what would happen—and because he'd always fantasized about taking the all-knowing Geuji down a peg or two—Flea twisted his klett and spat at Forgotten. The translucent blue-white glue hit the Geuji somewhere near his central core. Flea chuckled in delight as it dripped down the black flesh, then solidified as part the wall of slime.

Then the robotic hand Flea was standing on crunched down, deflating him again as it crushed his mass into an area about a quarter of its original size.

"I was pretty sure that it went without saying that, because the transformation of glue to flesh is very painful, you were not to spit on me when I take you into my inner sanctum," Forgotten said from the speaker across the room. He tightened the robotic fist with hydraulic force and Flea felt his legs twitch in reflex, his outsides effectively rubbing against his insides, "but it seems you make 'spitting' an option much more than you should." The robot hand tightened again. "*Much* more than you should."

"Sorry," Flea sputtered, which his translator flubbed due to the fact that the robot's hands were holding his wing casings down.

Forgotten seemed to understand anyway. "In any given scenario, there is only a point zero zero zero one percent chance that you will actually need to spit on someone to survive the coming days."

Weakly, Flea pressed his button.

"*Spitting is bad,*" the device told him.

"While you are thinking on this, I will simply upload the rest of your instructions into the chip I implanted in your brain and spare you the effort of further thinking."

Then Forgotten dropped Flea to the floor and, crumpled on the smooth stone of the Geuji's cold, clammy room, Flea felt his world begin to fade into darkness.

BACK TO YOUR OPTIONS: **page 28**

or

CONTINUE TO NEXT SCENE: **page 41**

OPTION 2

FLEA REJECTS THE GIFT...BECAUSE.

Flea looked down at the device, torn. He wanted to take it, he really did. And yet, if he took it, he would never know if the 'futures' he was seeing were real, or just some vision that the Geuji wanted him to have, yanking him around like strings on a puppet. Flea knew, by trusting the Geuji's device, he would just be opening himself up to be Forgotten's pawn.

Though it burned to refuse, Flea said, "You haven't told me a price, and I don't want to spend the rest of my life trying to figure out what it is, all the while dancing to your tune."

"My price, in this case, is to protect Joe Dobbs and see the Trith named Roq run away with his metaphorical tail clamped between his legs as he concedes defeat."

"Don't want it," Flea said. "Don't need it. You'd probably just tell me lies through it, anyway."

"I *could*, but I won't."

Flea *really* wanted to believe him. Really. But this was the same being who had utterly annihilated an entire Jreet clan and almost a quarter of the Dhasha just by tugging on those strings. "Sorry, man. I wish, but you lie by telling the truth." He turned to go.

"This course of action is highly unadvisable," Forgotten warned.

"I'll take my chances." Flea tossed the tiny charm into the great black mass that was the Geuji's body, making the slime-mold twitch in a tiny circular spasm where it hit. "Which way's out?"

"That way." Forgotten gestured with his robot arm to the door on the left, which opened for him obligingly. Flea took to the air and flitted from the room.

No sooner had he gone twenty rods into the second hallway did the door slam shut behind him and suddenly Flea felt a total loss of pressure.

Instead of the normal *de*flating, Flea was just realizing that he was *ex*-flating at approximately the same moment he heard a *pop* somewhere ahead of him and he went shooting out Forgotten's airlock and into the endless starry expanse beyond. His feet and antennae froze first, becoming totally numb and unusable in under a second. Then his wings, which he had yanked under his wing-covers in reflex, stopped responding to his mental commands. Then he realized his vision was changing, getting blurry, lined with shards of glass.

Then Flea's body couldn't handle the pressure anymore and he exploded, jetting internal gasses into space.

Flea's last conscious thought as he drifted through the abyss was that it probably would have been a lot more fun—and more longevitous—to accept Forgotten's offer…

END IT HERE

or

RETURN TO YOUR CHOICES: **page 28**

OPTION 3

FLEA ACCEPTS, FOR THE GEUJI IS WISE AND BENEVOLENT...

"Okay, I'll play your game," Flea said, putting the little charm around his neck.

"You shouldn't put it around your neck," Forgotten said.

Flea left it around his neck. "So. Geuji. What's my mission?"

"Excuse me?"

"My *mission*," Flea said. "You're the Master of Chaos—Daviin says that's what they've been calling you in the Regency. Obviously, you want me as your agent. Your agent of *chaos*." He shuddered a little with the glee of it.

"Noooo, I want to keep you alive," Forgotten said. "I *had* been hoping to pull an agent out of tonight's catastrophe in the casino, but I was forced to take you, instead, because I find intense pleasure in disrupting the plans of Trith, and in order to do that, I needed to keep you alive. I'll have to find another agent elsewhere. Even with my device, you only have a point-zero-zero-zero-zero-zero-six percent chance of actually getting anything done, considering your propensity for random tangents and penchant for life-threatening acts of impulsiveness."

Flea cocked his head, then hit the little button on the bottom of his charm.

"You have a miniscule chance of actually being useful due to your tendency to make misjudgments," the charm told him cheerfully. *"Approximately the same chance of surviving a space-walk unprotected."*

Flea frowned. Why did that seem so familiar for some reason...?

"You said this was about Joe," Flea said. "I wanna help."

"Actually," Forgotten said, "it's a grudge-match I'm currently having with a particularly annoying clan of Trith that want to kill off you and all of your friends in their attempt to quell the ripples of change you're spreading throughout the fabric of this dimension's reality, but sure, if you want to condense it into something more succinct, it's about Joe and my current attempt to keep him alive."

"Where do I fit in?" Flea demanded.

"You stay alive."

Flea rubbed his wing-covers in irritation. "There's no way I'm not going to use *this*," he held up the Pepsi charm, "to save Joe's butt. Tell me how or I'll figure out how."

Forgotten sighed, deeply. "Fine. But I will be sending you in *under cover* and for no reason whatsoever are you to drop Daviin, Jer'ait, Joe, or my names to random strangers, you understand? You keep this *under* the radar, because you will be infiltrating the assassins' very home. You will be creeping through their *lair*."

Flea loved the sound of that. Finally, for once, he could kick ass without languishing in the others' shadows. And they cast *big* shadows. "I can do that. What do you want me to do?"

"Spy on them."

Flea felt a little thrill envelope his wing-muscles, making them vibrate. "No problem. Then what?"

"Spy on them some more. It might take as many as twelve *hours* of spying on them."

Flea frowned and pressed his button. "*It might take as long as you sleep in one night to discover the information you seek.*"

That was less appealing. Flea frowned. "That's a long time. Can't I just stick them?"

"And this, right here, is why you have a miniscule chance of succeeding at this mission, and why I should find a truly gifted operative to infiltrate this planet."

"You're trying to manipulate me," Flea said, irritated.

"No, I am stating a fact. If I were trying to manipulate you, I would tell you that the planetoid the Trith and his assassins are using as their home base is a ruvmestin planet, and one can routinely find ruvmestin nuggets out in the dry desert creekbeds, if you can dodge the dust storms and heat spikes."

Ruvmestin...Flea immediately felt a pang of desire. Nuggets of ruvmestin could buy shuttles, and he needed to pay off a shuttle in order to make the bankers stop leaving nasty messages on his phone. He had *wondered* what that had all been about.

But on a ruvmestin planetoid, Flea could theoretically collect enough nuggets to go back to the Core and drop them in a pile at the Bajnan bankers' desks, right between their hundreds and hundreds of legs. He wondered what that would sound like, dropping millions and millions of nuggets onto expensive carved carbon. It would probably tinkle delightfully...

"Once again, you illustrate with stunning efficiency why I am more likely to succeed with a different agent."

Quickly, Flea made himself concentrate. "All right, so I go in real quiet, pretend I'm just some washed-out Congie Baga down on his luck."

"That shouldn't be difficult."

Flea scowled. "Then what?"

"Then you are to figure out how the Trith plan to lure Joe away from his training activities for the assassination to take place."

"Figure out their plan. Got it."

"Oh," Forgotten said, "and try to keep yourself from getting sent to work in the mines. They stay down there in rotation-long shifts, and I suspect whatever they're planning on this planet will be finished within the next sixty-seven days, giving you nine days to get your bearings, if you left now and account for travel time.

Squinting at Forgotten, Flea pressed his button.

"You will have as many days to unravel the plot as you have eyes, feet, and spitters. How long you spend in travel is inconsequential, since you will be unconscious for it."

Flea frowned. "Wait, who said I'd be unconscious?"

"Now remember," Forgotten said. "You don't know me, you don't know Joe, you don't know Daviin, and you *certainly* don't know Jer'ait. You will not contact any of them from the planet, because all outgoing lines are tapped and monitored by the company that holds the planetoid's mining contract. You will simply figure out how they plan to assassinate your friend Joe, and you will *not* warn him once you figure it out."

The little round nozzles along the outsides of the room started to hiss. Flea looked at them distractedly, then turned back to Forgotten and said, "Right, but once I figure it out, how do I contact you?"

Forgotten laughed. "That won't be necessary."

"Wait," Flea cried, indignantly lifting his front arms in the air. "You can't send an *agent* into the field without a way to contact you!"

"You're not my agent yet," Forgotten said. "Give it a successful mission or two. Then we'll see."

Then the odd scent of spices overwhelmed him from those hissing tubes in the wall, and Flea sank to the robot's palm as darkness swallowed him.

CONTINUE FROM HERE: **page 41**

or

GO BACK TO CHOICES: **page 28**

PART 2

FLEA S FIRST MISSION

(Or, if you aren't ready, RETURN TO PART 1 CHOICES: *page 28, or if you came here by mistake,* RETURN TO PART 3 THE TRITH: *page 205 or* RETURN TO PART 4 PANDEMONIUM: *page 243)*

Flea woke in a box. He was groggy, sluggish, and he had absolutely no idea how he had gotten there. Another confrontation with a druglord? Usually Daviin pulled him out of those. He remembered something about Daviin yelling through a commset—yeah, pretty sure he'd been helping Flea con Moxi—and then BOOM, nothing. There was a blinking light somewhere under his chin, but when Flea ducked his head to look, he saw nothing but empty floor.

The blinking light, he realized, was coming from under his *chin*.

It's a bomb! Flea thought. One of the best ways to kill a Baga—and the hardest, because miga routinely snipped Bagan heads off with their beaks, so Baga had evolutionarily developed a resistance to head-snipping—was to pop off their heads. So it wasn't a stretch that one of his many wronged druglord acquaintances would drop a bomb around his neck and then seal him in a box to keep the explosion from creating a mess in their living room.

Scrambling, Flea reached for the thing dangling from his neck, then froze when he saw the tiny charm and its two buttons. The blue, red, and white logo for an Earth drink that was wildly popular with the Ooreiki was flashing, causing the blinking light. He got this creepy-cold sensation when he looked at it, like hundreds of tiny mites crawling across his carapace. He could *almost* remember where he got it…*almost*.

He did, however, remember one very important fact: It granted three wishes.

Like one of Joe's genie-in-the-lamp stories from Earth, Flea could now have anything he wanted.

The very first thing he was going to do, once he got out of this box, was to find himself a casino.

…or was that how he'd gotten in the box in the first place? Flea frowned, trying to remember the events leading up to him being packaged like so much trash. He remembered being *in* a casino, and one of the Hebbut thugs kicking him, then the delightful feeling of stamping on their greasy faces.

But there were *two* buttons. Flea was sure—he counted. One for three wishes, one for…

Something was straining at the back of his mind, a lot like when he was trying to figure out the difference between seven and eight. His tutor had spent *rotations* trying to show him. *Seven* was how many legs he had, plus his head. *Eight* was…Flea's mind instantly went blank. It was *more* than seven, but when his tutor told him to count his *eyes* and not his *head*, that meant it was less than his head.

…the device has a built-in method for reducing numbers to quantifiable sums you can better understand.

Flea blinked. *Where* had he heard that before? He pushed the bottom of the tiny soda can.

"If you suddenly grew another head out of your ass, you would have two heads and six legs, which together makes eight appendages, which happens to be the same number of points on Commander Zero's star of rank. Imagine it as if you got squished on top of a huge Prime Commander's rank insignia, and that each point on Commander Zero's star becomes a leg or a head, keeping in mind you now have a head out of your ass."

The image was so vivid that Flea had to blink. So *that's* what eight meant…

He was about to push the button again, to get the device to explain 'nine', when he heard a muffled shout of, "Yeah, I think it was coming from here!"

A moment later, Flea stumbled as something picked up his box, then roughly shook it.

"Hey!" Flea cried, after he had righted himself again. "I'm in here!"

"Yep, definitely a stowaway." The alien—it sounded like an Ooreiki—set him down again heavily. Then, a few moments later, they were prying open the top of the box and Flea was blinking up at the sudden, searing light of a spaceship's cargo bay.

"Oh my sweet Hagra," a Jahul blurted, from the startled ring of crew surrounding him. "Please tell me that's not a Baga." He was backing away as if he was seeing something vile. "I *hate* Baga. Little worshippers of chaos, that's what they are."

"At least we don't stink like the Jahul," Flea muttered, already catching a whiff of the disgusting creature. But, because he didn't disagree, he didn't spit on him for it. Instead, he started crawling up the side of his box.

"Not so fast," the Ooreiki who had spoken earlier said, grabbing him with a stinging tentacle around his carapace and lifting him bodily up into the air. Directly into his face, the Ooreiki sneered, "You're not on the manifest, buddy. You're gonna have to pay for your ride."

Flea spat at him. The glob landed on the Ooreiki's wrinkly, boneless mouth, and the creature screamed, even as his mouth was now sealed together in the middle, delightfully making *two* mouths. The rest of the crew got out of the way as Flea took to the air and landed on the ceiling, to scowl down at his adversaries from above.

"Ashes!" one of the Ooreiki cried, holding the box Flea had come in between them like some sort of shield. "How do we get it off our ship?"

"'It' has no memory of getting *on* this ship," Flea said. "Where are we?"

"We're headed for Glaxxion," the Jahul said. It had started glistening with its own excrement—some sort of defensive technique—and the stench had increased tenfold. "We can drop you off there. Please just stay—"

It, like all Jahul, was a pussy. Flea spat at him a little, enjoying the way the six-legged creature danced away and shat himself even more, reveling in his superiority for a moment before the Ooreiki holding the crate said, "Burn this," and threw the box at him.

Normally, Flea would have been able to dodge it easily, but he was too busy harassing the Jahul. He hated Jahul. They could generally tell what he was thinking, and he hated that. He wanted it to be a *surprise*...

Thus, the box took him full in the side, knocking him from the ceiling and tumbling him down to the ground.

Immediately, the Ooreiki stomped on Flea's spitter. "I can see why someone shoved it in a box. What do we do with it? Is it like a trained torrak or something? Someone's pet? It could belong to one of the passengers..."

"The Baga are a recognized and protected sentient species," Flea snapped.

"Oh yeah?" the big brown Ooreiki demanded. "What Act was that under?"

Flea winced. He'd never been able to remember the number because it was so big. "Uh."

"Yeah, that's what we thought," the Ooreiki snorted.

Out of desperation, Flea pushed the bottom button on his charm. Immediately, it said, *"The Baga were recognized as a sentient species via Sentience Recognition Act Two*

Thousand and Thirteen. That was 1,906,732 Turns after the formation of Congress, the 204th Turn of the 718th age of the Huouyt."

"Yeah, that!" Flea cried, exhilarated.

"*In other words, they were recognized as sentient much later in Congressional history than most other sentient species because they are numerically impaired to the point of retardation and essentially look and breed like vermin.*"

Flea frowned.

"Huh." The Ooreiki did not lift his foot from Flea's spitter, which was really starting to hurt. "Well, you still didn't pay the fee."

"And you owe Rhogl for surgery," one of the Ooreiki noted, gesturing to the Ooreiki that was picking up a crate with obvious rage written across his wrinkly face. Which was now bisected with an added lump of flesh where Flea's spit had fused together the lips. Which was delightful.

"He messed with me," Flea said. "He got what he deserved."

"Maybe we're not being clear," the Ooreiki pinning him to the floor said. "You're not on the manifest."

Another Ooreiki loomed forward and said, "That means no one knows you're here."

"And no one will miss you," the Jahul finished.

Flea glanced up at the four goons, then sighed and decided to use one of his three wishes.

Instantly, it was like three pathways opened up in his brain, all three laid out in gruesome detail…

Option 1) Find a way to spit on them: **page 49**
Option 2) Use the names of friends as leverage: **page 54**
Option 3) Apologize for being a shit and ask if there's a way you can work off your debt: **page 59**

OR RETURN TO PART 1
CHOICES: **page 28**

OPTION 1

SPIT ON THEM, BECAUSE SPITTING IS FUN...

"Yeah, sorry about that," Flea lied. "It's an instinctive reflex when I'm afraid. You guys are all so big...I just couldn't help myself."

"Don't trust him," the Jahul said. "I was in a regiment with a Baga. They're smart and they're *nuts*."

"And nobody trusts us because we're so ugly," Flea whined.

Immediately, the big Ooreiki faces softened... because they, like Jahul, were pussies. "It's all right, little bud," the one stepping on him said. He pulled his foot away and squatted beside him. "Can't really imagine what it must be like to be so small and wandering around Congress."

"It sucks," Flea said truthfully, carefully maneuvering himself out of reach. "Everyone thinks I'm some sort of pest."

"Bad first impressions, probably," the laughably soft-hearted Ooreiki said. "I'm Prakk. This is Wryali, this is Rhogl, and this is—"

Flea, tired of the introductions, spat on the speaker first, because he had stepped on him and his klett still hurt. He aimed at the place where his booted foot touched the floor, fusing them together.

"I *told* you guys the Baga are crazy!" the Jahul cried. He turned and started to run.

Flea spat at him next, because he talked too much and he had called him nuts. The Jahul screamed and flailed as Flea went about fusing each of his gangly six feet to the floor.

Then, because it was amusing, Flea took to the air and landed on the disabled Jahul's back, riding him as he took aim at the next Ooreiki.

The next Ooreiki had a gun, and was aiming back.

Flea skittered around to the Jahul's face, putting its head between him and the Ooreiki. Putting the tip of his spitter against the Jahul's eye, he told his mount not to move, at which point, the Jahul went delightfully still.

“I see we are at an impasse,” Flea said. “I want off this ship.”

“Allow me to escort you to the airlock and I can ensure that happens,” the Ooreiki with the gun—Prakk?—said. His face had lost all amusement.

“You first,” Flea said. “*After* you plug in new coordinates. I want to go to the Core. I have friends there.”

Prakk snorted. “*You*? Friends?”

That wasn’t nice. Flea spat on the gun, clogging it. Then he spat on the Ooreiki’s hand, fusing it to the gun. Good luck with the surgery on *that*...He was just about to take to the wing again, to start scouting out the ship he was on, when several more crewmembers burst into the room with them dressed in full riot gear.

“Everyone stop!” Flea shouted, still clinging to the Jahul’s face. “You see this Jahul?” Jahul were most comfortable as captains on ships, feeling out the emotions of their crew, putting out fires before they could start, mediating, negotiating with buyers, acting as ambassadors in new places, and, in some cases, using their sensitive *sivvet* to get them into places where they shouldn’t. In short, they were perfect captains. “Your captain is *dead* if you don’t take me to the Core, right now.”

The Ooreiki looked at each other with bafflement. It didn’t take a genius to see that the whimpering Jahul that was even then sliming itself under Flea’s feet, giving him a perma-stink that would take *weeks* to wash off, was not their captain.

"That's the janitor."

Flea was appalled. "You hired a *Jahul* as a *janitor*?" He was trying not to touch as much of the rank alien and its putrid slime as possible. "Isn't that an oxymoron?"

"Not sure," the Ooreiki in crisis gear said. Then, to something over his head, he said, "You got him?"

Flea frowned and turned…

Just in time to see Two-Mouth knock him off the Jahul's face with a balled tentacle. A moment later, he was being stomped on by a dozen heavy thugs. Somewhere in the thrashing that followed, the charm's bottom button got pressed, and it helpfully said, "*You are being trampled by the equivalent of six medium-sized melaa.*"

He was barely conscious, his whole body making involuntary muscle twitches, when they peeled him off the floor and carried his deflated body to the airlock.

"Sayonara, burnbag," the Ooreiki who still had a useless gun fused to his hand said. He tossed Flea inside, then, a moment later, Flea heard a whooshing *pop* and he was tumbling out into space.

As his eyes were freezing over, blotting out his vision in tiny crystalline lines, Flea heard a vaguely familiar voice say, *But it seems you make 'spitting' an option much more than you should…*

Even as his brain died, Flea had a sudden surge of memory. *Forgotten!* He thought. *Forgotten gave me the—*

The rest was lost to the Void.

END IT HERE

or

GO BACK TO YOUR CHOICES: **page 47**

OPTION 2

USE THE NAMES OF YOUR POWERFUL FRIENDS TO MAKE THEM SHUDDER IN FEAR AND GIVE YOU ANYTHING YOU WANT

"My best friend is the Peacemaster," Flea said, because that was the only way he saw himself getting out of this situation without kowtowing like a pussy. "And I am blood-brothers with the Jreet Representative."

The Ooreiki glanced at each other. "You are?" the one pinning him down asked. "What's his name?"

Flea flinched as a memory struck him, seemingly out of nowhere…

But I will be sending you in under cover and for no reason whatsoever are you to drop Daviin, Jer'ait, Joe, or my names to random strangers, you understand?

It had been a Jahul's voice, but for some reason, Flea was pretty sure it hadn't been a Jahul. Some sort of voice-altering software, then?

"Uhhh," Flea said, hesitating. He was pretty sure it was someone *important* who had said that, arguably even more important and dangerous than Daviin, which was hard.

Flea wracked his brain trying to figure out who was more important than Daviin. There were only three Tribunal members—Daviin, Aliphei, and Mekkval—and *they* were the most important people in the universe. There was also the Peacemaster, who technically answered to them but who could also arrest them for crimes, but Jer'ait wouldn't have bothered using voice-altering software. There was *Joe*, who somebody said was going to destroy Congress, but Joe probably would have been here *with* him if he was going to send him on a mission.

Flea had this nagging sensation there was someone he was missing, something really *obvious*, but it slid through his mind's grasp like wisps of smoke.

On the plus side, this meant he was on an undercover op. Which was *cool*! Now if only he could remember what he was supposed to do…

"Yeah, I didn't think so," the Ooreiki pinning him said.

The Jahul said, "What are you, a runaway Congie?" He pointed to Flea's carapace, which had been painted black for the military, which Flea had never bothered to get refinished because it was easier to hide in the shadows and spy on druglords when one was all black.

"Uhhh," Flea said. He *wanted* to blurt out that he was best friends with three of the most powerful creatures in Congress, but that unknown *fourth* mysteriously made him nervous. The kind of nervous he felt when he was sitting on a rock, looking up at the impending doom of a starliner's landing gear about to crush him.

"He's a runaway," the Ooreiki holding him sighed. "Okay, what do we do with the little asher?"

"There's a Congressional recruitment station on Glaxxion," the Jahul said. "We could turn him in. Make some serious credits."

That was just like a Jahul ship captain, to think about turning guys over for credits. Unfortunately for them, Flea was also a famous war-hero, and the moment those guys at the recruiting station ran his chip and realized who he was, they were going to throw all of his aggressors to the Peacemakers for abusing a champion of Neskfaat.

"No," Flea mimed, "please don't send me there! They'll send me back! Please!"

"He's right," the Jahul captain said. "We should keep this from the captain."

Flea twitched. "You're not the captain?"

"I'm the sanitation engineer."

Flea felt his mandibles fall open. "You're the *janitor*? Isn't that an oxymoron?!"

"Did you just call my friend a moron?!" a Hebbut snapped, because Hebbut had the intelligence of slime-covered rocks. Flea had only met one smart Hebbut, and he'd been imprisoned for trying to run a blackmarket karwiq ring in one of Flea's—

Slime-covered rocks! That had something to do with—

Then the Hebbut's ubiquitous club was coming down, and all the processes of Flea's mind were overloaded with the singular fact that his life was about to become a lot more painful. At the last moment, the Ooreiki holding him to the ground let him up, seemingly to avoid ending up with Bagan entrails all over his foot.

"He said *oxy*moron," the Ooreiki cried, wrapping a tentacle around the thug's arm. "Chill out, Pozi. We need to sell him to the recruiters to get any money out of this."

"I was just gonna smash him a little," Pozi muttered.

Flea, who had used the moment to clamber back up onto the ceiling, stared down upon his adversaries in interest. Were *they* the ones he was supposed to infiltrate? He'd been told undercover, so obviously he needed to spy on someone. But who?

Then the Ooreiki who had been stepping on him seemed to realize Flea had made his escape, and immediately groaned when he saw Flea's new perch. "Oh man. He's back on the ceiling again."

Before they could start hurling things at Flea's direction, however, Flea said, "Don't worry. I'm out of spit and I'm tired of running. They'll be glad to see me at the recruitment station." He flitted down and landed on the Hebbut's shoulder, making the big, stupid creature flinch. Offering his two forearms out in supplication and bowing his head, he said, "I'll go quietly."

CONTINUE FROM HERE: **page 65**
or
RETURN TO YOUR CHOICES: **page 47**

OPTION 3

WHEN IN DOUBT, APOLOGIZE...

"Oh burn me!" Flea cried, using the Ooreiki vernacular to endear him to them. "I'm sorry! Sorrysorry! I have this reflex when I'm spooked, and I literally have *no idea* how I got here. I think I ran afoul of some nasty types. I had this gambling habit, see, and this guy named Moxi roughed me up with a couple of his goons and—"

"Ugh. Moxi." The Ooreiki towering over him, holding his spitter to the floor, made a face. "You pissed off Moxi?" He sounded almost sympathetic.

"I...think?" Flea said. He honestly couldn't remember what had happened with Moxi. He *thought* he remembered the Jahul crime boss running around screaming, but maybe that was just wishful thinking. "Someone must have drugged me. I can't remember anything."

"Hmph." The Ooreiki glanced up at the others, then back down at Flea. "Now we're past introductions, can I let you up without you being a little asher?"

"Don't do it!" the Jahul—who had to be the captain—cried, distracting the Ooreiki pinning him down. "Bagans are *crazy*!"

Flea immediately broke into a sob, snapping the attention of the Ooreiki—who were all soft-hearted pussies—back down to him. "It's so hard."

"Huh?" he said.

"Everyone thinks we're *vermin*!" Flea wailed. "That we can't be trusted!"

"I don't think I've ever seen a bug cry before," a big Hebbut off to one side said, cocking his head at Flea curiously. "So that's what it looks like."

"Kind of like he's humping the floor," another of the crewmembers noted.

Flea inwardly narrowed his eyes, but he kept up his façade. "I'm so ugly…everywhere I go, people hate me! They don't even get a chance to *know* me!"

"That would be easier if you didn't spit glue at them," the Ooreiki holding him said, though Flea could see delightedly that his adversary's resolve was beginning to waver.

"It comes out when we're scared," Flea cried. "I couldn't help myself!"

"Hagra's balls," the Jahul said. "I spent some time around a Baga. It actually fuses two materials together, making them one in the same. Hurts like a Dhasha paw, and they know it." He glanced at Two-Mouth. "Doesn't it, Rhogl?"

"I'm gonnath desthroy the wlithle asther," Two-Mouth mumbled around his fused lips.

"*Please* let me up," Flea said. "It was just reflex."

The Ooreiki holding him down grunted. "Fine," he said, "but you stick any of us again and we'll eject you into space." He then reluctantly lifted his foot off Flea's klett.

"Thank you!" Flea cried, immediately flexing his klett to make sure it still worked. "It won't happen again!"

"There's still the issue of you being on this ship without a ticket," the Ooreiki who had freed him said. "You said you got some debts...You got some credits tucked away somewhere Moxi don't know about? Say, six thousand of them?"

Because that went over his head like a cloud in a megastorm, Flea squinted and pressed the bottom button.

"*Six thousand credits is approximately the same amount it would cost to feed Daviin for half a rotation,*" the device said. "*Or the price of one night with the famous Bagan prostitute Xissxishikaln.*"

Flea immediately perked up. "*Really*?" Then he realized he'd never spent a night with Xissxishikaln because her agent had said he couldn't afford her, and that Daviin ate like...a gigantic Jreet. "Oh."

Seeing his reaction, the Ooreiki glanced at each other. "We *are* headed to a penal colony," the Jahul captain said. "You could sign us an IOU and go work off your debt there."

"Sure," Flea said, because he knew he wouldn't spend more than a few tics in the penal colony before he found a way out.

"Ships only land on that planetoid once every rotation, unless it's a special delivery," the Jahul warned. "They'd send you straight to the mines."

"No problem," Flea said amicably. "I love mines."

The Jahul sighed. "He's going to try and escape."

"Yeah," the Ooreiki with the gun said, analyzing Flea, "but I figure we drop him off, claim our IOU, and he's someone else's problem."

"Yeah, we just gotta keep it on the down-low," the Jahul said. "Forget to mention he's a spitter."

"I'll act like Hagra herself while you hand me over," Flea said.

The Jahul frowned at him. "Hagra is an all-powerful male deity of chaos, and he's a renowned prankster and rabble-rouser when he's bored, legendary for bringing down entire civilizations for the sake of entertainment."

Flea did not retract his statement.

The Jahul groaned. "Whatever. If the little guy is okay with going in willingly, fine. We get our money, he gets to spit on the warden and anyone else he likes."

"I'll go in undercover," Flea said, getting excited, now. "I'll pretend to be the sweetest, most loveable little Baga ever, totally not there to spy on anyone and figure out their evil plan for murdering one of my friends."

The Ooreiki, Hebbut, and Jahul all looked at each other.

"He's got a screw loose," the Hebbut noted. He thumped his club into a huge hand. "Want me to smash him now?"

Flea, meanwhile, was frowning, trying to figure out where that last little burst had come from. He remembered something about going undercover, and that there was something horrible about to happen to… Joe? Yeah, he was pretty sure it was Joe. He was going to get shot by a Trith.

Then Flea frowned. He'd *seen* a Trith before, and they probably weren't going to do a lot of shooting with those gangly little arms and top-heavy heads. Which meant he had to have a band of minion assassins under his command…

"Ugh, just get him to the captain so we can write up an IOU and make it all official-like."

But if that was the case, Joe was dead already. Trith could see the *future*…

The Flea blinked down at his little charm. Then again, *he* could see the future. Which made him…

…anti-Trith. Like, if the two of them ever found themselves in the same room together, one would have to explode! Now who could have made something like that…

As the others were drawing up the paperwork, Flea decided to make it his mission to find the Trith, completely forgetting to use his little device to ensure that the numbers they were quoting on his IOU were reasonable and accurate.

"All done!" the Ueshi captain cried, once Flea had signed. "With the pain and suffering and transport container repairs taken into account…Five million credits!" The rest of the crew bobbed their heads eagerly.

Flea had assumed that five, being less than six, was them cutting him a deal, but the Ueshi seemed a little *too* enthusiastic. Suspicious, he pressed his charm's bottom button.

"You now owe the cost of a small interstellar to Captain Oglu and his crew," the translator said cheerfully. *"Congratulations on the signing of such a brilliant and financially feasible contract without my input or advice!"*

"Get him to the loading bay," the Ueshi captain ordered. "Before he has second thoughts."

Flea was flabbergasted. "You *lied* to me!"

"Hey, we needed to be properly compensated," the Ueshi captain said. "Your wrongful presence onboard our ship caused lasting physical and psychological damage."

Flea narrowed his eyes and was about to start spitting when one of them dropped a sack over him and roughly shoved him inside, then cinched it shut.

GO BACK TO CHOICES: **page 47**

or

CONTINUE FROM HERE: **page 115**

OPTION 2 CONTINUED

RETURNED TO THE FORCE...

"So yeah, we caught this little guy stowed away on our ship and he's obviously a runaway, so we're hoping to get a little compensation for bringing him back to you guys." The Ooreiki that was holding Flea by the spitter cocked his head at the recruiter behind the desk. "*Will* you guys compensate us?"

The recruiter, a Hebbut who looked like he would rather go back to watching a televised match than dealing with the spacers' interruption, sighed and, with visible reluctance, took his big, bare feet off the counter. His uniform was dusty and unwashed, and he wasn't even wearing a rank symbol. He leaned forward to give Flea a good look. "Kinda puny. Doesn't look like it'd be very useful in the Force. What is it?"

"I'm a Baga," Flea said, irritated at the way he was being talked over. "Just hurry up and scan my chip, okay? This guy's got a death-grip on my klett and it hurts." He was sure that this whole misunderstanding would be fixed the *moment* they looked at his file and saw some of those big names.

"It wouldn't hurt if you hadn't tried to use it on us."

"I *told* you I could *fly* here," Flea snapped. "And you tried to put me in a *box*."

"So you were in the Force?" the Hebbut asked in the middle of the Ooreiki's response, obviously not alert enough to even be paying attention to their conversation. He looked Flea over with mind-numbing slowness. "You can fight?"

"I'm a *war hero*," Flea said, deciding that, burn it, he was going to get out of this before these bumbling goons ripped off his klett. "I was in Commander Zero's groundteam on Neskfaat. Look it up."

The Hebbut seemed to find that amusing. "Sure you were." He did, however, pull out a scanner and wave it over Flea's back.

"Huh," the Hebbut said, once the chip readout came back. "Gives me some really long name I can't pronounce. Nickname 'Flea.' Made Battlemaster when you served. Impressive." Flea could tell he was impressed that *Flea* had made Battlemaster, not that Battlemaster was impressive in and of itself.

"I *told* you," Flea gritted. "I fought with Zero."

"Mmm-hmm." He kept reading. "Minor commendations here and there—the obligatory medals, really—with a twelve-turn history of personality conflict."

"They started it," Flea said.

He pored through Flea's record. Then he raised a big, drooping brow. "Seventy-two cases of documented personality conflict."

"*All* of them started it," Flea insisted.

The Hebbut snorted, but continued. "Got special permission to volunteer before the minimum age because he had impregnated a hivelord's daughter and needed money to fund her first hatch..."

"Erm," Flea said, "it was her idea."

"Got his first enlistment extension when he assaulted a Dhasha Prime Commander in his own home..."

"He ate my battlemaster," Flea said. "So I followed him back to his den and glued his ass to his head while he was sleeping, then plugged one of his nostrils so he started to choke and stuck out his tongue. Then I brought my Small Commanders back the video of him licking his own asshole and they posted it for the whole battalion to see. They refused to tell him it was me, so he gave the entire battalion a term extension."

"Says you followed that up by getting caught thieving a ruvmestin medallion from the Ooreiki Representative on a diplomatic visit to your duty station."

"They weren't paying me enough," Flea said. "A hivelord's daughter has millions and millions of children. *Millions.*" For emphasis, he pressed his charm's button.

"A hivelord's daughter, being a potential Bagan queen, can produce billions of young from one mating, effectively making Flea a hivelord himself, should he ever decide to return to his clutch."

"Oh no," Flea said, shaking his head vigorously. "Nononono. She tried to *kill* me last time. They get fat and they get *vicious*—it's all hormones until BOOM, they turn the size of a space freighter, then they blame you for *everything* and threaten to sic the hive on you if you ever return. No way. Her eunuchs can take care of her. She just has her money-man take what she needs from my accounts."

"*Which are currently negative in the form of a small interstellar spaceship and a medium passenger shuttle*," the device reminded him helpfully.

"She can't expect me to support her forever!" Flea snapped. "She has a *hive*, now."

The Hebbut grunted, then went back to his file. "You glued your superior officers into their clothes over a hundred times before—"

Impatient, Flea said, "Just find the part where it says, 'Received a kasja for kicking ass on Neskfaat.' Then do the math. How many people survived Neskfaat?"

"Two groundteams," one of the Ooreiki holding him said obligingly. "Everybody knows that."

"*Yes*," Flea said. "Two groundteams. Mine and Rat's."

"Here we go. Says you're a deserter off Rhiso with an incredible talent for lying about connections to famous people, namely one Jreet Representative, Daviin ga Vora, and his two friends, the Peacemaster Jer'ait Ze'laa and the notorious Commander Zero."

Flea jerked. He'd never even *been* to Rhiso. "What?! Let me see that."

The Hebbut commander handed it over. "Looks like you'll do fine here, kid. Mine shifts start at oh-three-hundred." He started to lean back into his chair, returning his attention to the fight on the vidscreen.

Flea's mandibles fell open. It was his file, for sure, but everything from Neskfaat afterwards had been heavily edited.

Instantly, his carapace crawled. There were only a handful creatures in all of Congress he knew to have the capability of editing a personnel file like this, only two of which he had ever met or known personally. First was Jer'ait, who, as one of Flea's only real friends, wouldn't have done it, even if he *did* shoot at him every once in a while. The only other one was…

Suddenly, the dangerous Jahul voice made total sense. Forgotten. The last free Geuji. He didn't *have* vocal cords, so he had to use computers to talk for him.

Instantly, the Geuji's words came back to him. *But I will be sending you in under cover and for no reason whatsoever are you to drop Daviin, Jer'ait, Joe, or my names to random strangers, you understand?*

So he was on a mission for Forgotten? A *spying* mission? That meant he was an *agent*. On a *mission*. That was so…*awesome*!

"You know what?" Flea said quickly, "you're right. I made it all up. I was never friends with anyone famous. I have a lying habit and a gambling habit and I woke up in that box because some druglord shoved me in there because I couldn't pay off a debt."

"Like I said," the old Hebbut said, yawning, "mine shifts switch out at oh-three-hundred. Each shift lasts a rotation."

Getting a sudden, overwhelming urge *not* to go to the mines, Flea hesitated. "Uh. Is there anything else I can do?" An agent had to have access to the major players, and he had this uncannily strong feeling the major players weren't going to be at the bottom of a ruvmestin pit.

"Nope," the Hebbut said. "Go put him in the brig until shift."

Because he knew his next move as a secret agent was important, Flea pressed the top button on his charm. Instantly, like a Hebbut's club rendezvousing with his temple, Flea saw the following three choices spread out in painful detail…

Option B1) Find a way to spit all over the Hebbut at the desk, because that will change his mind: **page 71**
Option B2) Allow them to put you in the brig and hope for a chance of escape to present itself: **page 76**
Option B3) Try to talk them into complacency, then flee when they least expect it: **page 93**

OR RETURN TO CHOICES: **page 47**

OPTION B1

FLEA SPITS BECAUSE SPITTING IS FUN

As an agent of Forgotten, Flea knew that he would be protected no matter what he did. So, just as soon as the big, dumb furgs finished their conversation about how many credits they would get from Flea's incarceration, Flea twisted and clamped his snipping mandibles down on the Ooreiki holding him by the klett.

The Ooreiki, who apparently hadn't realized that Flea could have snipped off his arm at any time, now looked down at his truncated appendage in horror. "Burn me, that little asher just cut off my—"

But then Flea was spitting. He spat on the Hebbut, gluing his extra-large ass to his seat, then he spit at the Ooreiki closest to him, gluing his foot to the floor. Then the Ooreiki and the Hebbut were screaming, and Flea was chuckling as he glued them to the floor, the walls, the desk, the chair, each other…

He was on the ceiling, reveling in the chaos that he had created, when one of the Ooreiki he'd pinned to a wall bent down and pulled off his boot. Flea cocked his head, not having remembered spitting on that one's feet.

"Diiiiieeeee!" the Ooreiki screamed, the muscular creature hurling it at him with the approximate force of an interstellar freighter. Flea dodged it easily, then climbed out the hole it put into the ceiling, exiting via the polymer roof.

Flea crawled out onto the white, sun-baked sheeting, still chuckling. "Furgs," he said. And, for once, his choice of spitting hadn't ended in doom and disaster.

Then he froze, because, as he turned to get a panorama of the surrounding town, he found himself facing another Baga. A blue one.

Flea frowned. He was pretty sure that Baga didn't come in blue…

"Blarg ugh!" the Baga cried, the sharp rattle of his wing-casings snapping Flea out of his thoughts. "*Ugh*!"

"Yeah, you're one to talk," Flea snorted. This one was so butt-ugly he couldn't even tell if it was male or female. He skittered sideways to get a better look. Definitely a case of some massive inbreeding. "So they abandon you on this planet 'cause you look like a Hebbut's toejam?" he asked.

"*Mogruogh!*" the ugly Baga shrieked at him, vibrating its casings again.

"Yeah, uh, I don't speak furgling," Flea said. Still, though, he was curious. He hadn't seen another Baga in millions of turns, and he found himself looking forward to some intelligent conversation, maybe even a night in a proper hive. "Where's your queen?" He glanced around. "There a hive on this planet?" It seemed a little dry, but not beyond the realm of possibility.

"*Herble triggit!*" the ugly Baga screamed, skittering towards him sharply. "*TRIGGIT*!"

Flea blinked. He had nothing against ugly Baga, but this one just seemed...dumb.

Because he was getting a bad feeling, Flea decided to test out Forgotten's little device again. As he was in the process of retrieving the charm, the Baga opened its wing casings and displayed enormous multicolored sails where there should have been wings.

Flea's mandibles fell open and he forgot about the charm.

"I'll be damned," he managed. "We *do* look alike!"

"*TRIGGIT! HERBLE TRIGGIT!*" the torrak shrieked. It stood up on its hind legs, the sails taking up three digs in a full semi-circle around him, displaying a ridiculously tiny stinger just above its asshole. It started skittering sideways—faster, Flea realized uncomfortably, than Flea himself could move. As he spun to face the amorous torrak, finding the whole situation highly amusing, his view over the rooftop shifted to reveal a cluster of bigger torrak with egg-clusters stuck to their backs gathered in a group behind the lone, sail-flying torrak. Flea frowned.

Then the torrak skittered sideways again, distracting him by *swishing* the sail to the opposite direction. As Flea was expecting the creature to go left, it slid right, then skittered on top of him.

"*Hey*!" Flea cried, trying to squirm out from underneath it. The torrak, disgustingly, continued to ride him. "That's *so* uncool! Stupid thing, I'm not a girl—"

"*HERBLE TRIGGIT*!" Then the torrak stabbed him right in the carapace with the tiny, almost microscopic stinger in its butt.

Despite the heat of the day, the landscape took on a violet hue as Flea's vision instantly turned various shades of purple. He felt his legs start to twitch involuntarily, until he was running in all directions at once, his legs thrashing on the ground in spasms.

The torrak dismounted and skittered over to its harem, then spread its sail again. "Herble," it said, nuzzling one of the egg-clutching females. It 'herbled' and nuzzled back.

Flea's convulsions continued, his legs scrabbling until he had accidentally flipped himself onto his back, watching the torrak upside-down. The purple hues, Flea realized, were getting darker, until all that remained was the incredibly vivid, almost neon-bright patterns etched across the torrak's sail. Then, like a beacon in a storm, the torrak slapped its wings closed and the lights went out.

END IT HERE

or

RETURN TO CHOICES: **page 70**

OPTION B2

GO WILLINGLY, ESCAPE LATER

Obviously, Flea was facing superior numbers and mass, if not brainpower. As a newly-minted agent of chaos, he decided to calmly let them throw him in the brig and wait for an opportunity to strike.

For his part, once Loog had paid the Ooreiki spacers their ill-begotten blood-money and sent them on their way, the recruiter spent most of his time grunting and snorting with amusement as he watched Rock Crusher the Enormous pulverize a series of new opponents.

A Hebbut match pretty much went on until the Hebbut champion was dead or nobody else wanted to challenge—meaning all the opposition was dead.

Oddly, people actually signed up for that. Flea watched the vidscreen from his prison cell, trying to puzzle out the weird, brutal cultures of the less-endowed species. Sure, it was fun to *watch*, but what kind of greasy-eyed jenfurgling went up against an undefeated champion for the chance to be a champion—until defeated? And, in the Hebbut culture, 'defeat' was basically the same thing as 'brutal, horrific death'. Sometimes, when the defeat was bad enough and death wasn't coming fast enough, some of the fans or security guards would hasten the process, all the while cheering and carrying the champion around on their shoulders. It was madness.

"You like to fight?" Loog said, during a Congressional news break—apparently Daviin ga Vora, the hothead warrior-prince who had spent the last eighteen turns shaking up Koliinaat and its 'quivering puddle of fat politicians,' as Daviin put it, had disappeared, and the Regency was whispering foul play.

"Not especially, no," Flea said, distracted.

"Shame," Loog said. "I bet you'd make a good death-clip."

A death-clip, Flea had come to discover after watching a few Hebbut matches out of morbid curiosity, was a close-up of some body part twitching in death-spasms. Congressional law had expressly forbidden showing the faces of sentient creatures as they died on public waves for the purposes of entertainment, so the Hebbut had circumvented that for their traditional arena fights by showing *other* parts of the body at the moment of death. Usually legs, or, in Rock Crusher's latest opponent's case, a zoomed-in hand that kept spasming into a fist and back.

"I don't think I'd make a good arena fighter," Flea said.

Loog glanced over at him. "Well, it's either that or the mines. Commander Halperi won't want you at the station, since you already ran away once. He doesn't have time to babysit furglings."

Flea *hadn't* run away, but he didn't feel it was going to be productive to try and explain to the Hebbut squader that a hyper-intelligent, sentient mold barely smarter than Flea had hacked its way into Flea's supposedly un-hackable government file and made a few choice alterations.

"I'll take the mines," Flea said, still distracted by the Congress-wide manhunt that was going on as Peacemakers tried to find the Jreet prince, who had disappeared from Koliinaat with no warning and no ship's manifest to document his departure almost a rotation ago.

Damn, Flea thought, grimacing. *He's probably wreaking havoc on Akest, hunting down Moxi's children, siblings, parents, grandparents, friends, coworkers, pets…*Jreet princes, when in the throes of a revenge-massacre, got pretty focused and meticulous about carving the source of their fury out of the societal tapestry. He'd heard of one who had ransacked his victim's favorite restaurant, taking out the waiters, the cooks, the manager, and even the stockholders of the establishment for their part in pleasuring the dead guy with his favorite foods.

"Mines are tough," Loog said. "You can't lift a pickaxe, you get 'lost' in the tunnels. Shifts are a rotation long."

Flea chuckled the idea of anyone 'losing' him anywhere. "I'll be able to take care of myself." Though the idea of getting stuck down there for an entire rotation unnerved him a little. The spacers had told him that Marshi, the Ueshi in charge of the planet, ordered the huge metal doors to be locked until the miners produced enough ruvmestin ore to trigger the mechanism for the doors to unlock—usually about a rotation. Sometimes, if they were really lucky, it took a few days less. Sometimes, when the mineral deposit they were following depleted unexpectedly and they had to find another, it was closer to two rotations.

On those shifts, miners usually died.

Still, Flea rarely needed to eat, and he was fast, and a few dumb Hebbut with pick-axes weren't going to present a challenge to his escape. Mines usually had ventilation ducts, shafts for the drainage of water, air circulation systems…He would find something.

Thus, he didn't put up much of a fight when Loog called Marshi and two of her Ooreiki goons came up the bone-littered road to the recruitment center to collect him.

Unfortunately, it seemed that *somebody* had warned them about the many talents of a Baga, because one of them put a stinging tentacle death-grip on his spitter and didn't let go until they were safely inside the mines, at which point Flea got carefully transferred to an airtight holding cell and locked inside.

Time passed. *Way* too much time. Entire *millennia* passed as Flea waited there, trapped in a hermetically-sealed box. He started pacing, watching the exodus of dirty, thin, haggard-looking miners from the mines and the fresh meat flooding in, determined looks on their faces under their gas masks. A couple other fresh-eyed young Humans got shoved into the cell with Flea, but Flea didn't have a chance to spit on his captors before they slammed the cell shut again and locked it.

Meanwhile, Flea discovered by reading the pamphlet embedded in the wall that the underground air was naturally toxic, and that the miners were expected to breathe air that they brought with them in order to survive. Even then, huge pressurized bottles were being carted in and left against one side of the huge metal door—bottles that, Flea had discovered in horror—were only engineered to last the miners a rotation. The mines didn't *have* air holes because Marshi apparently thought that was too much of a security risk, and that she might lose some of her precious ruvmestin up a ventilation duct.

They're going to seal me down here, Flea thought, the crappiness of his situation finally beginning to dawn on him. If he got stuck in the mines, he was going to fail his mission, and he had a strong feeling that people who failed a mission for Forgotten had their own 'death-clips,' probably in private, as a sentient mold lectured them on his vast superiority.

Flea glanced again at the Glaxxion Mines Operating Procedures pamphlet that had been thoughtfully etched into the wall. At the bottom, in bold letters, it was written, *ATTENTION: ANYONE WHO WANTS TO SKIP THIS SHIFT CAN VOLUNTEER TO FIGHT IN THE GLADATORIAL PITS FOR A NO-HOLDS-BARRED MORALE-BOOSTING MATCH WITH THE CURRENT CHAMPION.*

Below that was a number for the local Bajnan lawyer for will-finalization and liability procedures.

Because they were getting ready to close the doors and he was running out of time, Flea started hammering on the glass and screaming for the foreman, who was standing with a clipboard nearby, checking people off as they arrived for their shift.

After several tics of Flea making his displeasure known—and the huge metal doors slowly inching shut—the foreman irritatedly handed the checkoff sheet to another elderly miner and turned to open Flea's enclosure.

"Yeah?" he demanded, wrenching the glass door open just far enough to talk through.

"I wanna fight in the gladiatorial pit!" Flea cried, scuttling up to straddle the crack between the door and the wall. "Don't let them close the door—I wanna fight!"

The miner's response was lukewarm. "Yeah?" He looked him over. "You're an exotic, which is always fun. But they'll make you clip your wings. You O.K. with getting your wings clipped? That's an unfair advantage."

Sure, because going up against a Hebbut two million times his size was totally fair. "Of course!" Flea lied. "Just lead me to the wing-trimmer!"

The miner gave him a dubious look. "You settle your affairs? Marshi *hates* unsettled affairs."

"All taken care of!" Flea cried.

"Even the Intentional Death and Dismemberment Waiver?" the foreman insisted. "And the Incomplete Corpse Good-Faith Collection Clause? You're probably going to need that one. You're pretty small, and when Kroeg starts pounding, stuff starts flying, and the whole arena's made of sand, you know? So kinda hard to find, say, fingers, when they get sprayed around like that."

Sprayed fingers? "You mean *splayed* fingers?" Flea said.

The miner foreman gave him an odd look, like Flea was confusing him. "No, *sprayed*. As in they fly everywhere and then get buried in the commotion. Oh, and eyeballs, too. They're usually the first to go."

It took Flea a moment to realize that the miner was totally serious. Swallowing, Flea reached up and clicked the top button of his charm.

Instantaneously, his choices lighted up his consciousness, three distinct pathways stretching out ahead of him…

Option B2a) Flea spits at the mine foreman, because that is the best way to facilitate a rational and productive discourse: **page 83**
Option B2b) Flea decides to deathmatch! **page 88**
Option B2c) Flea chickens out and decides that the life of a miner is better than getting sprayed across bleachers in a Hebbut death-pit: **page 90**

OR RETURN TO PREVIOUS CHOICES: **page 70**

OPTION B2A

FLEA SPITS, BECAUSE SPITTING IS FUN!

Now that the miner foreman was distracted, Flea subtly twisted his spitter to take aim at the old Human's pale blue eye while he continued to talk about wills and liability waivers.

The foreman was obviously going to receive some sort of bonus for Flea's participation in the death-pit, because he was *way* too excited. "It's all gotta be legal," the foreman said. He gestured at the Ooreiki in desert combat gear standing outside to stop closing the mine door. “Marshi doesn’t want any problems down the road if—”

Sensing the ideal opportunity, Flea spat.

The miner flinched backwards and stumbled, allowing Flea to push his way out of the holding cell.

He wasn’t, however, expecting the old, arthritic Human’s arm to lash out, Jreet-like, and grab him by the charm around his neck.

“Agg,” Flea gulped, as the Human tightened his fist, choking him.

“You. Little. *Shit.*” The Human yanked him out of the holding cell by his neck, his one good eye filled with death. “Close the doors!” he snarled to the Ooreiki with the guns. “We’ll deal with this one.”

Flea began to get a sense of foreboding as the huge metal door started to move again in its automated runner, blocking out more and more of the light from the outside.

Then, with a resounding clang that echoed eerily down the mines, it thundered shut.

Still holding him by the charm around his neck, the Human slammed him against the wall a few times, making Flea’s neck-tendons strain with the effort of keeping his head attached to his carapace. “Ugh!” The Human threw Flea aside and started clawing at his eye. “What the hell *is* it?!” The two of them were drawing a crowd of curious miners.

“Pretty sure that bug just jizzed in your eye, Craig,” one of the kids snickered.

"It was probably just scared," a big, dumb Hebbut said.

"Yeah," another elderly miner said, squatting down beside Flea and holding out a hand aggressively. "We're *all* miserable down here, little guy. Some of us've been here for decades. It's all right."

"Just chill out," another agreed. "We work together, everyone survives this."

Flea, out of self-defense, started spitting at everything with eyes.

Predictably, the big, stupid creatures started screaming and running in circles, and Flea skittered to the ceiling, feeling his innate superiority as they scrambled around beneath him.

They look like vaghi scattering from a shipping crate, Flea thought delightedly, watching the cluster of miners seek refuge.

But then he realized they were 'fleeing' to piles of 'pickaxes' leaned in clusters against the walls.

"There he is!" one of the miners he'd globbed in the eye screamed, shoving a pickaxe into the air and pointing at the ceiling where Flea crouched. "*Get him!*"

And Flea quickly discovered that, sealed underground with millions of angry miners and toxic fumes, there was literally nowhere to run. He had just started to get down a tunnel when a sickly yellow haze settling along the ceiling cut him short. On the walls were signs that said *DANGER: TOXIC AIR*, *WEAR MASKS*.

Under that, someone had scratched into the paint *Or Die.*

Flea was considering whether or not Bagan physiology would withstand whatever toxins were in the air ahead when a rock hit him from behind.

Though Flea normally could have withstood the attack with ease, the rocks at the edge of the toxic cloud were treacherously damp and slimy with the yellow stuff in the air. He had just regained his footing when another rock hit him and he slipped.

He hit the floor hard, and the jolt accidentally jostled the charm. As Flea scuttled along the floor, avoiding the first hail of picks sparking against the stone where he had been, the device said, "*You have exactly eight hundred and seventy angry miners chasing you, which is approximately the same number of angry miners that would completely fill a Congressional Ground Force regiment.*"

Flea screamed and buzzed to the side as one of the picks came a little too close and flattened one of his feet, squirting it off to *plop* against the wall.

"*Then again, if you were looking for a mass comparison, eight hundred and seventy angry miners is approximately the same mass as forty medium-sized Dhasha princes or twenty-five ancient Jreet.*"

A pick came down on his left antennae, ripping it from his head. Flea howled and scuttled sideways, between a miner's legs.

"*Or, if you would rather have that converted into the mechanical force equivalent, you're looking at the sheer kinetic energy of eight medium Congressional tanks.*"

Someone stomped on Flea's klett, drawing his escape up short. "We've got him now!" There was an angry cheer and the thunder of boots. Flea started to scream and claw at the foot holding him to the floor, desperate to reach something he could get his mandibles around.

"But if you're asking about the number of pickaxes, *there's only eight hundred and sixty-nine of those. One of them broke when he threw it at you earlier. To clarify, that's approximately the same number of pick-axes as—"*

Flea felt the first pick go through his carapace, pinning him to the stone. Squirming on the floor, Flea had just enough time to see another pick come down between his eyes before he felt a sudden jolt and all conscious thought fizzled suddenly out.

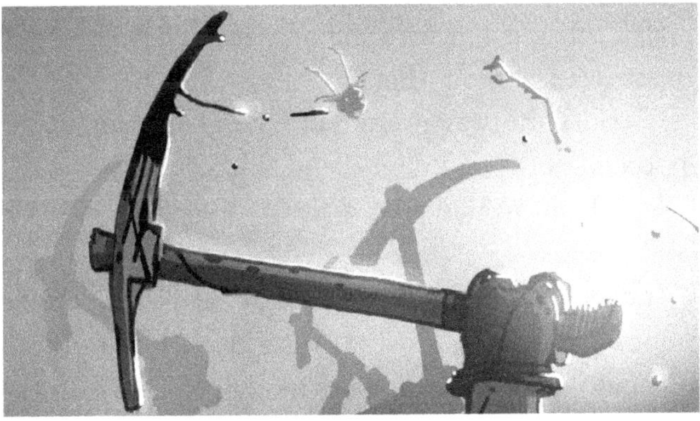

END IT HERE

or

RETURN TO CHOICES: **page 82**

OPTION B2B

FLEA FIGHTS, BECAUSE DEATHMATCHING IS FUN!

"I'll do it!" Flea cried. "I don't need my wings!" *Anything* to get out of the mines before the tunnel was sealed for an entire rotation. He had Joe to save, a Trith to kill, and a group of assassins to infiltrate and annihilate. He was a secret agent of chaos, and it was his *job* to face death without fear, regardless of the odds!

Besides, he was pretty sure he could spit in his opponent's eyes and then spend the rest of the match riding them around like a beast of burden. Which would be *fun*.

Lots of fun. Flea could see it now—the crowd chanting his name, howling with glee as he rode his opponent like a Borgian Racer…

The mine foreman gave a huge grin. "Sounds great!" he cried. "Let's get you out of here before they close the doors."

"Yes," Flea said, chuckling inwardly as he smacked a Hebbut—his third opponent for the day—in the ear, ordering it to run faster, "let's do that."

CONTINUE FROM HERE: **page 169**
or
RETURN TO CHOICES: **page 82**

OPTION B2C

ROCKS FALL AND EVERYBODY DIES...

"Uh, never mind," Flea said, finding the idea of coating an arena with his insides less than appealing. Besides. He was a *scout*. Fighting really wasn't his bag...Heck, maybe it *was* more fun and fulfilling to be a miner stuck grubbing in the dirt underground for entire rotations at a time than it was to be a secret agent and go with the flow. "I think I'll try mining, instead. Because that's obviously what I'm supposed to be doing right now."

The mine foreman gave him a disappointed look. "Ah, okay. Guess we'll just have to find something for you to do." He gestured for the Ooreiki at the big metal door to finish sealing them inside. Once the door was shut, the miner gestured to a stack of hard hats, masks, and picks against one side of the entrance. "There's your stuff. It's all the same, just grab something."

"Uh," Flea began, looking at the enormous gear. "I really don't think that will—"

"Everyone gets one," the miner said darkly. "*Rules*."

So Flea dutifully grabbed a pick and scuttled under a hard hat, though he couldn't fit one of the masks to his face and had to drag it behind him. He shuffled under the oversized hat, the big green dome acting like a second carapace as he pushed the pick ahead of him and dragged the mask with the other.

He couldn't help but think, scuttling down the tunnel under the hat that would separate his head from his body the moment something heavy fell upon it, that this probably wasn't what Forgotten had in mind when he sent Flea to Glaxxion to be his agent of chaos, but it was too late now.

Besides, he'd grown tired of the intrigue, the danger. Life had become way too exciting, too fast. The stress had started to overwhelm him, the anxiety of not knowing which way to turn, who was enemy or ally, was taking over his dreams, paralyzing him. For *so long*, he'd been forced to remain constantly alert, ever aware of his surroundings, totally prepared for anything that might come his way, or die. It had, quite simply, become too much to handle. The lonely nights, the drinking, the grueling weeks spent scouting out his targets, the look in their eyes as their lives slid away…Flea knew he probably had developed some form of mental malady from the strain, but he was forbidden from exposing himself or his employer in any form of therapy.

Thus, after such a punishing existence as a spy, Flea was looking *forward* to a life of a miner, obediently hacking away at rocks in the dirt, toiling away so some rich Ueshi could add a ruvmestin coating to her mansion. It wasn't a glamorous life, and it wasn't exactly fulfilling, but at least he was still alive, *not* risking his life in a gladiatorial pit.

Thus, he was meekly picking away at the stone, prying at a particularly stubborn nugget, contemplating his new, infinitely more wholesome existence, when rocks fell and he died.

(If you are a Dungeons & Dragons player,or especially if you've been a Dungeonmaster trying to herd chronic pain-in-the-ass players through a great storyline when they decide they're going to go do something utterly stupid and random instead—like chronically make love to sheep—you will get this. If not, just assume the abrupt ending is intentional, for it showeth the powereth of ze Dungeonmaster…)

END IT HERE

or

RETURN TO CHOICES: **page 82**

OPTION B3

TRY TO TALK YOUR WAY OUT OF IT, FOR YOU ARE SMARTER THAN A DUMB HEBBUT

"Holy *ash*," Flea cried, twisting to get a better look at the fight on the Hebbut's vidscreen. "Is that Rock Crusher?! She's my *favorite*!"

"She's getting old," the Hebbut said, sounding disappointed. "Now Kroeg, *she's* a fighter."

Flea frowned. "I knew a Hebbut called Kroeg. She was a *beast*."

That seemed to get a slight twitch of interest from the Hebbut manning the desk, but then the Ooreiki still holding Flea by his klett jiggled him and said, "So we get a reward for bringing him back, right?"

"Standard reward's three hundred credits," the Hebbut said distractedly. On the screen, Rock Crusher was hefting a boulder over her head, roaring as she barreled down on her opponent, a much smaller Hebbut on her back.

"Three *hundred*?" the Ooreiki gathered cried. "But that won't even pay for Rhogl's surgery!"

"Not my problem," the Hebbut said. To him, the conversation was obviously over.

"So did Kroeg get into professional fighting?" Flea asked. That seemed like something Kroeg might have done, once she got out of prison. "She was certainly big enough for it. In the fight on Isst, I saw her crush a Jikaln's skull with her *fist*."

The Hebbut at the desk gave Flea a sideways glance. Then, to Flea's Ooreiki escorts, he said, "Leave the little guy here. He can't hurt much."

The Ooreiki glanced at each other, then the one holding Flea pointed to his klett and said, "Uh, but he's got this butt-tube that shoots—"

"Ooreiki really *are* pussies, aren't they?" Flea demanded loudly. "I'm what, like the size of your *head*? What could I do, really?"

"Rhogl's still in surg—"

"Rhogl was a pussy," Flea said. "He got beaten by a *bug*."

The Hebbut chuckled, gesturing. "Just set him on the desk and leave. It's not like he can go anywhere, anyway."

But the two Ooreiki still looked unsure. "Yeah, but he can fly..."

"Where's he gonna fly to?" the Hebbut demanded. "This is a desert planetoid with *one* settlement and no surface water, and temps get over sixty-nine grads at the end of the light cycle. He flies away, he'll come back before the burning starts. They always do."

Flea didn't need surface water, and heat really didn't bother him, but he wasn't about to mention it.

"Okay," the Ooreiki said warily, "but don't say you didn't get warned..." He set Flea down carefully on the desk, allowing his legs to gain purchase on the surface, but still maintained a grip on the spitter. Then he inched his body away, still gripping Flea's klett in a deathgrip.

"You know I use that thing to mate with, right?" Flea asked, as the Ooreiki took his sweet time letting go. "So in effect, you've had a death-grip on my dick for the last three hours. How's it feel, Ooreiki?" It wasn't true—Flea's genitalia were stored safely inside his carapace, so as to better endure the gruesome act of violence that was mating with a hivelord's daughter—but he knew the Hebbut—who as a culture were very crass and crude, sexually-driven creatures—would find that amusing.

Indeed, the Hebbut chortled as the Ooreiki froze, looking down at his fist on Flea's klett in horror.

"So yeah, *stand* there," Flea said, "and keep stroking it, big boy."

The Ooreiki released him and stumbled backwards, barreling into his fellow reward-seekers in his hasty attempt to get away. Which, of course, the Hebbut found even more amusing.

"Three big Ooreiki afraid of one little tiny bug," the Hebbut said, tisking.

"You *sure* you don't wanna join the Force?" Flea goaded. "I'm pretty sure we could find a good battle-master to grow you some balls..." Which, of course, made the Hebbut chuckle again. For some reason he still didn't completely understand, Flea had a way with Hebbut that he actually considered somewhat alarming.

But useful. Very useful. The big, dumb brutes made great muscle, when properly directed.

"So for our reward..." the Ooreiki suggested. "That's three hundred each, right?"

The Hebbut snorted. He reached under his desk, found a chit, flipped it over, and wrote something on it, then flipped it to the Ooreiki, who fumbled to catch it—without bones, their arms and hands just ropes of muscle, Ooreiki weren't good with moves that required quick dexterity.

The Ooreiki squinted at the clumsy Hebbut handwriting, then, in dismay, cried, "This is just an IOU!"

The Hebbut shrugged and went back to his fight.

Seeing they weren't going to get anything else from the dirty old recruiter in the dusty office, the Ooreiki made disgusted sounds and filed out the door, slamming it behind them.

Flea skittered around to stand on the Hebbut's shoulder to get a better look at the match. "Wow," he said, "it's a *deathmatch*? I didn't think they allowed those anymore."

"Hebbut law," the Hebbut said. "I'm Loog." He was still watching the match.

"I'm Flea," Flea said.

Loog grunted. "You really know Kroeg?"

"She tried to squeeze the life outta me when we first met," Flea said. "Kinda left an impression."

Loog grunted again. "She want you dead, then?"

"Oh, no," Flea chuckled. "We got over that and we were best buddies. I helped her with her karwiq operation, until the Peacemakers got wind of it. I was her delivery service."

Loog still hadn't taken his eyes from the screen. "Kroeg harder, now. Glaxxion's been hard on her. She's the town champion in the war-pit."

Flea cocked his head. "How does one become a champion in a Hebbut war-pit?"

"Not die," the older Hebbut said. He reached out and dug out a little tin of some unidentified shredded plant and offered him a pinch. "Want some?"

"Huh-uh," Flea said. Half the stuff aliens offered him was poisonous, even with the best of intentions. "So how often she gotta fight in the ring?"

"Each time she doesn't wanna go to the mines," the old Hebbut said. "Anyone who don't wanna go, they gotta fight." He glanced at Flea, a single heavy brow raised. "You fight?"

"To the *death*?" Flea said. "Probably not."

The Hebbut grunted. "Guess it's the mines, then."

"So those are my options?" Flea demanded. "Go to the mines or fight?"

"Or fly away," the Hebbut said. "But you'll be back, and then they put you in the mines for two rotations, instead of one."

Some deep, burning part of Flea recognized that going to the mines would make it difficult to do his job as a secret agent for the greatest criminal mastermind in the galaxy. Which would be a lot more cool if *failing* to do his job wouldn't be failing the greatest criminal mastermind in the galaxy.

Trying not to think of what would happen if Flea couldn't complete his mission, Flea pushed the top button of his charm.

Like three blazing paths lit up in a void, the choices—and the repercussions—burned their way into his brain in an instant…

Option B3a) Flea spits on Loog: **page 100**
Option B3b) Flea escapes: **page 102**
Option B3c) Flea fights to the death in the Hebbut war-pit: **page 107**

OR RETURN TO PREVIOUS CHOICES: **page 70**

OPTION B3A

FLEA SPITS, BECAUSE SPITTING IS FUN

Flea, who didn't like to be pushed around, twisted his spitter around and spat on the Hebbut. The Hebbut let out a startled cry, then, while Flea was chuckling and skittering onto the ceiling, the Hebbut pulled the biggest laser rifle he'd ever seen from under the desk in front of him.

In a horrifying instant, the rifle barrel swiveled to face him. Flea didn't have time to move or duck, still pinned in a corner of the room, and a moment later, the Hebbut sliced through him with the rifle.

Stunned, Flea dropped to the floor, twitching.

The Hebbut slung his big rifle over his shoulder and smugly walked up to him. "We get lots of pirates in these parts. Ruvmestin planet has lots of thieves. You get good with guns 'round here." He cocked his head. "If they let you carry a gun. Most don't carry guns."

"Need. Doctor." Flea managed.

"This place don't got doctors," the Hebbut said. Loog lowered his gun again, this time taking aim at Flea's head. "You wouldn't do no good in the mines anyway. Too small." Then he pulled the trigger, and Flea's world exploded into darkness.

END IT HERE

or

RETURN TO PREVIOUS CHOICES: **page 99**

OPTION B3B

FLEA FLEES

Flea decided he wasn't getting anywhere with the Hebbut and decided to go sightseeing, instead. He made small-talk about full-contact fighting until someone came through the front door, then launched himself off the desk at full speed towards the exit, blasting past the startled Huouyt in the entrance at millions of marches a tic.

He got out the front door and shot up into the sunny sky, gaining altitude and therefore advantage.

The first thing he noticed was that the planet where the Ooreiki had dumped him was a dusty craphole. The reddish stone looked baked into place, and what little vegetation there was actually looked like living weaponry, obviously engineered to keep predators from stealing its precious water reserves.

The town proper was really just a cluster of gray box-buildings that had been prefabricated in space and slapped down upon colonization, all laid out in identical rows, with equal spaces in between and dusty little yards fenced off behind each house. The 'road' through the middle of town was really just a track that ran from the mine through the house-cluster—which seemed to be centered around a walled fighting pit—and up to the landing strip, where a single black Congie interstellar squatted on the carved stone airfield. A much smaller brown shuttle sat opposite it, but it was clear that it was not a long-distance vehicle. The Ooreiki traders, then, had already departed.

Flea climbed higher, noticing that what the Hebbut had said was true, and that there appeared to be no roads out of the tiny town. The desert beyond the tiny settlement was completely untamed, with dust clouds rolling across the wind-whipped landscape. Reddish dunes complimented a red-orange haze. Even the sun itself seemed to burn hotter than it should, a deep orange as opposed to the whites and yellows that Flea was used to.

Flea circled the town and came to a hover over the mine. The huge metal door was sealed, and guardtowers speckled the landscape in all directions leading up it. Flea was about to get closer—land-lubbers never bothered to look *up*—when he noticed a cluster of

Jreet-sized auto-turrets casually swinging to face him from the top of every tower, following his movements.

Flea hastily backtracked, landing on a stony outcropping overlooking the town. Off in the distance, he saw a dust-storm sweeping across the horizon. Up on the opposite cliff across the town from him, a small com array sat in disarray, the ramshackle building having a visible hole in the roof. Two of the satellite dishes were lying face-down on the stone, and the third was swinging mildly with every gust of wind.

Flea took that moment to consider his lot in life. He was ninety percent sure he was a secret agent of the Geuji…and he'd figured it out *despite* the fact the Geuji had obviously drugged him and wiped his memory of their time together. Which was exhilarating.

Unfortunately, Flea didn't have the first idea where to start as an agent for vigilante justice. All he remembered—and it was more a feeling than an actual image—was that someone on this planet wanted to kill Joe.

And, because he had nothing else to go on, Flea realized that was probably where he should start. He jumped off the cliff and flew down into the town itself, ready to begin his career as a secret agent.

He was halfway back to the town, totally minding his own business, when he heard the unmistakable buzzing of a Baga at full-speed. Which, because a Baga's full speed was *almost* as fast as sound, reached him only a split second before something black slammed into him from the side, sending him tumbling through the sky and almost knocking his head off his carapace with the impact.

"*Engaging the enemy!*" a female Baga using a Congie voice-projector screamed. "*I'm taking him down!*"

A moment later, Flea got the heady rush of pheromones that told him, unequivocally, he was dealing with a virgin princess.

Then she was bashing at his face with her toes, screaming the traditional Bagan war cry:

"Dieeeeeeeeee!"

Flea screamed and started pounding his wings to get away from her, tugging them higher into the air, but she then crawled onto his back and clamped down on his casings, apparently intent to craterize them into one of the roofs below.

Flea, in his horrified flailing, accidentally clamped his fist on the charm's top button out of sheer.

Immediately, three choices splayed out before him, illuminating new pathways through the shadows of his mind...

Option B3c1a) Flea spits at the princess: **page 135**
Option B3c1b) Flea tells the princess she looks familiar…: **page 140**
Option B3c1c) Flea finds a way to escape her hold: **page 157**

OR GO BACK TO PREVIOUS CHOICES: **page 99**

OPTION B3C

FLEA DEATHMATCHES TO AVOID THE MINES, BECAUSE BAGA ARE NATURAL BADASSES

"I am a natural badass," Flea said. "I'll fight in the ring."

The Hebbut chuckled. "Can you win?"

"Define 'win,'" Flea said.

"Kill your opponent."

Flea didn't precisely like killing people for no reason. "How about I just make it so they can't fight back?"

Loog cocked his head in confusion. "You mean kill them?"

"No, I mean *disable* them."

"Kill them," Loog agreed.

Damn the Hebbut and their brick-stupid assumptions. Flea waved it off. "There's more than one way to descale a Dhasha. You'll see. Where do I sign up for the ring?"

Loog grunted and thrust a sign-up form at him. "Oh, and they'll wanna shave one wingtip, make sure you stay and fight."

Flea, who was already starting to sign, hesitated. "Say what?"

"Wouldn't want you flying away," Loog said. "Would give you an unfair advantage." He shrugged. "Not my rules. Marshi's pretty strict about fliers. Kroeg can't fly."

Mandibles still open, Flea pressed the button on his charm.

Immediately, he was overwhelmed by a searing flash of his immediate choices and their repercussions...

Option B3a) Spit on Loog for trying to deceive him, then escape: **page 100**

Option B3X2) Stall and hope someone else volunteers: **page 109**

Option B3X3) Fight in the death pit anyway, wings be damned! **page 169**

OR RETURN TO THE RECRUITMENT CENTER: **page 54**

OPTION B3X2

THERE MUST BE ANOTHER WAY...

Flea was staring at Loog, strongly considering sticking him for not making that clear earlier, *before* he'd started to sign his life away, when a young Huouyt burst through the door. "Squader Loog," the three-legged Huouyt snapped, "I've been sent by Commander Halperi."

"Hey Ka'neth," Loog said, without looking up from his vidscreen.

The Huouyt—who had a small star, one of those ones that, if Flea grew a head out of his ass, would have three fewer points than his legs and heads—brushed Flea out of the way dismissively, his full attention on the Hebbut. "According to our records for the last three turns, you haven't sent a *single* recruit up to the station." He glanced around at the dusty room. "Congressional algorithms put this as a *hotbed* for recruiting. The inhabitants are miserable. Their food is rationed. They have no entertainment. They live in shacks with hardened criminals. They're looking for *any* way out. What have you been *doing* down here?"

"Marshi made her and Commander Halperi's wager all legal-like, so Marshi won't let me into her town unless I have one of my champions beat her champion," Loog said, with a big Hebbut shrug. He continued to watch his match.

The Huouyt's slit of a mouth fell open. "We've sent you *six*!"

Loog shrugged again. "It's Kroeg."

The Huouyt's big, reflective blue-white eyes scowled back at Loog. "What is Kroeg?"

"That's the name of their champion," Loog said. "She's big."

"Big means nothing in a fight," the Huouyt Small Commander said.

Loog looked over the much smaller Huouyt, whose pale skin and two tentacle arms were writhing with tiny white cilia, then snorted and went back to his wrestling match.

"This is a Congressional-owned planet," the Huouyt snapped. "Marshi can't stop us from recruiting here."

"Probably not," Loog said. "Marshi's pretty small. Kroeg can, though. Oh, and the security turrets they've got on those towers. She said I leave the recruitment station before we've beat her champion and she shoots us. Same goes for anyone who tries to walk up here—they get shot. And he's not joking, 'cause some have tried. Heads explode. *Pop.*" Loog made a big motion with his hands. "You see those skeletons on the road out there? Pop, *pop.*"

"Oh for the ghosts'—" the Small Commander stopped and squinted at Flea. "Who the hell are you?"

Flea gave him his blankest, buggiest-eyed stare.

"Merciful dead, I'm surrounded by jenfurgling leafcutters. Where's the sign-up form? *I'll* do it." He reached out and yanked the paperwork out from under Flea's foot, then squinted at the list. "Who the hell is 'Fl'? It says they signed this morning."

Loog raised an arm and pointed at Flea, who cocked his head up at the Huouyt Small Commander with the dumbest, most furglike expression he could manage.

"Oh for the love of—" The Congie scratched out the start of Flea's name and put down his own. He tossed that back at Loog. "There. Get Marshi on the line and tell her I'm coming down to put an end to this. That squirrely Ueshi shit has delayed as long as she's going to get."

"Commander Halperi *did* make that bet with her." Flea could tell that the Hebbut was enjoying the Huouyt's frustration. "And just like she promised, her champion hasn't lost. She's got lawyers saying the planet's all hers until Halperi can deliver a worthwhile opponent."

"We'll see about that," the Huouyt said. "Call her."

Loog grunted and reached for a comm. He connected, then said, "Marshi? Yeah, I got another one. What, no, not the bug. Commander Ka'neth himself. Yeah, he knows it's no rules."

But Flea was watching the Huouyt, finding something oddly familiar about him. He crawled up onto the ceiling to get a better look, expecting the sudden movement to make the Huouyt flinch, but it didn't even look Flea's direction. Seeing that, Flea began getting weird tingles of unease about Ka'neth. It was rumored that Jer'ait had killed off the entire city of Va'ga in order to escape his training, having no mercy for students, teachers, or bystander staff alike, but since then, the city had recovered and was once again producing assassins, albeit lesser-quality ones. *Those* were easy to spot, because they sucked, and they were getting picked off like lice wherever they went.

But this one was different. He was good. *Very* good. And, if it hadn't been for the 'Merciful dead' comment—and the way he'd shown absolutely no fear of Flea—Flea would have missed it. Even though his expressions and body demeanor showed frustration and aggression, his eyes were totally flat, giving nothing away except what he wanted the Hebbut to see—a young, indignant, arrogant Huouyt Small Commander that was way too proud of his greasy assignment in the middle of nowhere.

But the Hebbut obviously wasn't seeing what Flea was seeing. He was busy discussing a wager on whether or not the Huouyt would win against the town champion.

"She doesn't like the idea of Kroeg going up against a Huouyt," Loog said to the Small Commander. "She says no shape-changing and no weapons. You pick a form and fight in it, no changes."

The Huouyt bowed in acquiescence.

"He says he's good with that." Loog cocked his head. "Yeah, it's sanctioned. Halperi sent him down here. There will be no retaliation if he dies."

Listening to that, Flea's mind was going dozens of marches a tic. With the glaring exception of the Peacemaster Jer'ait Ze'laa, Va'gans were mercenaries, so Small Commander Ka'neth was probably dead or tucked away somewhere.

Which meant there was an agent of evil on this planet, and it was Flea's job as an agent of chaos to follow him and figure out who he was working for, then decide whether or not to stop him. Which meant, should spying on him fail, he would have to interrogate him.

Working for Forgotten was *fun*!

Loog put down the receiver. "She says you can come in. Match is in four hours. Might want to settle your affairs first."

Ka'neth snorted with typical Huouyt arrogance. "That won't be necessary," he said to Loog. "If anyone goes looking for me, I'll be in the town. I hear the bartender on this planet's decent." The Huouyt turned and walked out.

Before he could get away, Flea pressed the top button of the charm. Instantly, three options blazed new pathways through Flea's mind...

Option B3c1) Flea spits on the assassin, because Va'gans are arrogant pricks: **page 131**
Option B3c2) Flea interrogates the assassin at the first opportunity: **page 165**
Option B3c3) Flea follows the assassin at a distance in the hopes he will lead Flea to his evil cabal: **page 199**

OR RETURN TO PREVIOUS CHOICES: **page 99**

OPTION 3, CONTINUED

APOLOGIES ONLY GET YOU SO FAR...

Flea spent the next few hours in a stuffy, airless sack. It probably would have killed a lesser species, but the Baga were innately superior, and thus mostly immune to that sort of thing. Still, when they finally dumped him out onto the prison warden's desk, Flea was ready to spit at the first thing that moved.

He didn't, though, because he had this weird feeling that Spitting Was Bad. Maybe it was the way the last option to spit had left him getting shoved out an airlock, but it almost like it felt like something deeper, like the warning had come from someone very important.

...like maybe the same person who had given him the charm?

That thought made him hesitate as the violet-clad Ueshi clinking with ruvmestin jewelry came into focus from where she dubiously peered at him behind her desk, surrounded by her three big Ooreiki thugs, Flea hesitated.

"Here's his IOU, Marshi," the Ueshi pilot said, holding out the document to show to the Ueshi, who looked more interested in petting her indifferent, spotted green-and-red torrak. "Five million credits!"

The torrak, meanwhile, was taking an unhealthy interest in Flea's presence, lifting its head and wing-casings in an aggressive stance. Flea skittered to the side uncomfortably.

"I'd be buying him more for the exotic value than anything," the Ueshi said, still squinting at Flea. "He couldn't lift a pick if his life depended on it, so I wouldn't be able to get a return on his contract by putting him in the mines." She squinted at Flea, still petting her agitated torrak. "Are you *sure* it's sentient? It looks like an ugly version of Peg, here." Marshi continued to pet her little monster, which did not look *anything* like Flea, because it had a sloping, inbred face and a *polka-dotted* carapace. How she could overlook something so obvious made him buzz his wings in irritation.

At Flea's wing-buzz, the Ueshi's pet lunged to its feet and screamed, "*Triggit*!" It flared its sail, showing a pattern resembling the pretty huge-tailed blue birds that Flea had seen on Earth. "Herble triggit!"

The Ueshi sighed and lifted the torrak up to one of her Ooreiki goons. "Here, take him for lunch. The little cretin is upsetting my baby."

"Triggit," the torrak muttered, now hanging docilely under the arm of an Ooreiki, still watching Flea as the goon carried him away.

Flea bit down the urge to spit. He was, after all, here to infiltrate an assassins' den to save Joe and couldn't go around spitting if he wanted to keep his cover. But he wanted to. Badly. In her *eye*.

To distract himself, Flea tried to think of who had the capability to build something like his charm. It had to be someone who knew the future, but all he could think of was a Trith. The answer felt like it was tugging at the tips of his antennae, almost like it was a huge ship looming inside the dust cloud of his mind, its shape *almost* tangible, but intentionally obscured by a dark, glistening, formless mass…

Forgotten!

As soon as he had the realization, Flea's wing-casings tightened on his carapace in nervousness. He remembered the chaos of Neskfaat and the panicked reshuffling of Congress following it. He remembered how Forgotten—the *master* of Chaos—had orchestrated the ascendance of two of Flea's three groundmates to bigwiggery in Koliinaat. And even *Joe*, a weak and squishy biped, had become a huge hero to the Ground Force, with his famous, greasy Human face on propaganda posters in recruitment centers across the known galaxy afterwards, regardless of planet or species. Flea had honestly felt a little left out.

Was this finally Forgotten giving *Flea* his chance at greatness?

His chance to become a *secret agent of Chaos*?!!

"So," the Ueshi said, leaning forward and steepling her hands on the surface of the table, oblivious to Flea's awesome revelation. "I hear you were in Planetary Ops. Can you fight?"

"Can I *fight*?" Flea snorted. "Does a miga have wet, greasy eyes?"

The Ueshi glanced at the three Ooreiki behind her, who shrugged. Turning back, the Ueshi said, "I… assume so?"

"I was on *Neskfaat*," Flea blurted. "I survived because—"

"Was that before or after the war?" the Ueshi said tiredly, as if she had heard the claim a thousand times before.

Flea straightened indignantly. "It was *during*."

Marshi gave a light chuckle, an irritating nasal sound that made Flea want to plug her nostrils.

But behind her, Marshi's Ooreiki thugs started laughing like that was *the funniest* thing they'd ever heard, guffawing loudly and holding their stomachs, making his carapace vibrate with the sound of their chortles. Flea's mandibles twitched as he scowled at them.

"It's really not funny," Marshi said, her men going silent with a simple flash of her palm. "And if I had a credit for every time some criminal or conman insisted they had been on Neskfaat during the war, or that they knew Commander Zero, or that their best friend was the Peacemaster, I could build myself a mansion." She hesitated, glancing around at the opulent building around her with faux surprise. "Oh, wait. I already have."

"It was *during*," Flea muttered.

"Uh-huh." Fiddling with a ruvmestin paperweight—for some reason, ruvmestin paperweights seemed to be popular with criminal overlords and rich wardens of miserable prison planets—she returned her attention to the Ueshi pilot and said, "Look. Soreet. My guys are in need of a good match, someone I can pit against the town champion and make those idiots placing bets actually wonder if she's gonna lose. As it is, I don't think purchasing this IOU really gains me anything." She slid it back across the table towards the Ueshi.

The pilot's head-frill trembled a bit. "But…There were *costs*!"

"Uh-huh. *How* much space did he take up inside that crate in your hold, did you say?"

"One of my men needed surgery!" the spacer captain cried.

"Then he was clumsy," Marshi said. "But if you insist, I'll give you three hundred credits for the IOU."

"But—" The space captain hesitated at the way the three Ooreiki thugs started to move closer, hands moving noticeably closer to the weapons on their sides. "Uh…yeah, maybe his ticket wasn't worth all that much anyway."

"Indeed." Marshi made a dismissive gesture with her near-translucent hand. "One of my men will see you properly compensated for your time." She nodded at the Ooreiki closest to her, who immediately came around the desk and put a big, tentacle arm on the Ueshi's narrow shoulder. "So do you want those on a chip or over the waves…?" he asked the much smaller creature, as they wandered off.

"And the rest of you, stop *hovering*," Marshi said. "Go find that thief who raided my pantry and cut off his hand or something." She made another dismissive gesture.

"But boss," one of the Ooreiki behind her complained, "what if he tries to hurt you?"

"*Look* at him," Marshi snapped, gesturing contemptuously at Flea. "*How* is he going to hurt me, again?"

Flea could think of about two dozen different ways, but he kept them carefully to himself as he sat there, motionless, on her desk, his best bug-eyed stupid Grekkon expression on his face that he could manage.

The Ooreiki looked like it wanted to argue, but after staring at Flea and Flea staring motionlessly back, he clasped his hands in acquiescence and waddled off to go do something more thuggish.

"So let me get this straight," Marshi said, once Flea was left to face her alone. "You fell in with Moxi, and instead of taking a couple of feet, Moxi stuffed you in a box and sent you to me." She cocked her head at him, her face and body totally at ease, but her eyes much too alert. "*What's* your name again?"

Realizing that someone had tried to *kill* him at Moxi's, and that he was now on the planet from whence the assassins had originated, Flea cocked his head like a torrak and said, "Neskfaat?"

"No, your *name*," she said irritatedly.

"Traxxalihania," he said, intentionally making it impossible for the Ueshi to understand half the Bagan syllables, which included wingbeats and clicks.

The Ueshi made a face. "You got a nickname?"

Flea cocked his head in his impression of vermin stupidity. "Nickname? What means this word?"

"Ugh!" Marshi snapped. "Never mind. I'm sending you to the ring. You win, I tear up your IOU. You lose, you die. Oh, and we'll clip your wings so you can't escape. Sound good?"

Realizing he *really* wanted to spit at her and that, as Forgotten's newly-dubbed agent of chaos, this was as good a time as any to use one of his wishes because maybe he was missing something, Flea pushed the button on his charm.

Immediately, three new pathways blazed through his mind, illuminating his future in disturbing detail…

Option 3a) Flea spits at Marshi, because she was petting a torrak: **page 122**
Option 3b) Flea mentions his important friends, because their names will bring clarity to the situation: **page 125**
Option 3c) Flea agrees to fight, if only to get out of a room that smells of the sex hormones of a disgusting polka-dot torrak: **page 169**

OR RETURN TO PREVIOUS CHOICES: **page 47**

OPTION 3A

FLEA SPITS, BECAUSE SPITTING IS FUN.

Anyone who willingly touched a torrak in rut definitely had a few bolts loose, and Flea had always been a proponent of tightening loose parts with glue.

So, calmly taking aim at her eye while Marshi calmly watched him back, Flea spat.

Instead of traveling to its intended victim, the glue smacked against an invisible barrier on the desk with him, separating him and Marshi. When Flea took a closer look, it was some sort of electrostatic shield that extended subtly around and behind the desk, creating almost a booth for Marshi to sit behind. Even then, his glue was bubbling down the surface to dribble into a sizzling, smoking mass on the surface of the desk.

"I see," Marshi said. "Guns?"

Flea frowned. *Guns*? What gu—

Seemingly out of nowhere, four huge autoturrets rose from hidden flaps in the floor and ceiling, and swiveled to face Flea, their tips crackling with blue-white energy. Desperate, Flea started jabbing his button, trying to figure out how to get free.

"You have exactly four autoturrets aimed at your face," his charm said, when he jammed the wrong side. *"Surely this wasn't worthy of my attention."*

Marshi yawned, already getting out of her chair. "On second thought, you wouldn't be worth a bag of sand in the ring, anyway. Too small. Crowd can't see your moves. Would only be good for comedic effect, as Kroeg hops around trying to stomp on you." She gestured at the turrets. "Fire."

Flea, already knowing what was coming, lunged off the table at full speed—

The burning started in his klett and less than an instant after that initial agony, Flea was no more.

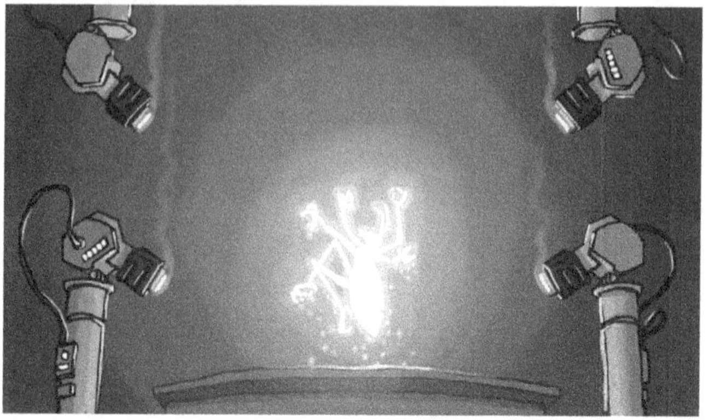

END IT HERE

or

RETURN TO YOUR CHOICES: **page 47**

OPTION 3B

FLEA TELLS HIS LIFE STORY, BECAUSE MARSHI LOOKS LIKE A GOOD LISTENER...

Flea decided he was tired of playing dumb. *So* tired. *Nobody* in this universe appreciated just how hard his life really was. Even when presented with his greatest acts of heroism, they would merely blow it off as a fluke, like he was actually some agent of chaos, determined to bring civilization down around him or something, and his heroics were merely a situational accident.

Which was *so* not true. Flea didn't want the entire *civilization* to crumble, just *pieces* of it. Mainly the pieces of it he happened to be wandering around in at the time.

So, armed with this heavy knowledge, Flea said, "It's hard to be me."

Marshi, who was looking as if the matter were sealed and he were about to calmly go flitting off to die in the gladiatorial pit because she said so, paused. "Excuse me?"

"It's *hard*," Flea said. "I mean, I was *on* that mission that saved the world on Neskfaat. *I* lured Prince Bagkhal into that pit. I was *part* of that shake-up in the Regency that ended with Rri'jan Ze'laa losing his Tribunal seat to a Jreet. I was *there*. I played major parts. And what kind of acknowledgement do I get from the world?"

When Marshi just narrowed her wet Ueshi eyes at him, Flea vehemently said, "None!" He made a cutting gesture with his hands. "I get cast aside! Forgotten!"

Then it occurred to him that maybe that's why Forgotten had chosen him as a secret agent. After all, he went unnoticed in most places, able to be overlooked and underestimated. The perfect spy for the Master of Chaos.

Huh, Flea thought. *Maybe he did have a plan, after all...*

"You were there, huh?" Marshi said, jolting him back out of his reverie. She had a narrow look on her greasy face that Flea did not like. "Mind if I check that?"

Flea snorted and gestured dismissively. "Go ahead. It's all in my file. Chip Number AGENT666FLEA." After Neskfaat, he had bribed the three-man Jahul chipping crew to re-chip him with something more fitting of his status as an agent of chaos than some arbitrary number he couldn't understand or remember. Flea had originally offered dozens and dozens of credits, but the Jahul had been so awed when they looked up his file that they'd done it for free, as long as he posed on each of their heads for a picture for their kids.

But that seemed to make Marshi's face darken even more. Like she didn't believe him. They *never* believed him. "Yeah, let me just check that…" She pulled her datapad across her desk and started tapping in an entry.

Because he knew what Marshi would find, Flea said, "I'm actually here because someone's trying to kill my friend Joe." Then, when she just lifted a brow at him, he added imperiously, "You know… *Commander Zero*?"

"It *does* say you were there," she said, sounding satisfyingly shocked. "Sins of the saints," she cried, staring at the screen in obvious awe. "A Congressional hero. *Here*. In my very *office*."

Gratified, Flea puffed up and raised his wing-casings a little. "I wasn't going to say anything, but I've had so many people blow me off I just got sick of it," Flea said.

"It says here you actually earned a *kasja* by killing a Dhasha *prince*." More awe poured off of her sticky Ueshi face, and Flea felt almost heady with the respect he was finally receiving, almost twenty turns after the fact.

"I did," Flea said. "That was only my first one. I got another when I helped Zero take out Prime Sentinel Raavor ga Aez when he—"

"We won't be needing *this*," the Ueshi said, picking up his holoparch IOU and ripping it in half, her head-frill trembling in excitement. "What kind of sand-loving *crap* was that, anyway? Five million credits for a ride in a *crate*?"

Flea snorted. "I know, right?" According to his charm, he could have bought the *ship* for that much.

Throwing the sizzling IOU aside, she cried, "We need to get you something to *drink*!" She pressed an intercom button and said, "*Hwill, get this Baga something to drink!*"

Flea, who seemed to have an immunity to most liquors, toxins, and other drugs that most species used recreationally to relax, started to say he wasn't really interested, when an Ooreiki with a flat, unnerving expression stepped into the room with them. The odd stare—which reminded him way too much of Jer'ait for his liking—pulled him far enough out of his pride that he actually took a nervous step backwards.

"Enjoy," the Ooreiki said, setting a bowl of amber liquid under his face.

That's a Huouyt, he thought, watching the Ooreiki nervously. He might not have the same 'spidey senses', as Joe called them, but it was easy enough for Flea to notice a *bad* assassin when he saw one. It was too…creepy. It hadn't yet mastered the art of social camouflage.

"Drink up," Marshi said, her sea-blue eyes flat.

Flea got the carapace-crawling realization that it wasn't a request. He took another step backwards. "Hey, I…"

He bumped into a Hebbut, who had stepped into the room behind him, its pot belly right up against the desk itself. "Now?" it asked.

"Now," Marshi said.

Something sharp punctured his carapace from above, then deflated him as it went straight through to the other side, ramming home into the desk, pinning him in place.

"Oh *come on*," Marshi cried, jumping up. "I said to *skewer* him, not *maul* my *desk*!"

The Ooreiki grunted and yanked, and Flea came off the desk, squirming on what felt like a blade. "So you want him in the head room or the hand room?" the big Hebbut grunted. Then he cocked his head down at Flea, who was desperately trying to get his spitter pointed at an eye. Almost curiously, the Hebbut said, "And you want me to dehydrate him first or just toss him up on the wall with the rest?"

"Definitely dehydrate him," Marshi said. "Don't want him starting to stink up my collection."

"Okay, Boss," the Hebbut said. Then, without another word, Flea got marched from the room and into a nearby room with a big, lidded vat in its center.

"Okay, little dude," the Hebbut drawled. "Sorry, but this is gonna sting a little." He pried off the top of the vat.

Instantly, Flea smelled the overpowering aroma of Bantonax, the moisture superconductor.

"Hey, wait!" Flea cried, as the Hebbut lifted him out over the vat—he was on a *spear*, he realized—where Flea could see the barrel of white, fluffy nannite mix rolling with the air currents. "I can pay!"

"Boss pays," the Hebbut said, then plunged him, spear and everything, into the mix. Flea's last thought was, *Ha! Little does he know that a Baga's carapace is utterly moisture proo—*

END IT HERE

or

GO BACK TO YOUR CHOICES: **page 121**

OPTION B3C1

FLEA SPITS, BECAUSE THE HEBBUT NEEDS TO KNOW HE'S DEALING WITH AN IMPOSTOR

Flea waited until the Huouyt's front foot was contacting the floor of the exit, then spat, gluing him into place. "That's not your Small Commander!" Flea cried. "He's an assassin. He's with the Trith!"

"He's what?" Loog was reluctantly turning from his wrestling match when the Va'gan whipped out a small handgun that had been hidden under his shirt, and, with very little hesitation, began firing at Flea.

Flea skittered out of reach and spat back, fusing the gun to his hand.

Then the Ooreiki pulled out *their* guns and started yelling—yelling at Flea, yelling at Loog, who was reaching for an enormous laser rifle under the desk—and, with Flea randomly spitting into the center of them, the whole room became an explosion of chaos.

Flea took the moment to exit through an open window, gaining the high ground.

Not a moment later, the polymer roof erupted in a spray of plasma…which dislodged a cluster of little blue Baga-shaped creatures from the roofing. Flea skittered backwards as they all went tumbling into the gaping hole the weapons-fire had made, screaming something that sounded like, "*Herble triggit*!" as they plunged into the room below.

Immediately from below, Flea heard screams, then more weapons-fire. He skittered even further up the room, onto the ridge.

"Torrak!" the Ooreiki were shouting. "Torrak, run!"

Then all eight of them—Flea was pretty sure it was eight, but he counted the hypothetical head out his ass anyway—went barreling from the building below.

"He's an assassin!" Flea shouted at the loudest setting his translator would allow. "He's a Va'gan Huouyt!"

On the ground, the Hebbut was giving Ka'neth a measuring glance.

"So when are you going to kill Joe?" Flea demanded. He spat at the assassin, fusing one of his three tentacle legs to the reddish stone. "Where's the Trith? Did you already kill Small Commander Ka'neth?! Where's the assassination planned?!"

Loog was blinking at the Huouyt assassin. "You're an assassin?" he said, with about the same mental dexterity as a glacier. "But you came down in the ship..."

The assassin sloughed off the piece of flesh that Flea had glued and, giving the Hebbut an exasperated look, reached out and grabbed him by the arm.

The Hebbut's eyes went wide only a moment before he collapsed into a pile in the orange dust. Even from this distance, Flea heard him say, "No one said there was a Jreet-loving Baga already on this planet."

"*I say we let Klick take care of him,*" Flea heard a voice say. "*Though I've got a decent shot, if you want me to take him out.*"

The assassin peered up at Flea, who had immediately begun dodging and weaving on the hot roofing. "No, he said something about the Trith. We need to bring him in, see what he knows."

"Ha!" Flea shouted. "Good luck with that, greaser!" He launched into the air, aiming to get as much altitude as possible so whoever had a bead on him had to look at the sun through the dust-haze to take their shot.

He'd gotten maybe a few million marches before something fast and black hit him from the side like a cannonball. Flea felt the air leave him in a startled *whoosh* as his attacker barreled them back towards the ground, its legs clamped around his wingcases.

No, not 'it'. *Her*.

Another Baga, and not a sterile one, at that. He could smell the overpowering pheromones of a virgin queen even as she was driving him into the earth at approximately the speed of sound.

"Wait!" Flea cried, seeing her black wing-covers. The smell of her was so heady it was making it hard for him to think. "I'm a Congie!"

"Sure you are," she growled, still hanging on. "Don't worry. It'll be over soon."

Flea got a wing loose and started to change their trajectory, grappling with her as they continued their descent, but it wasn't going to be enough.

Because she was driving him towards the ground and the waiting Ooreiki, and because Flea wasn't going to be able to gain altitude before they grabbed him, Flea pressed his button.

Instantly, three options played out in his head, searing their paths into his brain in a blinding rush…

Option B3c1a) Flea spits at the princess: **page 135**
Option B3c1b) Flea tells the princess she looks familiar…: **page 140**
Option B3c1c) Flea finds a way to escape her hold: **page 157**

OPTION B3C1A

FLEA SPITS AT THE PRINCESS, FOR PRINCESSES APPRECIATE THAT SORT OF THING...

With the Bagan princess clinging to his carapace, clamping down on his wing-casings, driving them towards the ground as her mere presence overwhelmed his baser instincts, Flea panicked and started spitting. Too late, he realized it was the *instinctual* kind of spitting...

"What the—" the princess cried, blindly trying to pull away from him, but failing. "Did you *seriously* just—"

And then, in a moment of horror, Flea realized he had used the time-tested technique to subdue a hormone-crazed queen in her mating flight…by fusing them together at the crotch. "Uh," he said, "sorry, I, uh…"

"You disgusting *insect*!" she screamed. And then she was buzzing her wings, trying to rip away from her, which happened to take them skyward again. Because that was the opposite direction of the ground—and therefore the Ooreiki waiting with guns—Flea obliged her, adding his wingbeats to hers, much like the crazed pirouettes in the final stages of a mating dance….

"Don't you *dare*," she snapped, grabbing him and leaning forward and levering her snipping mandibles around one of his eyes. "Don't even *think* about it."

"Not thinking about it," Flea babbled, as his eye picked up mandible on all sides. "*Really* not thinking about it." Even though he *was* thinking about it, because one of the side-effects of fusing one's crotch to another's crotch was that they became the same crotch.

And, now that he was getting a *very* good look at her face through the uncomfortable frame of a set of mandibles, Flea had a startling realization. "Wait. *Klick*? As in *Rat's groundteam* Klick?"

"Ugh!" the princess screamed. She steered them up to a rocky ridge, where Flea thought he spotted a red-orange shape shift momentarily before the princess hurled them down amongst the towering rocks. Immediately upon landing, something big and colored like an orange boulder grabbed Flea by the head and slammed him to the stone.

"Which one's which?!" a gruff Human voice demanded.

"Get him *off* me!" the princess screamed, writhing. "Use your knife! Quick! Before he has a chance to finish it!"

"I'm not going to—" Flea started.

A big gloved fist immediately punched him to the ground, cutting off the rest of what Flea was going to say.

"Hold on," a Human said, from somewhere in the hologram of the boulder. Flea had only enough time to realize he recognized the voice before he heard the sudden sizzle of a laser scalpel, then he was being dragged inside the hologram, and he was looking up at an angry Human woman with a knife who was none-too-gently prying them apart with the blistering edge of her blade.

"Ow!" Flea cried, sucking in his gut as the sizzling knife slid down between them, cutting them apart at the waist. "Ow, ow, ow, *ow*!" Then he was being tugged away from the princess and shoved flat against the stone, a heavy Congie boot pressed hard on his spitter.

"You hurt?" the Human asked. She was not asking Flea.

"I'm fine," the princess said, sounding shaken. "The leafmunch asher."

Over the comm, he heard, "*Is Klick okay?*"

"She's fine," the Human said. "Just shaken up.

"Wait," he said, giving a little start as he realized what duo was assaulting him. "Rat? *And* Klick? You're both *here*?" They were two members of the only other groundteam to survive Neskfaat with him and Zero...only to supposedly go rogue and die assaulting Representative Mekkval's deep den soon thereafter. Which Flea had always thought stank like flake. "You're working for Mekkval now, aren't you?!"

Crouching above him, Rat's expressive Human face darkened. "Yeah, I think I'm just going to shoot him so he doesn't endanger the op," Rat said into her comm, reaching for one of the plasma pistols on her hip.

"Wait!" Flea cried. "I'm Flea. Zero's groundmate. We partied together after Neskfaat."

"Got enough to worry about with that Trith running around—" Then Rat, who had been talking into the comm, froze. "*Flea*?"

"Wait, so you're here to save Zero, too?" Flea demanded.

But she seemed more angry than anything else. "What in the burning ash are you *doing* here, Flea?"

And Flea, because he recognized that dangerous tenseness to the Human's face, that look Joe got whenever he was about to kill something he thought might not actually deserve it, decided it was an excellent time to use his charm. He reached for the device dangling from his neck...

"*Bomb*!" Klick cried, scuttling away from him.

Flea flinched, turning to her and holding out the blinking charm. "Wait, no, it's—" Flea had only a moment to realize that laser knife in Rat's hand and coming down at his head before he had the odd sensation of bouncing against the rocks and boulders, completely free, rolling like a ball, before he tumbled off the edge of the cliff and went sailing into eternity.

END IT HERE

or

RETURN TO YOUR CHOICES: **page 134**

OPTION B3C1B

FLEA REALIZES HE KNOWS HER FROM SOMEWHERE...

"Wait," Flea said, as the Bagan princess drove him towards the ground. "Don't I know you?"

"Not likely," she said, all business. She was keeping them on a crater-making course towards the recruitment center, which was at the end of the road that terminated at the airport, set apart from the village itself. Now that Flea was getting a good look, there really *were* autoturrets posted all over the town, especially over by the mine, aimed outward from the huge metal doors planted into the side of a rocky, cliff-covered mountain. Cliffs surrounded them on all sides, the town having been built inside a depression in the dusty orange rock. As they hurtled towards the ground, spinning, he caught sight of a lone, run-down comm station clinging to the top of the cliff-face the only structure Flea could see outside the town.

Wow, Flea thought, seeing the rocky clusters on all sides, *that* would *be a good place for a sniper*...Had it been

Joe hiding up in those boulders, he could have wiped out the entire *town* before anyone figured out where he was.

Thinking of Joe made Flea remember where he had seen this particular Baga before.

"Hey, I *do* know you!" Flea cried. "You're Klick! From Rat's team. You don't remember me? I'm Flea! Commander Zero's groundmate. We partied together after Neskfaat."

The Baga, who had been seemingly intent on driving them into the stone, jerked and brought them into a hover. "Flea?"

"So wait," Flea said, glancing down at the Huouyt and the six 'Ooreiki' beneath them. "Is that Sol'dan? Is Rat and Benva around here, too?"

Klick released him and buzzed backwards, until they came to an even hover and were able to see each other clearly. "Flea, are you *part* of this?" she sounded stricken.

"Part of what?" Flea asked. "Someone's trying to kill Joe. I'm here to stop it."

Klick blinked at him, sounding confused. "Kill… *Joe*…? He's here, too?"

"No, but there's a Trith working on—"

"Shhh!" Klick cried, slapping her front foot over Flea's mandibles. "Do you know where he is?"

Flea frowned. "Joe's already on the planet?"

Klick blinked at him, then glanced to the rocky outcroppings around them. "Come on," she said. "We need to get out of sight so we can talk."

"Pretty sure there's torrak all over the planet," Flea said, finding her anxiety suspicious. "If anyone sees us, they won't think anything of it."

"No, *listen*," Klick said. "There's a Trith on this planet. It can see the *future*. All it has to do is look out the window and if it *sees* us, it's going to see what we plan to *do* to it. Let's *go*." She grabbed him and tugged him towards the cliffs, giving him the choice of either being dragged or spitting on her.

Since it was *incredibly* rude to spit on a virgin queen—so culturally heinous that the spitter could actually be brought up on sexual assault charges—Flea let her drag him to a cluster of rocks overlooking the town.

Immediately upon landing, the boulder reached out and grabbed him. As Flea screamed and twisted to spit, something heavy slammed down on his klett and the barrel of a Huouyt-made Rodemax came to rest against his braincase. "Don't."

Recognizing Rat's voice, Flea swallowed hard and said, "Okay." He still couldn't see Rat through the hologram that the assassin's gun was projecting around her.

"How much did you hear?" Klick asked the Human.

"Enough," Rat said. To Flea, she said, "Is Zero here?"

"No way," Flea cried. "Somebody here's gonna kill him, and I've got to stop it!" Then he froze. "*You're* here to kill Zero, aren't you?"

"Don't be stupid," Rat said.

"You said something about a Trith," Klick insisted. "Where's the Trith? We've been here for three weeks and can't find it. We know it went down *to* the planet, and it hasn't come back *off* the planet because there's been no ships travelling back and forth."

"There was a Ueshi freighter," Flea said.

Rat scoffed. "Yeah, and it's in lockdown in the belly of a Congressional supertanker right now. *Nobody's* going on or coming off that ship until we figure out where the Trith is and kill it."

Flea glanced at Klick. "I can help."

"Yeah, before we go there, let's just back up a second," Rat said, still holding the gun tight to his head. "*Why* did you say you're on this planet again, Baga?"

"I, uh…" Flea remembered quite clearly that he wasn't supposed to name-drop, and he assumed it was probably a bad idea to tell an assassin who worked for Representative Mekkval—who had a personal vendetta against Forgotten—about the Geuji's involvement in sending him here. "I got attacked by some guys in a casino. Jer'ait told me they belonged to a mercenary group called the Shard, and that I could find them here."

"What's that got to do with Joe and a Trith?" Rat demanded warily.

"I've been listening in the shadows, talking to people," Flea said. "You'll be surprised at how much a Baga can learn when he puts his mind to it."

The gun reluctantly lifted from his head and the hologram came down, revealing Joe's former groundmate in camouflaged desert-colored gear. Rat glanced at Klick. "Actually, no, I wouldn't."

"What's that blinking thing around your neck?" Klick demanded. "It looks like a bomb."

Flea froze, trying to figure out how to explain Forgotten's device without revealing it came from the Geuji. "It's to help me with numbers," Flea said. When Klick just gave him a skeptical look, he said, "I'll show you. Rat, how much did your gun cost?"

"More than you will ever have or understand," Rat said, pulling it away from him warily.

"Come on, humor me," Flea said.

"My *boots* cost twelve thousand three hundred credits," Rat said. "I'm not telling you what my gun cost."

Flea pushed the can's bottom button. Immediately, the device said, *"Rat's boots cost the equivalent of six tickets to the Core and back."*

Flea felt his mandibles fall open. "No *way*." He immediately moved forward, to get a better look at what kind of footwear could possibly be worth that much.

"Back off," Rat growled, raising one desert-colored boot in warning.

"So you're here to stop the Shard, too?" Flea said, examining her boot anyway. He could see several slots for weapons and hidden electronics that most Human boots didn't have. Skittering up her leg and onto her shoulder—stopping only long enough to take the laser knife from her pocket and sliding it under a wing casing—he said, "I would've thought Mekkval would be the kind of guy to *hire* these guys..."

Rat snorted, but didn't brush him off her shoulder. "Not a chance. The Shard's got its fingers in every pie in Congress, pulling Representatives' strings like puppets. Mekkval's trying to put an end to that, to put the integrity back into politics."

"Or at least his nephew is," Klick said. As she spoke, Flea couldn't help but notice how utterly *sleek* and *sexy* the other Baga was as she cleaned dust from her wing casing with one leg. "He's the one who sent us." She started cleaning the other wing casing, stretching the leg facing him out to its fullest, then sliding it back up the ribbed carapace once more. Working discreetly for Representative Mekkval must have been good to her, because Klick looked *good*...

"Flea?" Klick stopped cleaning herself.

Shaking himself to get back on task, Flea rewound Klick's words and remembered Keval from hunting down Prime Sentinel Ravvor ga Aez with Joe fifteen turns ago.

"Keval wouldn't have sent us without his prince's permission," Rat said. Flea thought that was a little naïve, but Humans struck him as naïve creatures in general. Not as stupid as a Hebbut, but not much smarter, either.

Apparently, Klick was thinking the same thing, because the look she gave Flea—readable only to another Baga—was akin to a Human eye-roll.

"Anyway," Klick said, "looks like we're on the same page, so why don't we join forces? We could use another eye in the sky."

Flea, knowing that he was going to about to make a decision that would probably help or hinder his hunt for Joe's assassin, pressed *both* buttons on the can, to keep the others from realizing what the device was really for. Immediately, the can said, *"A 'force' can be any number of people, machines, or other object, being, or animal gathered together with a similar goal. In this instance, it means joining Rat and her team, whose visible number has thus far been three, making the total 'force' four, which is approximately the same as a standard Congressional groundteam if a Dhasha ate two of its members.*

At the exact same time, three blinding possibilities slammed through Flea's brain.

Option B3c1b1) Spit on Rat, because you've always wanted to: **page 147**
Option B3c1b2) Join forces with Klick, because she's hot and you can't stop looking at her. Oh, and because it's better to work with a team than it is to try to fight a Trith solo on a desert planetoid with no way out and no backup: **page 150**
Option B3c1b3) Refuse and go solo. Because: **page 154**

OR RETURN TO PREVIOUS OPTIONS: **page 134**

OPTION B3C1B1

FLEA SPITS ON RAT, BECAUSE SPITTING ON BADASS ASSASSINS IS FUN

"Wow, what a glazed look," Klick chuckled. "He couldn't even make it past *three*..."

"It's a wonder Zero was able to work with him," Rat said. "I have trouble with you, and all you can do is seven."

Flea carefully considered his options. Then, because he was this close to Rat's face—and because he'd always wanted to see what happened—Flea twisted his klett up to her ear canal and spat in it, fusing ear shut. Then he launched himself into the air before she could throw him from her shoulder as she started to scream.

He was chuckling to himself, buzzing across the landscape as fast as he could go, when a horrible burning suddenly enveloped his back half, all the way to the wings, which started to sputter. When Flea glanced back, everything from his shoulders back was gone, and his carapace was still sizzling from the round of high-grade plasma that had hit him from behind.

He had just enough time to see Rat on one knee amidst the rocks, taking aim at him, Klick watching from her shoulder, when the second blast hit him in the chest, the round simply *appearing* on him, consuming him from the neck back.

And then without wings to hold himself up, Flea began to fall, spinning as he rolled through the air, heading for the town below.

He hadn't gone more than a couple feet before the next blast hit him, and Flea's world went dark.

END IT HERE

or

BACK TO YOUR CHOICES: **page 146**

OPTION B3C1B2

SHAMELESSLY JOIN THE TEAM, BECAUSE MAYBE THEY'VE GOT FOOD...

"Wow, what a glazed look," Klick chuckled. "He couldn't even make it past *three*..."

"It's a wonder Zero was able to work with him," Rat said. "I have trouble with you, and all you can do is seven."

"For your information," Flea said, "I can count to *eight*. It's the same as if you have a head out of your ass."

Klick blinked at him as if the heavens had parted and the world suddenly made sense to her now.

Feeling totally superior in every way, Flea said, "I'll join your team."

He certainly wasn't going to give back such a cool knife, though. He launched himself off her shoulder, keeping it carefully concealed under his body as he flew down to land beside Klick.

"Good," Rat said. "Klick's been putting eyes on the insides of every single building down there, but she hasn't seen the Trith anywhere. Maybe you should go take a look, report back when you find something."

Flea considered. "Yeah, maybe. Say, you guys have any food? I don't know how long I was locked in that crate, but I'm pretty sure I haven't eaten in a couple weeks."

"There's a chow hall down there," Rat said, pointing with her gun. "Slip the cook a few credits and he'll find something you can eat. Klick got some gidha there earlier."

"I don't have a few credits," Flea said. He held up his charm. "*This* says I'm in debt for the price of a small interstellar and a medium passenger shuttle."

"It can *do* that?!" Klick cried. "Where did you *get* it?"

"Desert pawn shop," Flea said. "The guy claimed there was a genie inside, but I'm pretty sure it's just an AI."

"Whoaaaa," Klick said. "Let me try! Rat, how much do I owe you and Benva?"

"Three million, seven hundred and thirty-nine credits," Rat said. She cocked her head. "*If* you're counting that ridiculous three million credit bet you made with him on ka-par."

"He says I have to pay him if I don't want to serve him," Klick said.

"I *won* my ka-par," Flea said. "We had millions of re-matches for supremacy. I won five out of ten." He remembered the number because 'ten' was the limit that Joe would let them rematch until he started shooting them in the eyes with a slingshot every time they tried, effectively ruining the match.

Klick gave an awed girly coo and said, "You *did*?" at the same time Rat said, "That sounds like a draw to me."

"I *won*," Flea said, "all *five*. Therefore I own him."

Rat sighed and glanced at the sky. "You guys are gonna have to work that one out on your own."

Klick was still staring at him in awe. "Benva says I owe him three million. How much is that?"

Flea obligingly pushed the button.

"*You owe* half *of a small interstellar to Rat and Benva*," the device replied.

Klick immediately looked stricken. "I do?"

"Now tell her how much she owes *without* that stupid ka-par debt," Rat insisted.

"*You owe Rat and Benva approximately the cost of a de-glanded torrak*," the device said.

"Oooh," Flea cried. "They *do* that?"

"*Glaxxion is one of the top exporters of pet torrak*," the device replied. "*Unfortunately, they still have not figured out how to keep the things from breeding, therefore creating unwanted intact torrak populations on every major planet around the universe.*"

"Wow, that's a really good AI," Rat said. "*Where'd* you say you got that?"

"In a spaceport gift shop," Flea said.

Both Klick and Rat frowned. "That's not what you—"

"*Anyway*," Flea said, "let's get to work! Time to explore the town and find us a Trith! I'll be back soon…" Then he got up and buzzed out over the town before they could ask him any more questions, gleefully intent on starting his new life as a secret agent with a badass new laser knife. And maybe sneaking a gidha or two from the town cafeteria because the path of a secret agent of justice was not always the path of luxury.

CONTINUE FROM HERE: **page 205**

or

BACK TO YOUR CHOICES: **page 146**

OPTION B3C1B3

TRY YOUR LUCK ALONE. BECAUSE.

"Wow, what a glazed look," Klick chuckled. "He couldn't even make it past *three*..."

"It's a wonder Zero was able to work with him," Rat said. "I have trouble with you, and all you can do is seven."

"For your information," Flea said, "I can count to *eight*. It's the same as if you have a head out of your ass."

Klick blinked at him as if the heavens had parted and the world suddenly made sense to her now.

Feeling totally superior in every way, Flea said, "Sorry, guys. I work alone."

He flew down from Rat's shoulder to land on a nearby outcropping, her laser knife safely stowed under his body, out of sight.

Klick and Rat glanced at each other. "Yeah, uh," Rat said, "sorry, but we've gotta keep this under containment until we get that Trith. That means…" She gestured at Klick, who immediately spat, sticking Flea to the rock he was standing on. "You get to keep me company for a while."

"Ow ow ow *ow*!" Flea cried, as his right back foot became one with the stone. "Ow that *hurts*!" He was so wrapped up in trying to pull his foot away from the rock that he didn't notice it when Klick twisted her lithe klett and spat at his other one.

"*Ow*!" Flea shrieked.

A moment later, Rat was trying to seal off his spitter with a piece of wire.

"Oh *hell* no!" Flea cried. He spat at her. Repeatedly. He caught her in the face first, then, when she screamed and started flailing, he twisted and spat at Klick.

As Klick was panicking, trying to contend with the fact Flea had glued her to her perch, Flea yanked the laser knife out from under his carapace and began sawing at the glue holding his feet to the rock. Which was effectively half-foot, half-rock. It hurt a lot.

But, knowing it was going to hurt a hell of a lot *more* if Rat got hold of him, Flea gritted his mandibles and made the final cuts, then spat at Rat's gun, fusing it to the rock where she'd dropped it. Then he took to the skies, knife in hand, to start his new life as a secret agent. Alone. Because that was even cooler than relying on pussies to do his work for him.

CONTINUE FROM HERE: **page 205**

or

BACK TO YOUR CHOICES: **page 146**

OPTION B3C1C

FLEA USES THE MASTERFUL WRESTLING MOVES HE JUST LEARNED FROM WATCHING ROCK CRUSHER WITH LOOG TO ESCAPE THE PRINCESS'S HOLD

"Hiyak!" Flea cried, kicking the princess in the face, then pounding his front feet against her throat in the death-dealing move he'd learned from the long-standing Hebbut Mistress of the Ring.

"What the—" the princess gasped. "Are you nut—"

Flea punched her again, this time in the eye. She gasped and released him.

"All hail Flea!" Flea cried, chasing her down and punching her again. "His Evilness and Master of Chaos, champion of the death pit for the last millions of turns, the Mountain that Kills!"

"Ow!" the princess cried, backing up some more. "Flea? *Ow*!"

"Take *that*!" Flea cried. "And *that*! And that and that!" He'd certainly picked up some tricks from sitting on Loog's shoulder, acting out every punch. He decided to make watching Hebbut death matches a priority from now on.

"Flea!" she cried. "Flea *stop*!"

"That's *hivelord* Flea to you!" Flea cried, kicking her again, then batting her with his wing-casings. It was a move he had modified for his own use after seeing Rock Crusher kill someone with her elbow.

"Ow! Flea, come on! You know me! I'm—"

"Silence, agent of order!" Flea shouted, impervious to her begging for mercy. "You dared to attack me…now face my wrath!" Following Rock Crusher's example, he began hammering her face, chest, wings, and legs in a jackhammer of punches and kicks.

"Ow! Ow ow ow ow ow ow ow ow!" Finally, she turned and buzzed away, and Flea gave chase, because it was fun.

"Flea, you stupid asher, stop it!" the princess screamed, as he pummeled on her sensitive back, which was exposed in order to remain in flight. "I'm—"

"Quaking in terror?" Flea demanded, kicking her again. "Begging for your life?"

"Going to *kill* you!" she screamed, turning on him again. This time, she renewed her attack, and Flea had the sudden, uncanny realization he was sadly outclassed. They began plummeting towards the ground again as Flea scrambled to get free, screaming as she clamped down on his legs, trying to snip them off. The only reason they *didn't* come off was she had too many in her mouth at once, and the added pressure was making it too difficult to get her jaws through.

That didn't stop her from trying, however. "Face the wrath of Klick!" the princess snarled around his joints. Flea screamed and writhed in her death-grip, desperate to free himself of the demonic cretin that was actively trying to eat him.

"Champion of good and light!" Klick shouted at him, finally giving up on snipping joints and pummelling his face and chest with her feet. "Mistress of the skies!"

At least she'd stopped trying to sever legs. That had been *so* uncool.

"Oh yeah?" Flea demanded, rapid-punching back. "You deceive yourself, agent of pussies! As a champion of chaos and therefore a master of darkness, I *must* defeat you!"

"Never!" Klick screamed at him, twisting to batter his braincasing with her wingtips. "Take *that*, evil one!"

"Your clumsy moves mean nothing to me!" Flea snapped back, kicking her in her exposed back, making her gasp. "I was trained by the greatest martial artist ever to *live*!"

"Oh yeah?" Klick snapped back. "I was trained by a *wizard*!" She spat at him, and it barely missed his eye.

"I knew the 'goodness' in you was just a ruse!" Flea cried, leaping away and tumbling to avoid her next two spits. "You stoop to dirty tricks!" He spat back.

"You vile monster!" she screamed. "No matter what happens here today, I will hunt you to the ends of the earth and *end* you!"

"You can't do that if you're dead!" Flea shouted back.

"I can if I turn into a *wraith*!" she snapped.

"You can't just *decide* to be a wraith!" Flea retorted. "You have to let the dungeon master roll for it!"

"She's *my* Prime Commander," Klick snapped back. "Of course she'll let me roll for it." Then, into her comm, she said, "Rat, would you let me roll to be a wraith so I can drag His Evilness into the realm of the dead where he belongs if he cheats and kills me?"

There was a very big, very long sigh on the other end. Then, "*Yes.*"

"Woohoo!" Klick cried. "I win!"

"You haven't died yet," Flea whined. "And it's His Evilness, Master of Chaos. You can't leave the last part out. I got *titled*."

"Rat," Klick whined, "I don't really have to call him that, do I?"

There was another huge, very long sigh. "*Yes.*"

"Score!" Flea cried, pumping his feet. "So who won the fight? I did, right?"

"*Just get down here*," Rat said. "*Before I put a plasma round through you both.*"

Flea glanced at Klick. "Shall we reluctantly set our differences aside and fight the oppressive Human, who would seek to end our fun?"

"I'm warning you," Rat said.

"The master of dungeons is full of hot air," Flea insisted. "We should take her down!"

"I have a Rodemax trained on your eyeball," Rat said.

"Her time as dominatrix over the universe has come to an end!" Klick agreed. "Look! Even from a distance, she threatens us!"

"Her petty words carry no weight here," Flea agreed. "We should join forces and destroy her together!"

"Agreed!" Klick shrieked. "My brains and your brawn!"

That gave Flea pause. "Nononono. It's *my* brains and *your* brawn."

Klick squinted at him. "*I'm* the wizard. *You're* the monk."

"I'm a *smart* monk!" Flea retorted. "If you hadn't spat on my character-sheet because I didn't let you steal my magic boots, I totally could prove it right now."

"She *said* I made the *roll.* That means the boots were mine. You were just a dumb monk that never saw me take them."

"But I rolled *after* that and I saw you *wearing* them to run away from that ogre," Flea cried. "Which reminds me! That was a close-combat fight just now! You *totally* didn't have a chance of winning that. I should get the xp, not you."

Klick frowned. "You didn't *beat* me, so you can't get xp!"

"Oh yeah?!" Flea demanded. "Then fight me, champion of pussies!"

"It's Champion of Good and Light!" Klick snapped. "If you get your title, I get mine."

"No way," Flea said. "Rat, do I have to—"

The plasma bolt exploded on the rock wall only a few million marches from them. *"And I, Good-Yet-Easily-Pissed-Off-and-Randomly-Malevolent Mistress of the Rodemax am trying to decide which of your legs to blow off first. Get down here or get squished."*

Flea blinked. "Wow, she actually sounds pissed."

Klick seemed to be equally as disturbed. "Yeah, we should probably go see what she wants."

"You first, agent of pussies," Flea said. "As agent of chaos, I refuse to have you at my back."

"We fly together!" Klick cried.

"You're certainly going to die together," Rat grated. *"This is an* op, *you ash-covered little furglings."*

Because Rat did, indeed, sound like she was about to shoot them, Flea sighed and followed Klick down to the rock outcropping that turned out to be the spot where Rat was huddled, once she dispelled the Greater Invisibility. "So why are you guys here?" he asked. "Are you here to save Joe, too?"

"We're looking for a Trith," Rat snapped. "Have you seen him?"

Immediately, Flea perked up. "Is this a…*quest*?"

He watched the muscles in Rat's jaw flex as she grated her teeth. "Yes," she muttered. "This is a quest."

"What do I get if I find the Trith's whereabouts before Klick?" Flea demanded.

"Experience," Rat said. "And treasure."

"Oooh." Flea buzzed his wings in excitement even as Klick said, "Wait, that's not fair! I should get it too! We're on the same team!"

"You," Rat bit out, "were already *paid* to do this mission."

Pouting, Klick said, "But you never said anything about experience."

"Yeah," Flea said quickly. "How much will it be if we find the Trith?"

"Billions. *Hundreds* of billions."

"Would that get me to level five?" Klick cried.

Flea, superior in every way, pushed the button on his charm.

"That would make you a god to the grandfathers of gods," the device said. *"In one mission. Good luck."*

Flea suddenly found it hard to breathe. "Are you sure we're ready for this, Rat? I mean, we still have trouble with *goblins*..."

"You're ready," Rat growled. "Now go. Retaining your title depends on it."

"I don't know," Flea managed, having second thoughts. "The last time you gave us a tough one, they pulled off legs."

A muscle twitched in Rat's neck. "You know what? Fine. Take this magic sword." She pulled her laser knife from her pocket and handed it to him. "It has a plus five bonus to slicing up Trith."

"Sweeeeeeeeeeeet," Flea chuckled, looking at it.

"Wait, why does *he* get the sw—" Klick started to whine.

"Too late, it's mine!" Flea cried, taking off immediately and heading towards the town, leaving the champion of pussies to bitch to the Mistress of the Rodemax as he began his deadly quest to usurp the gods.

CONTINUE TO NEXT SCENE: **page 205**
or
BACK TO YOUR OPTIONS: **page 134**

OPTION B3C2

FLEA FOLLOWS INCONSPICUOUSLY, BECAUSE PRIVACY IS THE BEST VENUE FOR INTERROGATION

Flea stayed on the ceiling until the Huouyt was gone, then slipped outside after him. Loog never even looked up from his vidscreen.

Chuckling to himself, Flea fell fully into his role of a super-secret agent of chaos, creeping amidst that shadows alongside the road as the Huouyt leisurely made his way down the bone-littered path overgrown with spiky, weaponized desert plants. It had obviously been a *long* time since anyone had traveled it.

But the assassin, ballsy furg that he was, walked right down the middle of the road, totally ignoring the three-story turrets swinging to face him.

Which was either a sign of a total wet-eyed jenfurgling…

…or a killer willing to act the proper part, whatever danger it put him in, if it allowed him to reach his target.

Flea paid extra attention to moving only when the Huouyt's head was turned, one with the very shadows themselves…

All hail Flea, Master of Darkness, immortal ninja of chaos!

He knew that back in his Dungeons & Dragons days with Rat and her Baga Klick, Klick would have complained about him switching classes mid-campaign—he was, after all, supposed to be a *monk*, not a *ninja*, but Flea saw very little difference between the two—but Klick wasn't here to whine to Rat, so Flea could therefore do whatever he wanted.

The greatest martial artist to have ever existed, ever! he thought, creeping along in the rocks within sight of the Huouyt. *So schooled in the secret arts that the shadows themselves part for him, offering him shelter where none other has passed…*

"Why are you following me?" the Huouyt asked, after Flea had stayed totally out of sight for millions of tics. The Huouyt had stopped and was staring off into the distance, as if surveying the town.

Flea clamped down in the crevice he was traversing, not about to be tricked out of hiding by a furgling.

After a moment, the Huouyt started to move again.

All hail Flea, the unseen stalker of ancient red dragons—

"So Forgotten sent insurance, did he?" the Huouyt said casually, as they walked. "He must not trust me with the body of a Trith."

Flea stumbled, but quickly recovered, taking hiding in a crack. *The great dragon has shown a propensity to talk to itself.*

"Smart of him." Then the Huouyt spun, and, aiming *directly* at Flea, fired a pen.

A...*pen*. Flea had just enough time to snicker when the pinprick of a dart hit him between the eyes.

"But not wise." Even then, like a vidscreen that was succumbing to static, Flea's vision was going dark. His hearing, however, remained totally intact. He heard the Huouyt awkwardly lurch up to him and squat beside him. "So." Flea felt a Huouyt's writhing tentacle settle upon his wing-casings. "Tell me what you know." He felt another sting, this one just under the sensitive cartilage of his shoulders.

And, because Flea was suddenly unable to help himself, he said, "I'm a secret agent of Forgotten supposed to find and kill a Trith that has gathered an army of assassins to try and kill Joe."

The Huouyt snorted. "They're not trying to kill Joe. They're trying to kill *me*."

"Why?" Flea asked, strangely unfazed by the fact he had a dart essentially buried in his brain, or that he couldn't see anything at all.

"Because they know that I'm going to kill them all." He felt a jerk as the assassin yanked the dart free. "And I'm going to ensure Zero fulfills his destiny on Earth."

Then Flea heard the weird sound of a heavy rock shifting against other rocks. "When you meet with the rest of those who have crossed my path," the Huouyt said, sounding further away, above him, "please tell the ghosts that I'm sorry, and that the things I do are out of necessity, to maintain balance."

"Okay," Flea said, feeling groggy.

The Huouyt made a grunt of strain. A moment later, Flea unexpectedly encountered oblivion.

END IT HERE

or

GO BACK TO YOUR CHOICES: **page 114**

OPTION B3X3

FLEA FIGHTS, WINGS BE DAMNED!

Flea decided what the hell, so he signed on the dotted line. Less than four hours later, his wings were nipped at the tips, and he was in the ring with the biggest Hebbut he'd ever seen, with instructions to kill her or die trying.

Or *was* she the biggest?

"No way," Flea said. "Kroeg, is that you?" That was just foul play—they wanted him to kill his old Hebbut *drinking buddy*?

The big Hebbut looked formidable as she walked out of the champion's entry and into the sunlight, her huge club held high. She turned to face the crowd that clung to all four walls overlooking the pit, and the miners cheered.

"Kr-oeg, Kr-oeg, Kr-oeg!" they shouted.

"It *is* you!" Flea cried. He scampered towards her. "Kroeg, you're *still* in prison for that karwiq bulb stuff? It's been billions of turns!"

Kroeg frowned down at him. Then she came after him with her club.

Flea screamed and took to the air...

Only to sputter and buzz on the ground because the disgusting furglings had cut his wings to make it 'fair'.

Because his life depended on it, Flea began an elegant dance with Death, darting this way and that to avoid her club, all the while trying to coax the massive Hebbut into realizing it was him.

"I'm your friend Flea!" Flea cried. "We were in the same battalion! I was your delivery boy on the karwiq project!"

The huge Hebbut flinched, and Flea saw his opening. But did he try to fight her, with all the miners watching and her freedom at stake, or did he try to find another way? He didn't want to hurt his friend...but he didn't want to die, either. In a moment of indecision, he pressed the button on his charm.

Instantly, like searing pathways lighting up in the darkness, Flea was given his three choices...

Option B3X3a) Flea spits at Kroeg, because this is a deathmatch: **page 172**
Option B3X3b) Flea allows Kroeg to hit him with her club, because he knows Kroeg wouldn't kill him for real: **page 177**
Option B3X3c) Flea tries to talk his way out of it: **page 185**

(Or, if you weren't ready to fight, try going to the RECRUITMENT CENTER: page 65 or MARSHI'S DESK: page 115 or the MINES: page 76, instead.)

OPTION B3X3A

FLEA SPITS AT KROEG, BECAUSE SHE WOULDN'T HAVE SIGNED UP FOR THIS UNLESS SHE EXPECTED TO DIE.

Flea, being an incredibly balanced and neutral agent of chaos, knew that it was up to him to stop the Trith from killing Joe, and with Kroeg being a no-name fighter on a no-name rock whose claim to fame was bashing in a few prisoners' skulls, not *saving the world* from a Dhasha rebellion, who also had the possibility of *destroying* it again in a few more turns, it was up to Flea to make the tough choices.

Thus, with Joe as the one most deserving of Flea's help due to his potential to wreak total chaos on the fat, pampered Representatives in Koliinaat later, Flea decided to go all-out.

"Your sacrifice will be remembered!" Flea cried, catching Kroeg by surprise and sticking her foot…to the sand. He blinked as she lifted her foot—and the clump of sand sticking to it—and roared a Hebbut death-threat.

"Sorry!" Flea cried, scampering away, because his wings no longer worked. "Sorry, I—"

The club came down hard beside Flea's head.

Flea shrieked and dodged through the Hebbut's legs, skittering across the sands towards the other side. He paused long enough to twist and spit at Kroeg's hand, fusing her fingers to the club.

…which didn't do him a lot of good.

"You don't want to kill me!" Flea cried. "I'm your friend!"

"*You're* the one that got me *caught*!" Kroeg shouted, burying her club into the sand beside him, just missing a foot. "You delivered *fifty-six million* bulbs instead of *nine*! You ran me out of stock!"

Jostled by his struggle to stay alive, the device helpfully said, "*Keeping in mind you have a head growing out of your ass, imagine you decide go to bask on a huge sheet of paper.*"

"Die, coward!" Kroeg's club came down, barely missing him again.

"Then, just when you're getting comfortable," the device continued, *"you get hit with a hammer the size of a spaceship. Because it's the only way to come back in one piece after you have been rendered into gore, you use a spell of Resurrection to revive yourself, then, because it's a* really *nice basking spot and you have this unhealthy optimism that—"*

Flea screamed as Kroeg's next blow tore off a leg, burying it in the sand. He scuttled faster, but without a back leg, scuttling was hard. "Kroeg, please don't kill me!"

"—if you repeat the exact same actions in the exact same situation you will somehow get different results, you do it again six more times, leaving seven Flea-splats on the paper."

"You ruined my *life*!" Kroeg screamed, giving up on the club and trying to stomp on him, now.

"No, wait!" Flea cried, crawling up a leg and onto her back. "It was a misunderstanding!" he cried, as he rode between her shoulder-blades, just out of reach of her burly arms.

"Now, because you've got this unhealthy curiosity about what your own insides look like, you start crawling through the gore to count the squished arms, legs, and heads of all seven of your deceased prior incarnations. Then you see another piece of paper in the distance that looks exactly like this one, covered in dead Fleas. Then you see another one. And another one. Until an entire city is wrapped in paper covered in dead Fleas. That *is the number of bulbs you delivered."*

Kroeg screamed in frustration and started scratching at her back with her club, trying to dislodge him. Flea immediately fused the club to her back. "Kroeg, listen to me!"

"I will *kill* you!" Kroeg snarled, grabbing hold of one of his mandibles and throwing him to the ground with the same force as a Congressional superliner. Then she screamed as she tore her club from her back, bringing skin and parts of her shirt with it.

"Now, if you were to grow another *head because you ate radioactive material and you now have another mutant Flea trying to crawl out of your abdomen, then you count all three of your heads and all six of your legs, that was how many karwiq bulbs you were* supposed *to deliver.*

Flea paused as his mind immediately began to go numb, unavoidably seeing the difference in what he had delivered and what he *should* have delivered. 'Nine' had been such a big number that he had assumed she meant all of it.

Realizing an apology was necessary, Flea said, "Look, I'm sorry I—"

The Hebbut's nail-encrusted club caught him between the eyes, and Flea had the odd sensation of his eyeballs separating from his braincase before they went bouncing across the sand and he was left in darkness.

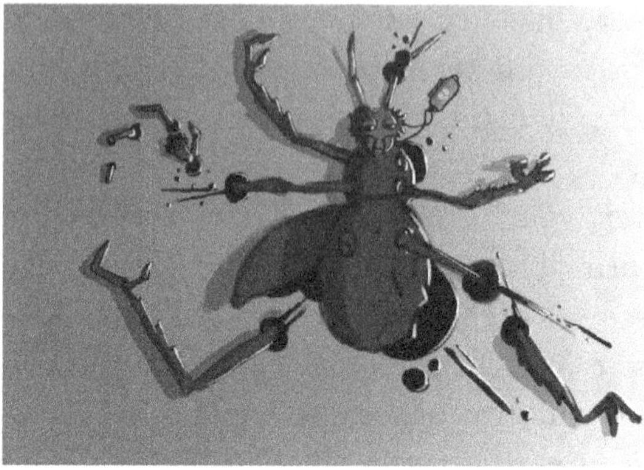

END IT HERE

or

RETURN TO YOUR CHOICES: **page 171**

OPTION B3X3B

FLEA ALLOWS KROEG TO HIT HIM WITH HER CLUB TO FAKE HIS OWN DEMISE, BECAUSE HE KNOWS KROEG WOULDN'T KILL HIM FOR REAL. REALLY.

"Yes, it's me!" Flea cried. "Flea!"

The look of building fury, however, was not the look of friendly excitement he had expected. "Flea?!" Kroeg roared. "You left me with *nothing*!"

"Huh?" Flea said.

But then Kroeg's club was slamming down at him, and it was all he could do to dodge the onslaught and dart away from her.

"They sent me to *prison*! To *this. Miserable. Rock*!" On each major syllable, she hurled the nail-studded club downward at him, each time barely missing his head, his klett, his feet…

"What do you mean?!" Flea cried. "You mismanaged your finances! You overextended and couldn't pay your bribes!"

"*You gave that bulbhead everything I had*!" Kroeg screamed, actively attempting to bury the club in his brain. "*My entire stock! On* one *deal!*"

Flea flinched. He had *thought* it was a little odd she had asked him to deliver all of her stock to a casual bulber, but she was the boss and he was just the delivery boy.

"I didn't know!" Flea cried. "You'd never asked me to deliver so many before!" Indeed, his wing-muscles had been hurting for weeks afterwards.

"I asked you to deliver *nine*!" Kroeg shrieked, swatting blindly at him. "*Nine* bulbs, not fifty-six *million*!"

"I don't know what that—" Flea began. Then he hesitated and pushed the little button on his charm.

"*Imagine a leg bursts out of your eyeball, then detaches from your head and crawls around and reattaches to your back*," the device said. "*You now have seven legs and two heads, for a total of nine appendages. That's how many bulbs you were supposed to deliver. Instead, you delivered the population of a small city.*"

Flea grew cold, almost missing his chance to skuttle away from Kroeg's next blow. "Oh, man, Kroeg, I had no idea…" He'd thought she was just a bad business partner. "I couldn't count past six, so I thought you meant them all!"

"Peacemakers showed up because the pile was *overflowing* the guy's *backyard*!" Kroeg cried, but she at least stopped trying to hit him, lowering the tip of her club into the sand and panting, instead. "You think I would have sent you to *fill* a guy's *backyard*?!"

"Erm." Come to think of it, it *had* seemed a pretty strange request. "No?"

"And yet you *did it anyway*!" she snapped, leveling the club at him. "You told me Bagans were *smart*!"

Okay, so yeah, that might have been a lapse on his part. "I'm sorry," Flea said. "I thought I was doing what you wanted me to do." She'd made sure he only delivered the small sales before that, and because she had been about to go on vacation, Flea had thought she was having him take over the big deliveries, too.

"You…" Kroeg shook her club, then reluctantly dropped the tip again. "You really didn't know, did you?" she muttered.

"Huh-uh," Flea said, still keeping a respectable distance between him and the club. "I thought it was all part of your plan, like maybe you were setting someone else up to take a fall, but then you went to jail."

Kroeg made a disgusted sound. "I can't believe this. I just can't believe this. I thought you sent me to jail on *purpose* so you could take over my business."

"Nope," Flea said. "Why would I want your business? I hate numbers."

Kroeg took a deep breath, glanced at the sky, then leveled her gaze thoughfully back at Flea. "You know I have to kill you now, right?"

Flea, who hadn't known that, flinched. "You do?"

"They only let one of us out of this ring alive," Kroeg said, gesturing up at the onlookers gathered on top of the wall, who were rooting and cheering and making bets.

"No sweat," Flea said. "I could just crawl out."

"Autoturrets," Kroeg said.

And, without a usable set of wings, Flea supposed that was a pretty valid concern. "Uh…"

"You wanna win this one, Flea?" Kroeg demanded, looking tired. "I've been fighting for six rotations. I don't want to do it anymore. I'm the executioner of this place. Miners put their name on the list so they can come in here to die—they don't even fight back. Only ones who fight back are the new ones or the ones Loog sends down. This place is a hell, Flea. I technically served out my time three whole turns ago, but they keep adding time to my 'sentence' whenever they can. I break a piece of equipment, I get a few more rotations. I hurt myself, I get a few more rotations. I get in a fight, I get a few more rotations. And Marshi stages fights! She sends goons after me so I have no *choice* to fight, then I get more turns on my enlistment. I'm tired, Flea. I'm never getting out of here. Marshi won't *let* me."

Only then did Flea really see Kroeg for the first time. She looked *old*. Her big body was even more muscular than before, but her face—especially her eyes—was *ancient*.

"I'm going to be here until I die," Kroeg insisted. "They know me. Marshi won't let me go anywhere else. But you kill me, it would give you a chance to get out."

Flea immediately scampered backwards. "Wait. *Kill* you? No way!"

Kroeg snorted. "You don't get it…*one* of us has to die here today, Flea. If we don't fight, it will be *two* of us that die."

Up in the stands, the miners were screaming at them to get on with the fight. Several of the town's security force, all of whom were carrying big, expensive-looking laser assault rifles, were giving them dark looks from the towers stationed at the four corners. Flea thought the gunmen looked a little better-suited to military ops than keeping a few miners in line on a no-name mining planet, but ruvmestin ore was expensive, so maybe Marshi had hired the best of the best.

"I've got a plan!" Flea cried. "You hit me with your club!"

Kroeg squinted at him. "What?"

"You hit me, I play dead, then we get me fixed at a medical facility and I go find someone who can help set you free!"

Kroeg gave him a long look. "Flea, I'd have to pay for your medical bills, and I'm already in debt to Marshi for the next two turns. An exotic like you, the doctor would probably charge triple. That'd give me another turn, at least."

"I'll get you out!" Flea cried. "It was my mistake—I should help fix it!" He didn't want to mention that he was a valued agent of Forgotten, and that, as such, great rewards would be his to reap at the end of the mission, but he *knew* he would be able to help her. "How much do you owe?"

"Six hundred thousand," Kroeg said. "Your medical bills would probably bring that up to nine. Even getting sick costs like forty thousand in medical bills, plus a thousand credits an hour that you're not in the mines on your shift. They make it so you can't leave!"

Flea pushed his button.

"Usually I would try to explain the numbers to you, but the essence to this question is much simpler: the medical costs are arbitrary, and are based on a creature's ability to pay. Essentially, Marshi's scheme is to keep the debt one step ahead of what Kroeg can repay, and whatever costs she owes now will quite possibly double or triple if she ever finds the repayment money, because Marshi will then charge 'interest' to keep control. In order to free her, you would have to find a solution other than cash, because Marshi will simply keep raising the bar until payment is out of the question."

"He's right," Kroeg said. "Only way I'm getting out of here is in a casket."

That didn't sound very fair.

"Listen," Flea said. "I'm not killing one of my friends. Hit me, knock me around a little, make sure I'm good and flat, then take me in to the doctor's when nobody's looking. I *will* get you out of here."

Flea saw a flash of hope in Kroeg's wet Hebbut eyes. "You really think you can?"

"Of course I can," Flea said. "I'm here on a mission for…" He hesitated, remembering in gory detail what happens to him when he mentions Forgotten's name in the choices. "…justice," he finished.

Kroeg blinked at him. "You came here to help me?"

"Yes," Flea said, because had he *known* that Kroeg was here because of him, he would have been there on the first flight in. He didn't abandon his friends. Even if he hadn't been here with that intention *originally*, he sure as ash had it now.

Kroeg seemed to consider that, then said, "Everything but the head, right?"

"Everything but the head," Flea agreed. Wincing at the spiked club she carried, he said, "And maybe use your feet? Restoration would probably cost less if you use your feet."

"Yeah, okay," Kroeg said. "But after we sat her talking for a couple minutes, we'll have to give them a good show or Marshi'll know something's up."

"Gotcha," Flea said. Subterfuge and deception, he could do. He was, after all, an agent of chaos.

"Okay." Kroeg took a deep breath, steeling herself, then said, "Run!"

Flea bolted, and Kroeg gave chase. Flea made a merry act of dodging and weaving and buzzing and, because he was really getting into the spirit, climbing up her leg and riding her face. The crowd cheered, then it roared, and when Flea managed to crawl under her shirt and she couldn't dislodge him, the crowd screamed.

Flea was actually starting to enjoy himself, clinging to her back under her shirt just out of reach, when the world flipped suddenly and, for a moment, Flea felt weightless. Then he connected with the ground on one side and the Hebbut on another, and he felt himself deflate with force of getting hit by a charging Dhasha. As he lost his grip on her back, Kroeg tore off her shirt and flung him aside, to the crowd's roar of approval. Then Flea had a split second to see her huge green Hebbut foot coming down at him before it connected and started grinding him into the sand. Sometime after she started stomping, he lost all conscious awareness.

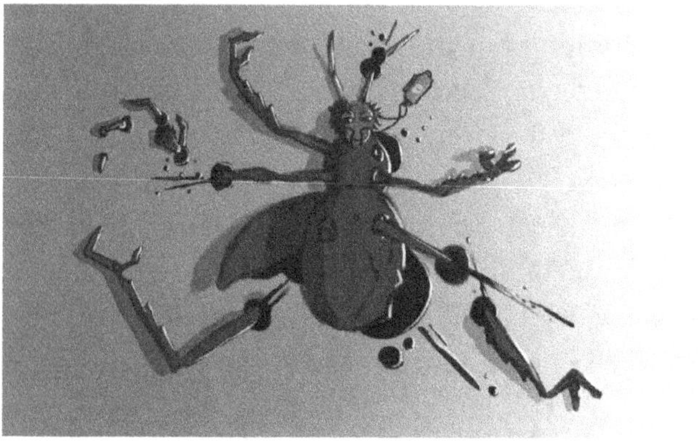

CONTINUE FROM HERE: **page 189**

or

BACK TO YOUR CHOICES: **page 171**

OPTION B3X3C

FLEA SPEAKS!

"It's me, Flea!" Flea cried.

The storm that immediately began to build upon the Hebbut's face was not what Flea had expected.

"I've come to rescue you!" Flea cried, as she raised her club and started towards him. "I have powerful friends! I can get you free!" Flea figured that as long as he didn't mention *names*, he wouldn't be violating Forgotten's rules and he should be okay…

"*You*," the Hebbut sputtered. "I lost *everything* because of you!"

Flea didn't think *that* was very fair. "You lost everything because you sold all your karwiq to a bulbhead that turned you over to the Peacemakers."

"Nine," Kroeg snarled. "I sold him *nine bulbs*. You gave him fifty-six *million*!"

Because those two numbers sounded very different, Flea blinked and clicked the button on his charm.

"Imagine you contract a horrible skin disease from your dubious sexual exploits where body parts start growing off your neck. First you see an eyeball, then mandibles, then a whole head develops, pushing aside your first

head, so now you have two heads sprouting off your neck. Keeping in mind that you still have a head growing out of your ass, you now have three heads and six legs, which is how many bulbs Kroeg had told you to deliver—essentially a small basket of bulbs. Instead, you delivered the equivalent of a single, medium-sized cargo bay filled to the brim with narcotics to a casual bulbhead, one by one, overflowing his yard, because you didn't bother to ask if that didn't seem a bit extreme.

Flea *had* been wondering what Kroeg had been thinking. "Whoa."

"You mean you didn't *know*?" Kroeg demanded. "You mean it was an *accident*?! You *emptied* out my *warehouse* on *accident*?!"

"Uh…" Flea didn't know what to say, because that was exactly what had happened.

"I've spent *six rotations* on this planet!" Kroeg snapped, breathing hard. "Because of *you*!" She shoved the nail-riddled club at him. "You ruined my *life*!"

And, looking around them at the dusty town and its shabby houses and armed guards and turrets in the distance, Flea suddenly felt really bad. "Sorry," he managed. "I never meant to give him the wrong number. I just couldn't count that high, so I thought you meant all of what you had. I'm here to help make things right and get you out."

Kroeg just shook her head. "I can't believe this."

"What?" Flea asked.

"You just think you can waltz in here, say you're 'sorry' and think you can waltz out again?" She was raising her voice dangerously. "While you were off whoring and gambling and spending your billions of credits, I spent six rotations fighting for my *life* in a *gladiatorial ring*, and every time I was forced to kill some innocent miner who was just too tired to work anymore, I imagined it was *you*."

Wow, put that way, Flea supposed he really *didn't* deserve to leave unscathed. He thought about his mission, and how he was here to save Joe, and then he looked at this deflated creature in front of him and realized Joe was billions and billions of miles away and Kroeg was *here* and he had wronged her more than he'd ever known. "I won't fight," Flea said. "Do what you want to me."

"I *want* to crush your *brains* out through your *skull*," Kroeg snapped.

Completely willing to let her do so for the trouble that he had caused, Flea wandered up and rested his head upon the sand in front of her huge green toe.

Kroeg scowled down at him for several moments, then said, "There's a hole in the wall in the northern corner. I bashed someone through it three turns ago and Marshi's too stingy to fix it—she just buries it with sand. Get out. Marshi won't kill me 'cause she needs me as her champion. I'll deal with the guards. They've got me fighting another guy here tomorrow, anyway. Just get out of sight before those turrets find you."

Flea pulled his head from the sand and frowned up at her. "You're letting me go?"

"You still think you can get me out?" Kroeg demanded. "It's gonna take force—Marshi doesn't *let* people go. This place is a death-trap. Anyone who comes in never goes out again. She orchestrates people's debts so they can't ever repay them, so they can't leave."

Looking up at her solemnly, Flea placed his front foot on her big toe. "Kroeg, I swear that I will help free you from this place. And, should anyone try to stop me, I will unleash chaos upon Marshi and her ilk, bringing this very town down around her knees."

"That's nice," Kroeg said. "You better start running. I think they figured out we're buddies and the guards are about to start shooting at you."

Saluting, Flea scuttled north across the sands of the gladiatorial pit, zig-zagging to avoid the laser shots that came only moments afterwards. He found the hole Kroeg had spoken of, half-buried in sand. It was already big enough that Flea was able to squeeze through with only a minimum amount of digging, and in a couple quick pushes, he was through, and scuttling across the deserted road on the other side. Taking a moment's sanctuary under a sunbaked porch, Flea then went looking for a doctor willing to fix his wings on credit.

CONTINUE FROM HERE: **page 189**

or

BACK TO YOUR CHOICES: **page 171**

OPTION B3X3

CONTINUED

Flea woke up after surgery feeling like he'd been hit by a superskimmer's windshield…Which probably wasn't too far from the truth. He rolled over and buzzed his wings to test them. The wings had been a simple fix, just a bit of QuickGro on the tips, but the 'doctor' had charged the price of a small skimmer anyway, credited directly to an account he made just for Flea, which the doctor told him he would hold off selling to Marshi until she came to oversee his books at the end of the week. Kroeg, it seemed, had been right in that—Flea saw no way, with all the gladiatorial matches and bar fights, that anyone would be able to pay off their debt. Even with the great expense of treatment, however, the 'doctor's' office was just a small shack near one corner of town, and from the dust clinging to the walls and floor and the makeshift implements on the table, Flea guessed that it wasn't exactly sanctioned by the Congressional Council On Physician Integrity and Treatment Standards Oversight.

But at least he was free of the fighting pit. He buzzed off the table and landed on a window sill to look outside. Nighttime on this planetoid was cold, almost too cold, even for Flea. There were ice crystals on the glass where the moisture from inside had condensed and then frozen.

Still, now that he was free—at least for a week—Flea had no choice but to brave the elements in search of the Trith and its group of assassins that planned to kill Joe.

...And, somewhere in the meantime, he had to figure out a way to save Kroeg. Money wasn't going to save her, not that he had any money anyway. It was going to take brute force or cunning, and whatever it was, he had to come up with it before they sent her back down into the mines for a rotation. He flew to the door, manipulated the latch, and crawled into the frigid air outside. Gingerly pulling the door shut behind him—which took more effort than he should have given, considering the doctor was ripping him off—Flea went looking for some sign of a group of assassins on Glaxxion.

He found them a lot sooner than he expected.

"Psst!" a Bagan voice called from up under the eave of a roof. "Flea? That you?"

Flea blinked up at the female huddled against the gutter, only taking a moment to recognize her because she, like him, had had her carapace painted black. "*Klick*?" It was Rat's former groundmate, one that he had played many a game of Dungeons and Dragons with during the days during and following Neskfaat.

Rat and Joe's teams were the only two teams to have survived that battle...

And then Rat's team had supposedly all died because they supposedly assaulted Representative Mekkval in his deep den for supposedly no reason at all. Hearing that, Flea had been less than convinced, thinking it was probably more likely Mekkval had 'killed' them so he could hire them as his own personal team of Dhasha slayers.

And, apparently, Trith slayers.

Then again, Mekkval seemed more the kind of ash-soul that would team up with a crazed Trith to use it to manipulate all his peers in politics rather than go out of his way to kill it. After what he had seen working with Mekkval's nephew, Keval, Flea was surprised that Mekkval hadn't been cast out of Congress for all the underhanded flake he was pulling. He hoped Keval challenged soon—Mekkval was starting to turn into one of those rotting sores that really needed a good surgeon before it took out the whole carapace. To that end, Flea had spent *millions* of hours practicing ka-par with Keval, getting him ready for when the challenge finally came. *Practicing*, mind you...Flea had yet to win a single match.

"Flea, what in the greasy ashes are you doing here?" Klick demanded from the shadows. "Is Zero here, too?"

Flea flinched, crawling up the side of the house to get closer. "No...Why are *you* here?"

"I could ask you the same thing," she snapped back, much too suspiciously.

For a moment, Flea was horrified. "You're working with the *Trith*?"

"I was going to ask you the same question!" Klick replied, sounding more suspicious than ever. "How do you know about the Trith?"

"How do *you*?!" Flea cried.

"Keval said this was a hotbed of assassin activity—a group that's been killing a bunch of Representatives in Congress, like ten in the last two rotations—and there's a crazy Trith backing it," Klick said. "We're here to kill the Trith., then take out the assassins."

"Is there anything else *you want to tell the random stranger about our* secret covert operation, *Klick?!"* Rat's voice demanded over the comm.

"It's not a stranger!" Klick said. "It's Flea! *Commander Zero's* Flea."

There was a weird pause. *"That can't be a coincidence."*

"Yeah, I don't think so, either." Klick was scowling at him from where she clung to the eave. "Who sent you, Flea?" she demanded.

Because Flea had already seen several options where dropping Forgotten's name had gotten him gruesomely killed—options that were still burned into his brain—he said, "I got attacked. Some guys working for something called the Shard tried to kill me. I escaped, then followed them. Did some reconnaissance, spent a few weeks on the ceilings, that sort of thing. Said they were working for the Trith and were going to try and kill Joe."

"*Joe*," Klick cried. "Why would the Trith give a crap about Joe?"

Flea thought about it for a moment. As much as the Ground Force loved him, Joe wasn't really a major player in Congress, yet this wasn't the first time the Trith had tried to kill him. Someone had said something about Joe destroying Congress, but Flea hadn't really put much stock in that. How could a *Human* destroy *Congress*?

Then again, maybe it was that vortex thing, the way Joe pulled all the different dimensions and possibilities together into one point, and the Trith just wanted Joe dead because Joe made it so they couldn't see the future.

"Do you know where to find the Trith?" Rat demanded. *"There's been no flights coming or going off this planetoid aside from ones we've caught and quarantined, and we* still *haven't been able to find him. Klick's been in every building and scouted out every crevice. It* has *to be inside some sort of shelter, because Trith physiology is incredibly delicate, but it's like he evades our every move."*

Flea thought that was pretty obvious that yes, that's exactly what it was doing because it was a *Trith*, and Trith could always see everything coming, all the time. He glanced at Klick, who was giving her equivalent of an exasperated, *Let's Humor The Stupid Human* look. "I'm sure there's a reason for that," Flea said. "You know...like maybe it sees the future and can just walk around the other side of a building at the exact right time somebody's coming the other way so nobody sees him at all?"

Rat was silent for several moments. Then, *"How do we fight something like that?"*

Well, Flea could think of one way—it happened to be around his neck—but he certainly wasn't going to tell the others, just in case they started getting curious about where he could get a device with that much capability in that tiny of a package.

"Just keep anyone from leaving the town," Flea said. "I'll find him for you guys."

"Right," Klick said, rolling her eyes. "Because you're *sooo* much better than me."

Flea, who definitely *was* better than Klick, wasn't going to say it because the last time he had, she'd spat at his eyeball and he'd had to go into three hours of surgery. "Just give me a week," he said. "I'll find you your Trith."

But first, he was going to find Rat. He flew off, keeping low, heading to the edges of the village. Rat, as a pretty much useless Human, was only good at sniping things from a distance. She was going to be up in the cliffs encircling the town somewhere, hiding amongst the rocks.

He had always made it a game to take something of Rat's each time he saw her, because Rat, like Joe, was fun to screw with. Humans always made funny noises and jumped around *hilariously* when they realized one of their oh-so-precious possessions had been lifted off their person, Rat especially. Rat liked to wear ridiculously expensive things, even more so than Joe. She always had the *cool* stuff. Little pieces of tech that cost as much as a skimmer, pressure knives, microscopic bombs, hologram pens, all *sorts* of fun things that Flea could swipe when she wasn't looking.

Mostly, though, it was the funny sounds she made when she found out it was missing. That was the *best*. Unlike Joe, Rat had a much higher-pitched voice that was delightfully squeaky. And it got *really* squeaky—and loud—when she was angry. Therefore, Flea loved to make her angry.

Therefore, because he could always find the Trith later, Flea was going to find whatever rock she was hiding under and relieve her of one of her expensive baubles. Because that was important.

It took relatively little effort to find her. All Flea had to do was figure out where *Joe* would have hidden in the rocky crags surrounding the town, then make it a little harder, because despite her squeaky voice, Flea was pretty sure Rat was smarter than Joe, which Flea made up for by being smarter than Klick, who was brick-stupid, especially because she a *wizard* and wizards couldn't *steal* things, and that natural twenty roll that she made to take his magic boots was a *fluke*, but Rat gave it to her anyway.

Flea wrote to the Dungeonmastering Society of Earth to try and complain, but all they'd come back with was, "Questioning the Dungeonmaster can bring with it great peril—the best course of action is to 'roll with it.' If the DM has stated your friend made the skill check necessary to take the boots, then her word is law, and you should move on, and try to find a way to destroy your thieving friend later."

That had been good advice, so Flea had waited until Klick wasn't looking and changed her character sheet, giving her warts and carapace-rot and the body-parts-growing-off-yourself disease. She, in turn, had spat all over *his* character sheet, and Rat had decided they'd had enough D&D.

Which totally wasn't fair because it was Klick's fault. So, from that point on, Flea had made a point of thieving from *Rat* until she revoked her ridiculous decree and gave him his boots back.

Flea watched Rat out of range of her Rodemax's proximity sensor for several minutes, trying to figure out the best way to approach her without getting shot. Like any Human in a combat scenario, she was huddled under a rock, with a holograph protecting her, waiting for the more capable members of her team to infiltrate the bad guys' camp.

Flea knew the reddish boulder was a holograph, though, because her Rodemax, while intelligent, wasn't creative—it was copying a boulder Flea could see on the far cliff-face, across the town from where Flea was crouching.

Like the patient, ultimate hunter he was, Flea continued to watch his prey, waiting for his opening.

It came when Klick came back to report. She made a long, whiny spiel about how Flea was better than her because he'd disappeared and she couldn't find him anywhere, and how the Trith was still in hiding.

Flea waited, listening to Klick's whining in quiet glee, then, when Rat told her to go back down there and 'find them both anyway', he struck. He waited for

Klick to buzz away, then buzzed down as fast as he could, entered through the illusionary boulder the same way he'd seen Klick do, then, as he came down under the hologram and saw Rat stretched out on the stone, overlooking the town, he scuttled over to her side.

Pockets, Flea had learned, were a Human's weak point.

As Rat was grunting and turning away from the town to look over at him with a gruff, "What is it now?" her Rodemax said, "*Unauthorized enemy presence.*"

But Flea was already yanking something fun-looking from her pocket—he was pretty sure it was a laser knife—and scuttling away.

"Oh goddamn it, not *again*!" Rat shrieked, getting up out of her prone position to pat at her pocket. "*Flea*! You thieving little *asher*! *Come back*! *I need that!*"

Chuckling, Flea took off, quickly putting a boulder between him and Rat and her gun. Then, mission accomplished, he began seeking out a place to stash his new trophy, so that he could always return to it a few turns later and gloat, like he had with all the others…

CONTINUE TO PART 3: **page 205**

(Or, if you're not ready, RETURN TO PART 2 START: page 41 or RETURN TO THE MINES: page 76 or RETURN TO MARSHI'S DESK: page 115 or RETURN TO THE RECRUITMENT CENTER: page 65)

OPTION B3C3

FLEA FOLLOWS THE ASSASSIN AT A DISTANCE TO UNRAVEL HIS EVIL PLOT.

Flea let the assassin leave first, then snuck out after him, when Loog—who apparently had written him off the moment Rock Crusher had started pounding some poor Ueshi slaughter-fodder into a predictably gruesome pulp—was busy with his vidscreen.

Flea took a perch on a high rock overlooking the town, watching from afar as the assassin brazenly walked down the middle of the unused, bone-covered road, seemingly oblivious to the big turrets that swung to face him as he approached the town.

For millions of minutes, Flea delightedly watched the turrets' barrels track their victim, anticipating an explosive finale.

Nothing happened.

How...*annoying*. Flea literally could have flown to the chow hall, had lunch, and returned in the time it took the assassin to traverse half of that path.

This time, seeing how much time it was taking, Flea *did* go get something to eat. He snuck a couple bites from pantry the while the big Hebbut cook was busy with his back turned, chopping meat.

By the time he returned, the assassin was still out in the open, only having crossed two thirds of the distance. He was also making no move to hide, so Flea following at a distance, in the air. The three-legged creature was so. Annoyingly. *Slow*. It was almost painful to watch the Huouyt's legs wriggle on the rocky, red-orange sand. But it also told him something about his adversary: Huouyt, which were naturally aquatic, hated the desert. It was like salting an Ueshi. Which was fun.

But it meant this one was *determined* to get into that town. Why?

Flea took up a position in the scaffolding of one of the ore-refiners, watching the Huouyt as it made its way into the town, then stepped into the first building on the right, which was only about the size of a shuttle cabin.

Flea waited.

And waited.

He waited *hours*. Flea couldn't give an exact time, but it was *much* longer than it should have been. Like whole days. Because he was getting annoyed, he clicked the button on his charm.

"*You have been waiting ten tics*," the device told him. "*That is approximately the amount of time it takes to—*"

Ten! Flea was outraged, not even bothering to listen to the rest. Obviously the assassin had decided to take a nap or something. Or maybe there was another assassin inside and he was dead. Or maybe he'd somehow noticed Flea and was cringing in terror. Or maybe there was a secret tunnel and the assassin had quietly egressed...

Because he had nothing else to do, Flea started hitting the button on the top of his charm, testing his options while he desperately tried to keep his mind from devolving into drooling furgocity as he waited *millennia* for his quarry to emerge from its hiding place.

"So what if I step with my *right* foot instead of my *left* foot...here..." *click.* One of his options was to spit at passerby—which really hadn't been his question—and get splattered with a high-impact mining hammer, while another option was slipping and falling to his death, which Flea took in stride. "Huh. Okay, what happens if I flap my wings in the direction of the *town* instead of the direction of the *desert*?" In the latter, a dust-storm wiped out the town, hundreds of millions of billions of turns from now. Flea immediately flapped his wings towards the desert, being careful not to spit on a torrak basking on a nearby roof, because in his set of options, it had launched itself at him like a possessed miga, catching him and stabbing him repeatedly with its tiny butt-stinger. "Okay, so what if I stretch out my *left* leg instead of my *right* leg?"

That time, aside when he spat on the driver of a passing skimmer—again, not really relevant to his question—*both* options had him getting suddenly slammed into from the side and tumbled towards the ground with something approximately his size attempting to claw out the facets of his eyes.

"Huh," Flea said, deciding not to spit *or* stretch out a leg.

Frowning, a little unnerved by his last set of options, Flea climbed through the scaffolding, putting a layer of metal bars between him and the outside world. He looked around, his carapace itching like someone was watching him through a high-powered scope, but saw nothing out there.

Tics passed. *Millions* of tics. Flea got bored again and clicked the bottom button on his charm. "Count the houses," he said.

"As I see no relevance to this situation aside from the fact that your infantile, concentration-deprived brain needs stimulation in order to prevent catastrophic cell-death, I refuse to act as a conduit for your personal entertainment. Count them yourself. It will be just as entertaining."

Flea had the disturbing feeling that the charm meant *Flea* was *his* entertainment. "Heeeey." Holding it out at arm's-length, he scowled at the charm and said, "Just what in the greasy ashes did you mean by tha—"

"*Got him!*" a female Baga using a Congie voice-projector screamed. A moment later, something black slammed into Flea from the side, and they went tumbling down of the refinery tower, towards the corrugated roofs of the town. "*Get ready for impact!*"

A moment later, Flea got the heady rush of pheromones that told him, unequivocally, he was dealing with a virgin princess.

Then she was bashing at his face with her toes, screaming the traditional Bagan war cry:

"Dieeeeeeeeee!"

Flea screamed and started pounding his wings to get away from her, tugging them higher into the air, but she then crawled onto his back and clamped down on his casings, apparently intent to craterize them into one of the roofs below.

And, like clockwork, the Huouyt had stepped out of the building he had been hiding inside, and was looking up at him in something akin to satisfaction.

Flea, who still had the charm in one hand, accidentally clamped his fist on the button out of sheer, unadulterated terror—his last run-in with a Bagan princess had *not* ended well.

Immediately, three choices splayed out before him, illuminating new pathways through the shadows of his mind…

Option B3c1a) Flea spits at the princess: **page 135**
Option B3c1b) Flea tells the princess she looks familiar…: **page 140**
Option B3c1c) Flea finds a way to escape her hold: **page 157**

PART 3

THE TRITH

(Or, if you're not ready, RETURN TO PART 2 START: page 41 or RETURN TO THE RECRUITMENT CENTER: page 65 or RETURN TO THE DEATHMATCH: page 169 or RETURN TO THE MINES: page 76 or RETURN TO MARSHI'S DESK: page 115. Or, if you came here in error, RETURN TO PART 4: page 243.)

Knowing that Rat and her team were in the area, hunting the same turf, gave Flea an incredible thrill. He began to turn it into a game, endeavoring to stay totally off their radar, while still doing his best to keep tabs on all of *them*. He found Sol'dan easily enough—the shapeshifter Huouyt wasn't even trying to hide in another species' body—he was walking around town hiding in plain sight, the only dressed-in-black Congie that Flea came across in all of his explorations trying to find a place to stash Rat's knife.

Rat was easy, because Rat was pretending to be a boulder, and boulders didn't move.

They did, however, have powerful, long-range hyperintelligent sniper rifles, and Flea had decided that it would be in his best interest to stay out of her sight until he could stash the knife, since she was *way* too possessive of her stuff.

Klick was hard, because Klick was hunting *him*, but he caught glimpses of her here and there, enough to know she hadn't found him yet.

Then there was Benva, Rat's Sentinel.

It wasn't exactly on Flea's list of priorities to tangle with a Jreet prince, but it was the planet's cold-cycle, and the Jreet notoriously hated the cold. Which meant the great Welu worm was probably coiled up shivering in some hole somewhere, waiting for the sun to come back out. Unfortunately, the Jreet also had that natural invisibility, so Benva technically *could* be anywhere, so Flea tried to keep himself to midway up walls or above, just to stay out of striking-range of an angry Jreet.

In his quest to find the perfect long-term hiding spot for his badass new bauble, Flea crept through every nook and every cranny of every building in the entire town, clicking his charm's top button each time he came across a likely spot, and each time not being satisfied with its long-term safety. He tried every rock, every hole, and every time, sooner or later, someone would always find the knife.

Frustrated, Flea started to try storing the knife up in the cliffs around town, but each time he clicked the button, someone *always* found his treasure. Either it was a miner trying his luck with the desert, or Klick out hunting him, or a random torrak, or a demolition crew, or pirates, or Congies out on their lunch break, or archaeologists, or there was an earthquake and that sent it tumbling down into the village, but over the course of millennia, someone *always* found it.

"Damn it!" Flea cried, yanking the knife from yet another perfectly good hiding spot where a Ueshi pilot millions of turns from now would discover it when the planet exploded and it knocked against the windshield of his spaceship. "There *has* to be a place I can put this!"

But apparently, at least on Glaxxion, there wasn't.

Frustrated at yet another dead-end after finding a perfect spot under a torn piece of flooring up in the abandoned comm center, Flea tore the charm off his neck. Holding it out and shaking it, he snapped, "I've tried *millions* of different places, and all you give me is dead-ends!"

"Actually, you've only tried to hide your ill-begotten bauble three thousand and twenty-three times, which is approximately the same number of times as could be expected from a neurotic chipmunk that somehow expects to return to the site after the universe implodes."

Flea's mandibles fell open. "That's *it*." He was running up the stairs to hurl it off the platform overlooking the edge of the cliff when he suddenly slammed head-first into a Trith.

The Trith stumbled, its huge black light-eating eyes blinking at Flea in surprise.

Flea blinked back. Already, he could feel the weird tug of the creature's too-big eyes, enveloping him, crushing him.

How did you get here? the Trith demanded, like a vice as it squeezed his mind in a fist. *How could I not see you coming?!* It was leaning forward, closer, *angry*, now. *Wait. What is that thing in your hands?*

It's going to kill me! Flea realized. He struggled in the Trith's mental grasp, his fingers fumbling for the button on the charm and failing. All he could think was he needed to spit. He needed to spit, to stop the Trith from eating him. He needed to spit, needed to spit, needed to spit…

But Forgotten had told him not to spit. But if he didn't spit, the Trith was going to come after him and find him while he *slept* and kill him.

Somehow, Flea found the button on the can, and he pressed it. As soon as he did, the Trith groaned and stumbled. Flea's choices remained splayed out in front of him like movies spreading out into the darkness…

Option 1) Flea spits.
Option 2) Flea spits.
Option 3) Flea spits.

Realizing that *all* of his options were to spit, Flea cried out and mashed the can button a few million more times, *desperate* for a different option.

Option 4) Flea spits.
Option 5) Flea spits.
Option 6) Flea spits.
Option 7) Flea spits.
Option 8) Flea spits.

Option 9) Flea spits.
Option 10) Flea spits.
Option 11) Flea spits.
Option 12) Flea spits.
Option 12) Flea spits.
Option 14) Flea spits.
Option 15) Flea spits.
Option 16) Flea spits.
Option 17) Flea spits.
Option 18) Flea spits.
Option 19) Flea spits.
Option 20) Flea spits.
Option 21) Flea spits.
Option 22) Flea spits.
Option 23) Flea spits.
Option 24) Flea spits.
Option 25) Flea spits.
Option 26) Flea spits.
Option 27) Flea spits.
Option 28) Flea spits.
Option 29) Flea spits.
Option 30) Flea spits.
Option 31) Flea spits.
Option 32) Flea spits.
Option 33) Flea spits.
Option 34) Flea spits.
Option 35) Flea spits.
Option 36) Flea spits.
Option 37) Flea spits.
Option 38) Flea spits.
Option 39) Flea spits.

Option 40) Flea spits.
Option 41) Flea spits.
Option 42) Flea spits.
Option 43) Flea spits.
Option 44) Flea spits.
Option 45) Flea spits.
Option 46) Flea spits.
Option 47) Flea spits.
Option 48) Flea spits.

The Trith screamed and grabbed its huge head with its tiny hands, which made Flea totally lose what little control he had left. Instinct took over and he spat.

Instantly, Flea knew he was going to die. He started scuttling backwards, trying to apologize. "It was just a little bit," he babbled, "and it wasn't even aimed at an eye, so you don't need super expensive surgery…"

The Trith was blinking at him, its little body going really stiff.

He's mad, Flea thought, horrified. *Oh grease and ashes, he's mad. He's gonna liquefy my brains or torment my dreams or—*

The Trith's tiny hands went up to its mouth and nose, which was now a hardened lump of Flea's spit.

"Sorry!" Flea cried. "A little bit of surgery can—"

Then he realized that it had *plugged* the Trith's mouth and nose, and his world came to a grinding halt.

"Oh ash." He stopped backing up and straightened in horror.

The Trith's tiny spasms, Flea realized, were because it was suffocating. Flea glanced down at the laser knife in his hand, thinking how easily he had seen similar knives slice through flesh before. Taking a deep breath, he pressed the button again. Then, because he didn't think *three* options would be enough, he pressed it again.

At the same time that the Trith gave another muffled scream and doubled over, then fell to its knees, Flea saw six more options splayed out before him...

Option B1) Spit again, because the Trith obviously needs another dose: **page 213**
Option B2) Use the knife to cut through the glue and get the Trith some air: **page 216**
Option B3) Let him die. (Flee): **page 227**
Option B4) Stab the Trith to make sure he's dead: **page 231**
Option B5) Capture it! **page 235**
Option B6) Let him suffer a little, then help him, then click the button some more, because that makes him scream, which makes it fun: **page 239**

OPTION B1

SPIT AGAIN, BECAUSE ASHES YOU SURVIVED THE FIRST ONE, SO WHY NOT TRY FOR TWO.

Because he'd already spat once and survived it, Flea decided he must have beaten Forgotten's curse and he spat again, this time at the Trith's foot, sticking its froglike appendages to the grating of the staircase.

The Trith tripped, ripping its foot from the grating with its top-heavy plunge down the stairs.

Flea, not expecting such a sudden forward attack, got hit in the chest by the Trith's big head and was taken down with the Trith's plummet. They rolled to the floor together, Flea upside-down under the Trith's forehead. Then the Trith's tiny hands were scrabbling around, reaching for something…

Flea heard the uncanny sizzle of a laser knife activating, then started to squirm, realizing the Trith planned to use it on him.

Unfortunately, the sheer *size* of the Trith's fat, bald head kept him pinned to the ground. Flea cried out as a searing pain shot through his shoulder and the knife made the unmistakable crackle as it started to eat through flesh. He screamed and flailed, but flat on his back, a Trith's head squishing him to the floor, Flea couldn't move, and could only lay there, spitting helplessly at the wall, as the Trith sawed at him.

The Trith grunted and stabbed him, repeatedly, heaving on its big head, then slamming it back into Flea's body, making muffled moaning sounds as it continued to drive the knife into Flea's body, towards its own face.

Then the Trith went limp above him, the knife still buried in Flea's carapace.

"*Forgotten sends his regards,*" the device said, even as the last tendril of tendon holding his head to his thorax fell loose and his head started to roll away. He got a grisly scene of his own headless corpse squished under a Trith—whose eyes were now *white*—before he rolled away from the scene, to stop facing a wall covered in his own spit.

And there, staring at a wall, he felt his vision fade, until all he could see were the discolored lumps he had created in the paint.

Then they, too, faded, and Flea slipped into the darkness.

END IT HERE

or

BACK TO YOUR CHOICES: **page 211**

OPTION B2

USE THE KNIFE TO SAVE THE TRITH.

Flea had always found it difficult to watch other intelligent creatures die when he could do something about it. Because he felt bad—not because it was necessarily the smartest thing in the universe to do—Flea crawled forward, making the Trith give a muffled scream and hold up a hand in terror.

"It's okay!" Flea cried, quickly climbing up the skinny creature's body and onto its head. He pulled out the knife and flipped it on, making the weird zapping sound as he held it awkwardly between them. The Trith gave a muffled scream and flailed.

"No, I'll save you! I—"

Too late, he realized that the Trith really *was* as top-heavy as he looked.

Clinging to the Trith's head, Flea cried out and scrabbled for purchase as the Trith started to teeter, then fell face-first down the stairs. To avoid getting taken down with it, Flea took to the air, wincing as the Trith's huge, rubbery head seemed to hit every single metal angle, then came to a sliding roll at the bottom, its neck at a *very* unhealthy angle to the rest of its gangly body.

"Forgotten sends his regards," the charm said.

"Uh…" Flea said, still holding the laser knife in one hand. Even as he watched, the Trith's deep, void-black eyes faded to a flat, opaque white. He glanced at it, then numbly shut it off. Then, dazed, he landed on the staircase, unable to stop staring at the little corpse at the bottom. *I just killed a Trith,* he thought, horrified. *That's not supposed to be possible…*

Immediately, he thought of all the horrible things that would happen to him if that little fact became public knowledge. The Peacemakers would immediately incarcerate and interrogate him, demanding to know every step he had taken, every tiny detail, then would confiscate his charm so they could replicate it themselves.

If the *Trith* found out, Flea would be as good as dead. He'd spend the rest of his life being hunted, having to watch his back every single tic for the rest of his existence, terrified the Trith's vengeful comrades would come for him in the night, or were hiding around the very next corner, knowing exactly when and how to cross his path to create the most pain and terror before death, then slip back into the darkness, completely unseen by the rest of the universe.

"Ashes and grease," Flea babbled, swallowing. "Ashes and grease, ashes and grease..."

Every instinct in him was screaming at him to run, to put as much distance between him and the dead Trith as possible, to keep anyone from knowing he had any hand in its death.

But if the dead Trith was discovered, ever, then Congress would scour the place top to bottom for genetic evidence, and they would figure out that Flea had been the culprit.

He had to do something. He had to hide the body. He couldn't let anyone *know*...

Immediately, Flea's mind returned to the nice, empty hollow space he'd found under the building, sealed off except for the peeling corner of one floor. If he dumped the Trith's body in there, the torrak would find it and pick at the corpse until there was nothing but scattered bones...

Desperate, Flea grabbed the Trith's leg and started to pull.

Unfortunately, while the Trith was smaller than even a Ueshi, compared to Flea, it was enormous. No amount of tugging and pulling would make the Trith's corpse budge. Flea, caught in indecision, returned to the charm that he'd dropped in his earlier struggle and pushed the button.

Instantly, three options seared through his mind where there had been darkness, creating new pathways of experience from which to choose...

Option B2a) Spit at the corpse, because it vexes you: **page 220**
Option B2b) Flee, leaving Rat's knife at the scene so the Trith will think she did it: **page 222**
Option B2c) Use Rat's knife to cut the corpse apart and hide the individual pieces under the floorboards of the abandoned comm center: **page 225**

OPTION B2A

SPIT AT THE CORPSE, BECAUSE IT MADE YOU BREAK A SWEAT.

Disgusted with how many hours he had just spent screwing around to absolutely no avail, Flea spat at one of the Trith's big white oblong eyeballs. It landed in the middle of one, as a puddle of blackness.

A moment later, there was a weird *humming* sound as it felt like the world itself was beginning to shrink and slide inwards, towards the Trith's eye.

"What the..."

The fabric of reality itself seemed to be pulling inward where Flea's black spit had hit the weird whiteness of the Trith's eye, like sheets of colored cloth getting tugged into the eye of a needle.

Flea recognized a singularity when he saw one.

Unfortunately, the split second that it took to recognize the formation of an infant black hole was too long to evade it, and Flea found himself sucked into the Trith's eye in a blinding instant of pain, twisting bands of light, and then total, complete darkness.

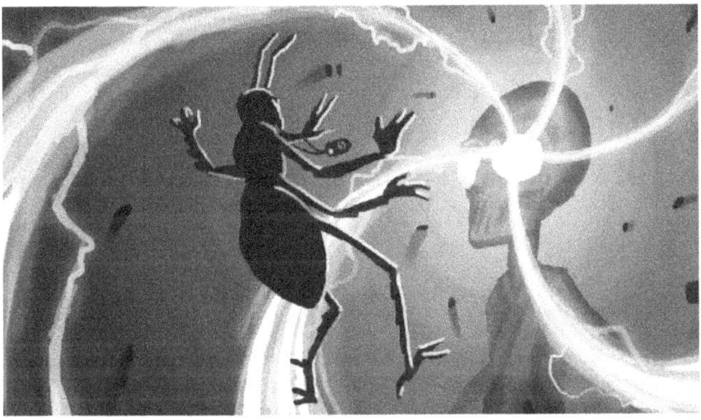

END IT HERE

or

GO BACK TO YOUR CHOICES: **page 219**

OPTION B2B

FRAME RAT FOR SOMETHING SHE PLANS TO DO ANYWAY.

Flea decided that wetwork wasn't in his job description and dropped the knife by the corpse. Besides, Rat planned to kill the Trith anyway, so why not let her take credit for the kill?

Then Flea realized the corpse didn't have any knife-wounds in it, and an autopsy—which Congress would without question do—would reveal that the Trith had suffocated to death, *not* stabbed to death with Rat's knife.

Because it was necessary—and because Flea knew this would be the *first* Trith the Congressional doctors ever autopsied—Flea decided to carry the knife into the air and let it drop on the Trith a few times, to give the corpse a legitimately freshly-killed look. They would never need to know that the nose and mouth were plugged. And, knowing Congressional doctors, who would rather pull something out of their butts than admit they didn't know, they would probably make up an excuse for why skin had sealed over the mouth and nose, chalking it up to vestigial, unnecessary processes, and coming to the conclusion that the Trith were so evolved they no longer needed to eat or breathe.

Once he'd dropped the knife into the Trith's chest a few times, Flea didn't even have the nerves to try to wipe his biomatter from the hilt. His whole body was shaking with panic, partially due to the blue lines of blood now seeping from the Trith's body, and partially due to the fact that every moment he spent here with the corpse was an added second that he could be caught with it.

Even more unnerving, the Trith's eyes, which had been a weird, almost glowing opaque white when it first died, had slowly turned almost sickly gray, the glow fading from them completely, leaving something...vile...behind. His carapace crawled just getting close to it.

I'm in an abandoned building with the body of a dead Trith, Flea thought. *An omnipresent being that can read minds and destroy Congressional fleets by the billions and billions.* It was the only thing he *could* think, and it was making him so paranoid he found himself wanting to spit at every gust of wind, every chitter of a nearby torrak, every flutter of metal sheeting against the comm station's frame...

Unable to stay in the same room with the corpse any longer, Flea hastily crawled out a ragged hole in the back side of the comm center—his instinct was to get back to civilization as quickly as possible, but he didn't want anyone to see him leaving the scene of the crime—and fled into the desert before doubling back and coming at the town from the opposite direction.

Once he was in the very center of town, Flea climbed up to the underside of a porch roof and hunkered down, staring out at the darkened town. Even stabilized by clinging to the polymer sheeting, Flea's legs were shaking. He kept seeing the big, light-eating black eyes, pulling him in. He kept hearing the creature's indignant rage reverberating through his mind...

One thing kept pounding in his brain like a hammer: If anyone linked Flea to the death, his life was over. Either he'd be interrogated until he died, or he'd be murdered slowly, but either way, he'd be hunted for the rest of his life.

CONTINUE FROM HERE: **page 243**

or

GO BACK TO YOUR CHOICES: **page 219**

OPTION B2C

HACK UP THE BODY, THEN STASH THE PIECES.

Because he needed to do something fast—and because he was already totally screwed—Flea collected Rat's knife and, grimacing and turning his head, started sawing off the Trith's arms, legs, and head.

I'm sawing off the limbs of a Trith, Flea couldn't help but think. *Grease and ashes, I'm sawing off the legs and head of a* Trith. *A creature that annihilated all the Congressional fleets that came after them, down to the very last ship, and I'm chopping it up like a melaa. If they ever find out who did this…*

But once he started, he couldn't realistically stop. The only way he was moving the body *anywhere* was in pieces, unless he wanted to call in Rat and Klick, and that simply wasn't an option. The moment that *anyone* knew that *he* killed the Trith, then the whole *world* had the potential of knowing. Just one slip, just one careless word, and Flea's life was over. This was a secret that Flea had to take with him to his *grave*. He couldn't tell *anyone*. Not if he ever wanted to remain free.

It was gruesome work, and by the end of it, Flea was covered in cold, congealing blue blood and viscera. He was shuddering as he grabbed the severed pieces of Trith and dragged them to the hole in the corner of the floor, then push-pulled them down into the crawlspace under the building with him.

When it was over, Flea spread sand all over the floor and rubbed it down in an attempt to rid the metal sheeting of the stain. Then he swept the clumpy blue sand into the hole with the Trith, pressed the metal flooring back into place, and got out of there as quickly as he could. Too shaken up to fly straight, he found a rocky crevice to hide in, climbed inside, and huddled in the darkness, desperately trying to stop trembling.

CONTINUE FROM HERE: **page 243**

or

GO BACK TO YOUR CHOICES: **page 219**

OPTION B3

GET OUT. GET OUT NOW.

The Trith gave a muffled croak and fell to a knee, one skinny gray arm reaching out towards Flea. Flea moved back on reflex, but the furious black eyes trapped him, swallowing him like the Void. *How… dare…you.* Each syllable was like a hammer hitting the inside of Flea's mind like a gong. It started to crush him, pulverizing his being from all sides.

Somehow through the terror, Flea managed to inch his fingers over to push the charm's button.

Instantly, at the same time Flea got three options splayed out in front of him, the Trith screamed, and its hold on his mind ceased like it had never been. In a panic, now, Flea started slamming his finger on the button, again and again, ignoring the options that popped into his mind as the Trith writhed, lost its grip on the railing, and tumbled down the stairs.

"*Forgotten sends his regards,*" the device said.

Flea bolted.

Blinded by instinct and terror, he was millions of marches out into the desert, buzzing over the dunes faster than a skimmer could travel, before he could get himself slowed down long enough to actually *think*.

It was possible he had just killed a Trith.

He, Flea, a single unarmed Baga without a credit to his name, might have just taken down one of the most formidable creatures known to Congress. Creatures that had thwarted entire Congressional armadas for millions of turns. Creatures so rare and powerful they were considered a myth by most, and a threat so severe to Congressional control that anyone who ever had *contact* with a Trith was immediately quarantined, often for the rest of their life, as Peacemakers tried to discern why a Trith would expend the effort to appear to that person, at that time.

To have *killed* a Trith—something that Congress had been fantasizing about since the planet of Trith had been discovered—Peacemakers would imprison and interrogate him every minute of every day until they revealed every single secret he had used to kill the creature. Which meant they would discover Forgotten's device. Which meant they would discover he was working with Forgotten.

Which meant Flea was dead.

Flea was *so* dead.

He buried himself in the sand of the crack of two dunes for several hours, with only that single, all-consuming fact rushing through his head.

He might have just killed a Trith, and he was dead.

Only after a few more hours had passed and Flea had watched a torrak make its slow march from the top of one dune through the valley connecting them, and to the top of another dune, did he finally find the courage to climb out of the little hole he'd dug for himself in the sand.

He was only dead, he decided, if he'd actually *killed* a Trith. If he hadn't, he was in a lot more trouble.

Suddenly, Flea had to know which it was going to be—Congress coming after him, looking for his keys to success, or the *Trith* coming after him, looking for vengeance for their fallen comrade

Unfortunately, the only way for Flea to figure out if he'd actually killed that Trith was to go back and look.

He didn't want to go back and look.

Time passed.

Flea made himself go back and look.

He crept up to the broken comm station's window slowly, half-expecting laser fire to blow him away as soon as he poked his head into sight.

Instead, when he found the courage to peek above the sill, he saw the very still—and very *dead*—form of a Trith splayed out on the floor at the bottom of the stairs, exactly where Flea had left him. Its big, once-black eyes were now a dull, sickly gray.

"Grease!" Flea cried, hunkering back down against the outer wall of the comm station. Beside him, the loose metal of the comm station wiggled in the desert breeze.

Flea listened to the creepy, lonely sound for several minutes, then fled for the town, unable to handle the idea he was *alone* with the body of a *Trith*.

CONTINUE FROM HERE: **page 243**
or
GO BACK TO YOUR CHOICES: **page 211**

OPTION B4

STAB THE TRITH WITH THE KNIFE, BECAUSE NOBODY'S EVER DONE THAT BEFORE.

In an act of killer reflexes, Flea's hand spasmed on the knife and the blade buzzed to life. As Flea was staring down at the knife in his hand blankly, he felt the Trith reach for his mind again. As the creature's mental fist started to lock down on Flea's being, Flea felt a surge of courage and screamed, "Face the wrath of Flea!" and stabbed the Trith in the eye.

"Forgotten sends his regards," the device said, as the Trith went stiff, then started to shake. *"Oh, and Flea,*

you will want to hold on to something and try to seal the wound before it eats this sector of space."

Flea winced and let go of the knife—he'd actually been aiming for the Trith's *chest*—and was just about to ask the device what the ash it meant when two things happened: The blade sizzled and sputtered out, and the room began to scream.

Not the Trith, the *room*. Flea stumbled backward, horrified, as the knife seemed to get sucked into the Trith's eye, leaving a gaping *blackness* in its wake. All around him, wind began whipping through the windows, doors, crevices, holes in walls, the roof…Flea felt himself being sucked towards the Trith's eye, and had to grab onto the floor to keep from being pulled inside.

Then, trapped with nowhere to go, the wind whipping past him, tearing at his legs and antennae, trying to rip his wings from his body, dancing the charm around at the end of its string like a marionette, Flea realized the only thing he could do was spit.

As the world shrieked around him, Flea steeled himself and began gathering up every ounce of glue he had in his abbas, building it into the biggest spitball he'd ever shot from his klett. Then, praying to the Jreet gods, he spat.

His wad of glue hit the Trith's eye dead-on, and for an instant, looked like it would get sucked into the wound with the rest. Then the glue solidified and the tear in the Trith's eye sealed as if it had never been, the entire body slumping onto the floor in front of him.

Still, Flea clung to the floor in horror, terrified the howling winds would start again, and he would be forever trapped inside a Trith's eyeball.

Once he was relatively sure the danger was over, Flea reluctantly straightened to get a better look. The Trith was sideways on the stairs, the one big oblong eye that Flea could see a sickly shade of gray.

Flea knew that no one would ever believe him.

Which was probably a *good* thing, he thought immediately. A dead Trith brought with it questions that he didn't want to answer. Questions that he would get *killed* for answering.

Perfectly willing to leave the Trith exactly where it lay, dead-yet-apparently-unharmed, Flea fled through the open door, rushing to get back to the town and establish an alibi.

Let Rat and Klick take the credit for that one. He didn't want the hassle that would come with it. First, there would be the Congies, looking to figure out how he'd killed the unkillable. Then there would be other Trith, looking to make an example out of him for killing one of their own, Trith that could show up when he least expected it, appearing when he was alone and vulnerable to carry out their gruesome and painful act of vengeance.

No, he would *much* rather stand back and let someone else claim this particular kill.

With that in mind, he went looking for a stiff drink.

CONTINUE FROM HERE: **page 243**
or
GO BACK TO YOUR CHOICES: **page 211**

OPTION 85

BAG YOURSELF A TRITH, BECAUSE NOBODY'S EVER DONE THAT BEFORE.

Grease and ashes, Flea thought, staring at the Trith that was suffocating on the stairs. *He's gonna die...*

But Flea *wanted* him to die, right? This was the creature that was planning to kill Joe. So it was *best* if it died.

Then, like getting hit with a sledgehammer, it occurred to him...*I could* catch *him and* interrogate *him and root out his accomplices! I, Flea, could be the very first Trapper of Trith!*

Buzzing with excitement, Flea scuttled up the stairs, circling around behind the choking Trith. Before it could stumble around to face him, Flea grabbed its two puny arms and yanked them together, then spat to fuse the tiny palms together. Then he spat at the Trith's feet, sealing them together at the ankles. Victorious, he climbed atop the Trith's head, chuckling to himself about how he, Flea, had bagged a Trith on his own when the full power of the entire Ground Force and its billions and billions of Jreet and

Huouyt and Dhasha and Humans and Ooreiki and Ueshi and Hebbut and Bajna and Jikaln and Trosska and Jahul and Grekkons and Ayhi and Dreit and Yugi and Dophin and all the other races he'd never seen or cared about had all failed. He really *was* Flea the Mighty, Champion of Chaos, Agent of Forgotten! He struck a heroic stance on the Trith's head, imagining what *his* propaganda posters would look like. In Joe's they always had him standing on a Dhasha's snout, a big gun in one hand, his head turned to stare majestically off into the distance.

In reality, Joe was usually hunched over a bar, drinking himself into a stupor, but maybe the cameramen missed that.

Flea's would be better! Flea had conquered the one being in Congress that could not be conquered! They would show an image of Flea stepping on their big squishy black eyeballs in every window, slap it on every wall, display it on every news reel, for *he* was the conqueror of *Trith*!

Or maybe it would be a picture of a Trith on its knees, arms up in supplication, Flea sitting stoically on the treads of a tank as it begged for mercy.

Or maybe—

Below him, the creature let out another muffled grunt, dragging Flea out of his reverie with a frown. When he saw the Trith's eyes half-closed, his body weaving as his chest struggled for air, its lips still sealed, Flea swore and jumped off the Trith's head to grab the laser knife off the stair above them.

The Trith, now unable to move his arms or legs, let out a muffled cry from Flea's sideways push and went toppling face-first down the stairs, landing in a crumpled heap on the metal floor below.

"*Forgotten sends his regards*," the device around his neck said, startling him.

Flea's mandibles fell open. "What the ash?"

The device did not reply.

The odd angle to its neck *couldn't* have been good, but Flea buzzed down to poke at one of its gummy black eyeballs anyway, on the off-chance the Trith was still alive.

It wasn't. Even as he stood there, squatting on its big bald gray head, the blackness seemed to get sucked out of his eye, departing inward, leaving a creepy, glowing whiteness instead.

Flea scampered nervously backwards, onto the Trith's chest. *That*...can't...*be normal.*

The white glow lasted about a tic, then it started to fade to a sickly gray that made Flea's carapace crawl. He backed up some more, until he was standing on the first step of the stairs.

Now that the Trith was unmistakably dead, the reality of the situation was beginning to really dawn on him.

He had killed a Trith.

Congress would want to know *how* he had killed a Trith.

Congress would interrogate him and take his charm so that *they* could kill Trith.

Flea couldn't let anyone know he had killed a Trith.

He did, however, have a sudden, brilliant idea on how to pay off Kroeg's debt. Congress had never actually *seen* a body of a Trith. They had no genetic material to work with, nothing to examine, no corpse to dissect.

A Trith's corpse would be worth Flea and Kroeg's freedom, easily.

All he had to do was convince Kroeg to help him retrieve it and get it to the recruiter up by the spaceport. *He* would get them off the planet, especially if they both said they saw *Marshi* kill it.

Chuckling to himself at his good luck, Flea buzzed out the window and back towards the town, knowing he was only hours away from making good with Marshi, Kroeg, and all of his debts in one fell swoop...

CONTINUE FROM HERE: **page 243**

or

GO BACK TO YOUR CHOICES: **page 211**

OPTION 86

PUT THE FEAR OF FLEA INTO THE TRITH.

Realizing this was the greatest opportunity for personal entertainment that he'd had in billions of turns, Flea screamed a war-cry and hit the Trith head-on, ramming the creature backwards into the staircase. Once the creature was down, struggling to lift its oversized head off the stair it had fallen on, Flea glued one of its tiny hands to the metal staircase. Then he glued its second hand to the wall where it was groping for purchase. Then, once he was sure his victim wasn't going anywhere, Flea whipped out Rat's laser knife, flipping it on with a sizzle as he stared down at the Trith over its humming green light. "You tried to kill me," Flea said, pausing for effect.

Immediately, the Trith started making muffled sounds of terror, shaking its head back and forth, its huge obsidian eyes filled with terror.

"And you planned to kill my friend," Flea leaned down until his face was inches from the Trith's big, Void-black eyeball. "Now you're *mine*." He pressed the button on the charm a few times, blasting out arrays of options into his head, enjoying the way the Trith wriggled and gave muffled screams.

As the Trith weakly tried to flail, Flea crawled atop his chest, and, stabilizing himself with two feet on the Trith's chin, he let out a cackling laugh and plunged the laser through the Trith's sealed lips. He yanked the blade free to the sound of the Trith screaming. Holding up the knife, its surface glinting with the blue blood of the Trith, Flea snarled, "Now face the wrath of Flea!"

The Trith started screaming in total, wild animal panic, and just kept screaming. And screaming. And *screaming*.

Flea, who felt a little bad, backed up and switched off the laser knife.

The Trith continued to shriek and thrash in complete terror, its little voice like the squeaky sound that came out of a balloon. Then that sound started to gurgle, like there was liquid caught inside the balloon. Specks of blue started sputtering out onto the walls and the Trith's face and chest as Flea's prisoner's screams turned into ragged, wet coughs.

"Uh," Flea said, as the Trith continued to flail helplessly on the staircase, spitting up blood. "Sorry?"

Azure liquid was pooling at the corners of the Trith's mouth, running down the sides of its head as it now struggled wetly for air.

The device around his neck startled Flea by saying, *"Forgotten sends his regards."*

Flea blinked.

"And by the way," the device said, *"the knife is coated with acute antimatter nanotechnology. You should probably put it down before you cut yourself."*

Mandibles falling open, Flea dropped the knife. "Forgotten?"

The device did not respond.

The Trith had stopped trying to breathe altogether, blood still dribbling out the corners of its mouth. Its eyes, which had originally been a deep, light-eating black, were changing, the blackness seeming to leach out of them like water draining even deeper inside its head, leaving a glowing whiteness behind.

Nervously scampering further up the stairs, Flea stopped on the top stair to survey the devastation below. The stairs were covered with a cascade of sapphire blood—more blood than he would have thought possible—slicking the entire surface of the second half of the rickety metal staircase.

"Ashes," Flea whispered. He had just killed a *Trith*. If its comrades didn't find him and torment him for millions of turns for what he had done, then the Peacemakers would, interrogating him for the rest of his life on how he had managed to kill what they couldn't, poking and prodding him to figure out what made him different. Once they figured out it was the device, they would take it, repurpose it, and discard him—permanently, so he couldn't tell anyone about it.

After one final look at the Trith's blood-soaked body, still pinned to the staircase, Flea turned and fled.

CONTINUE FROM HERE: **page 243**

or

GO BACK TO YOUR CHOICES: **page 211**

PART 4

PANDEMONIUM

(*Or, if you're not ready, RETURN TO PART 2: page 41 or RETURN TO PART 3: page 205)*

You!" At the same time as Flea heard the shout, he heard a pop and, as he was frowning and turning, a net caught him mid-air, knocking him out of the sky and dragging him to the ground.

As Flea struggled against the wires snagging his arms, legs, and wings, three Ooreiki came wandering up in combat gear. "Whoa. Wonder if Marshi will pay for a second one. She thought there was only one!"

Seeing their advanced operatives' gear, Flea realized why he hadn't seen Klick in a while.

These are the assassins, Flea thought. He wondered if they had any idea their leader was dead.

"My name is Klick!" Flea cried. "Not Flea."

The Ooreiki reaching down to grab him by the spitter glanced at the other two. "We don't care what your name is. All is marked on Marshi's collection sheet is *Vermin, Painted Black.*"

Then Flea was getting hefted up in the net, carried upside-down, a twist-tie around his klett.

"Hey," one of the Ooreiki said, "look at his charm! It's a little Pepsi bracelet!"

"I love Pepsi," another of his captors said, with a stupid chuckle. It reached for his neck.

Flea immediately grabbed it in reflex. "It's mine!"

The Ooreiki's big, wet brown eyes darkened. "You ain't gonna be alive much longer, so what do you care?"

Flea pressed the button.

"You have precisely three *Ooreiki thugs thieving your personal effects. Surely this wasn't a difficult one."*

"Hey, *cool*!" the Ooreiki standing to one side cried. "It talks! Grab it!"

Gasping, Flea flipped the can around and went to press the other side.

But the Ooreiki had grabbed the wire already, and with its tentacle wrapped tightly, a look of determination on its face, it yanked before Flea could find the button on the other side. "Give it, bug."

Flea, who had the wire around his throat, gagged as it tried to pull off his head.

He suddenly remembered Forgotten's warning: *"I don't suggest you wear it around your neck. For obvious reasons."*

Seeing no other alternative, he ducked his head and let them take it.

Chuckling, the Ooreiki lifted his charm up to get a good look at it. "Oooh!" he cooed, "it's got all the right details! It's even hollow!"

"How can it be hollow?" the other Ooreiki demanded. "It has an AI in it…"

"Dunno." The Ooreiki holding the tiny device pressed the button on top. Immediately, Flea got a flash of three different options, blinding him with their intensity. All of them had him end up in a cage beside Klick within the hour, but free again within a day.

Just as Flea was trying to make sense of that, the thieving Ooreiki frowned, its huge, oblong brown eyes squinting at the device. "I pressed the button. Why did nothing happen?" He pressed a few more million times.

"It's the *bottom* button!" Flea cried. "The top one emits a sex pheromone only Bagans can smell!"

The Ooreiki stopped pushing the button like it had suddenly caught fire. "Eww."

"And *torrak* are a distant cousin of Baga," Flea added, hoping that would get them to give him back his charm.

"No they're not," the third Ooreiki said. "The taxonomical classifications are completely different. One lays gelatinous eggs that grow into larvae and one has fully-developed babies crawl from hard shells." It cocked his head at Flea. "Further, they evolved on different planets over two hundred million marches apart. It would seem the little insect would like to keep his bauble more than he is letting on, to compare himself to vermin in order to manipulate us."

And that's when Flea realized that the third Ooreiki was actually a Huouyt.

"Greaser," Flea muttered, at the same time the Huouyt in Ooreiki pattern held out his tentacle and said, "Give it to me."

Apparently the leader of the trio, the first Ooreiki dutifully handed over the charm. The Huouyt looked it over, then said, "This wasn't made by a Congressional mind." He cocked his head at Flea. "Where did you get it?"

"Off a dead Trith," Flea muttered. "I think it let it see the future."

"A dead Trith," the Huouyt snorted. "Where?"

"Up in the comm station," Flea said dutifully. "Someone had done a number on it."

The Huouyt blinked, then glanced up the towering cliff surrounding the town at the abandoned comm station. Frowning, he glanced back. "You're lying."

"Maybe," Flea said. "Then again, maybe I killed the crap out of it and you'll never know."

The Huouyt-dressed-as-Ooreiki narrowed its brown Ooreiki eyes, but even they couldn't hide the sadistic, sociopathic nature of the creature wearing them. And the greed. Flea knew what a dead Trith was worth.

"Get him to Marshi's," the Huouyt said, his boneless fingers clamping around Flea's charm.

Despite Flea's protestations, they dumped him in Marshi's mansion in the center of town, near the back in a cage.

Klick was already there, and fuming. "This is *your* fault!" she snapped, jabbing an arm at Flea through the bars of her own cage. "They think I'm you!" Her wings had been clipped. Flea winced.

"So *there's* our favorite escapee," Marshi said, walking in flanked by the three Ooreiki, one of whom was actually a Huouyt. The Ueshi was wearing a skintight purple drysuit, which Ueshi preferred because they were amphibious in nature. "Which one are you? This one is insisting she's a refugee looking for her wayward brother."

Flea glanced at Klick, who gave him a look like she would *end* him if he said otherwise.

"She's an assassin sent here to kill a Trith," Flea said, deciding to see what the Ueshi's reaction would be, because that would tell him a lot about this operation as a whole.

Marshi gave Flea a startled look, then glanced at the Huouyt. "Why would a Trith be here?" he asked, his response a bit too cultivated.

"He says he already killed it," the Huouyt-dressed-as-Ooreiki said. "Up in the comm center."

"He's lying!" Klick cried. "I checked there a million times, there's no Trith."

"Guess you should've checked the *last* time, champion of pussies," Flea said. "As promised, I found it and killed it, for I am Flea, agent of chaos!"

The look on Klick's face told Flea that she would have spat on his eyeball again, had her klett not been wired shut. Still, she reluctantly said, "Your lies deceive no one, agent of darkness! If anything, you would *protect* the Trith and its machinations of evil. As a champion of Light and Order, it is my duty to destroy you both!"

"You can try, champion of pussies!" Flea cried. "And you will fail, for I am Flea the Powerful, the single most powerful wizard in the universe, and I will rain fire and grease down on all of you in my fury!"

"Wait, no, you're a *monk*!" Klick cried, jabbing at him through the cage. "*I'm* the wizard. You can't just *switch classes* like that, asher!"

"I can and did!" Flea cried. "No more am I Flea the Material, Champion of Chaos, Monk of Black Puddle. Instead, I ascended and I became Flea the Ethereal, Champion of Chaos, Wizard and destroyer of Trith! This is my third one *today*! And I got *billions* yesterday. That means I win."

"Ugh," Marshi said. "*Bagans*." She shook her head in disgust.

"Still, I want to check it out," the Huouyt said, giving Flea a narrow look.

Marshi made a disgusted gesture. "Take a skimmer. But *after* you clean up your mess in the other room. I said *dispose* of him, not *leave a body hanging from the rafters in my study*."

"You have maids for that," the Huouyt gritted.

"*My* maids *were not hired to clean up* corpses," Marshi growled. "*Besides. My torracks are hungry. Cut him up and stuff him in the pen. Oh, and* please *get rid of the plastic on the floor? It's revolting. I'm not paying you to leave random wetwork lying around in my home.*"

The Huouyt narrowed its eyes, then said, "Fine." Then it nodded its head at the two Ooreiki and turned from the room.

Klick, who had been paying attention to the conversation, flinched when Flea shouted, "You are *not* a wizard. You said you were an *assassin*. Talk about *changing classes*! That's not fair!"

"I can be an assassin if you can be a wizard!" Klick snapped back. "I can be the greatest Trith-killing assassin ever!"

"*I'm* the Trith-killer," Flea retorted. "You have to be something else, like a Dhasha-killer."

"No way!" Klick cried. "Dhasha smell like—"

"*Enough*!" Marshi snapped. "What are you two, siblings?"

"Groundmates," Flea said. "We came down here because someone said you needed to be brought down a peg or two in your ring. We're supposed to kill a Hebbut or something." He made a dismissive gesture.

Marshi's slick, translucent eye-ridge lifted. "*Are* you now?"

"Yeah, but then he found out it was one of his old buddies and he didn't wanna fight," Klick said. "So *I* was sent as backup for the pussy."

Marshi cocked her head at the two of them. "Commander Halperi sent *you* to fight in the ring? *You're* his latest champions?"

"Her first," Flea said. "Give her something fun. She's killed a Dhasha prince with nothing but her spit."

That seemed to get Marshi's interest. Even as Klick was giving Flea an uncertain look, the Ueshi said, "Like good enough for Halperi to bet everything on her?"

"Oh, *absolutely*," Flea said. Already, of the hundreds of thousands of options that he'd seen with the Ooreiki's vapid clicking, he had narrowed it down to just a couple possibilities, with one in mind in particular. "He'll only bet on her if she can use her spitter, though." Klick, thankfully, didn't contradict him. "You seal off her spitter, that's like cutting off a Hebbut's arms and it's a foul."

Marshi grunted. "Fine. But not until the fight. Don't want you two furglings running away."

Flea snorted. "Run *away*? I am Flea, the Hobbler of Hebbut, the Terrorizer of Trith, the Destroyer of Dhasha, the—"

"Enough!" Marshi shook her head. "Fine. We'll give you a fight."

"Excellent!" Flea cried. "She's been bragging how she could take on six of your guys at once, as long as I stay out of her way."

Immediately, Klick gave him a suspicious look.

"Then she'll go first," Marshi agreed. "*You* go up to the recruiters' office and tell Halperi that I'm tired of him wasting our time. He already had one guy back out—that slippery Huouyt came down here a few days ago all gung-ho, then saw Kroeg and got on the first flight back to base. *So*." Marshi leaned an elbow against the table that held their cages so she could get a better look at them. "My guys win this fight, Halperi stops trying to take my miners from me and takes Loog back to base. All Congressional presence is removed from the planet. Period."

"And if we win?" Klick demanded.

"If you win, we will allow recruiting in the center of town," Marshi said, with the completely straight face of someone who had absolutely no intention of doing so.

"The Agent of Chaos and his weaker sidekick shall prevail!" Flea cried, holding a fist out and peering into the distance heroically.

"Yeah, whatever." Marshi shook her head. To her Ooreiki thugs, she said, "I hate Baga. Never met one that's not completely nuts. Get the smaller one out of the cage and take him up to see Loog. I want confirmation from Halperi he's willing to bet everything on these two little vaghi. If he's not, we'll give them to the pit anyway. Someone will have fun stepping on them."

Flea waited docilely as the Ooreiki opened his cage and reached in for him...

Then he bit down on the hand and snipped off one of the huge creature's tentacles. As it was blinking its gummy brown eyes stupidly and dropping its gaze to its gushing arm, Flea crawled up its arm and onto its head.

"Flea, the Agent of Chaos, is free to rain down terror upon your insignificant town!" he shouted, as he rode the screaming Ooreiki around the room atop its head. "I will return for you, agent of pussies, once you have defended our Commander's honor in the ring, thereby clearing a place for my triumphant finale!"

And then, as Marshi was just starting to turn around with a frown, he fled out the front door to find Kroeg.

He searched the entire town, top to bottom, and finally found her in a guarded room in the main guard tower of the gladiatorial pit. She was seated in a chair in one corner, watching a news broadcast from Koliinaat, something about Daviin yet again doing something to cause a furor in the Regency.

Beyond her chair, standing at the door with their backs to her, were two Ooreiki with expensive-looking guns and combat gear that made more sense on black ops than guarding a mining camp. They were laughing and looking out over the parapet towards the gladiatorial pit, where a couple of miners were being forced to finish their drunken brawl from the night before…to the death.

"Psst, Kroeg," Flea whispered, climbing in through the window near her chair. He immediately crawled down the wall, putting Kroeg between him and the guards. "Keep watching the vidscreen and listen."

Kroeg, who had started to turn to look at him, glanced at the two guards, then carefully went back to watching her show. As she did, one of the Ooreiki turned to look at them, but he missed Flea crouched just out of sight behind the chair.

"I'm going to get you out of here," Flea whispered, once the Ooreiki guard had gone back to watching the fight. "But I need your help."

"What's your plan?" Kroeg asked.

"I'm going to take out the autoturrets," Flea whispered. "Then I'm going to make the world's biggest distraction ever! I need you to use it to grab as many miners as you can and go get everybody out of the mines."

That seemed to make Kroeg angry. "What, you're just going to *disable* the auto-turrets?"

"Yes," Flea said, with complete confidence, for he had seen it.

Kroeg gave him a sideways look, then reluctantly went back to her vidscreen. "Okay," she whispered, "and what about the hundreds of guys with Planetary Ops grade weaponry? Don't think they're not trained in it. There's some serious flake going on here. That's why Marshi won't let any of us leave."

"It's a home base for a group of assassins calling themselves the Shard," Flea said. "And yeah, they're *really* good."

Kroeg squinted at him. "We've got *miners*. How in the ashes are you thinking we could take on hundreds of *assassins*, Flea?"

"Rat's better," Flea said.

Kroeg, who had heard him tell stories of Rat, raised both eyebrows in surprise. "*She's* going to help us?"

Though Flea hadn't actually *asked* Rat to help them, he was pretty sure that, once the shooting started, she wouldn't really have a choice in the matter. Besides, he was pretty sure she still wanted to kill him for taking her knife.

Kroeg's big tusked face darkened. "You didn't ask her."

"She'll help!" Flea cried. "I have something she wants, so she'll help."

Kroeg wasn't convinced. "Could she get that something by *killing* you?"

Technically, she could, but that was beside the point. "Just get out of here, get to the miners, and watch for my sign. When you see it, it means the turrets are down and it's time to strike."

"What am I looking for?" Kroeg asked.

"Oh, believe me," Flea chuckled to himself. "You'll know it when you see it." Then, because he'd used up his allotted time, he said, "Excuse me! I have to go take out those turrets before a Huouyt finishes chopping up a dead guy."

Kroeg cocked her head at Flea and frowned. "You mean Her'ruth? Marshi's second-in-command? Who'd he kill this time?"

"No idea," Flea said. He shook his head. "Just go get the miners, then attack when you see my distraction, okay? The more chaos, the better."

Kroeg rolled her eyes with a groan. "*Please* tell me this isn't that 'Agent of Chaos' flake again."

"For I am Flea, Agent of Chaos!" he cried gleefully, because she had said it. Then, because the guards were turning at his yell, Flea spat in their eyes and escaped out the window to the sounds of their pissed-off shouts. Behind him, he heard Kroeg give a full-throated Hebbut howl as she bum-rushed her two guards and sent them careening over the edge of the parapet.

His next task was harder. He had to get close enough to the turrets so as to not set them off, and for that, he needed a disguise.

He found a blue cloth dangling from one of the miners' clotheslines and tied it around himself like a cloak. Then, at a walk, he scuttled across the ground towards the first turret along the path to the mines.

"Herble triggit!" Flea called as he walked, remembering his possible 'futures' that ended with death-by-torrak. "Triggit!"

It took several minutes, but eventually, he had a torrak scuttle out into the open and flash its multicolored, patterned sail at him. "*Herble triggit!*" it snapped.

"Triggit!" Flea snapped back, flashing his own 'sail'.

The torrak flinched at the size of the cloth, then screamed its war cry and charged.

Flea bolted, keeping low to the ground and half-flew, half-ran to stay ahead of it. He watched the auto-turrets follow them as the AIs ascertained their threat level.

"*Herble triggit!*" Flea cried, once he was close enough to launch at the turret. He spat.

The turret seemed to hesitate a moment, then it tried to fire back. The round got bottlenecked at the ejection point and the turret, unexpectedly backed up, exploded, shooting bits of metal into the air in all directions.

The explosion seemed to draw the attention of every male torrak within range, because suddenly Flea had an entire herd of them running behind him, screaming their little war cry. Praying the next turret didn't learn from the first one's demise—or consider the unexpectedly huge number of torraks a threat—Flea approached the next turret along the path to the mines.

This one apparently *did* learn from its predecessor, because it began shooting.

"*Herble triggit*!" Flea screamed, taking to the air and letting the torraks keep running forward in front of him. Several of them got picked off by the turret by the time Flea was close enough to spit, but there was safety in numbers—he got a good spit off and the second turret, like the first, exploded.

"*All hail Flea, Agent of Chaos!*" Flea screamed, as the broken bits of turret rained down around him and his army marched on the next turret.

He and his minions took out millions of them, and by the time he'd finished, he had enough torraks gathered to his flag that they could have filled a small building.

...so that's exactly what Flea did. He marched his army back to town and into the Security Headquarters building, to the delightful sounds of screaming within. Then he took to the air, headed towards the comm station, to steal a skimmer from a greedy Huouyt.

• • •

"*Just stay calm,*" Rat told Klick through the private comm. Klick's Prime was mingling with the miners, hiding in plain sight. "*Benva's up in the battlements and I've got a bead on the entrance—whatever they send at you's gonna get splattered. Sol'dan's in Marshi's estate, looking for our escape vehicle. Just hang in there.*"

Klick didn't *feel* like hanging in there. Flea, that *asher*, had cheated at Dungeons & Dragons again and left her to fight the evil hordes alone. What she *wanted* to do was go hunt him down and glue him for being a wet-eyed greasebag.

A sudden explosion rocked the air with a concussive blast that made Klick's carapace tremble. Klick, who felt exposed squatting out there on the sand in the middle of the gladiatorial arena, flinched and hunkered down. "Uh," she said, "what was that?"

"*Hold on.*" There was a long silence from Rat, then a reluctant, "*Benva says the turrets around the mine are being taken out by a herd of angry torraks.*"

Klick, still been fuming about the fact that Flea couldn't just *change* classes, slowly broke into a grin. "Really?"

"*Yeah, hold on. I don't see how—*" As Klick watched, Rat jostled in the growing crowd gathering to watch the oncoming fight. Her Prime struggled up the stairs to the top riser, then set Max—disguised as a regular assault rifle, because in this town, it was assumed that anyone with a gun was *supposed* to have a gun—on the wall to peer through the scope. More explosions followed the first, but Rat just stared for some time before she said. *"Herd…of torraks."* Then Rat raised her head from the scope. *"I'll be burned. They're coming this way."*

"Can someone tell me why an army of torraks just ran into the security barracks?!" Sol'dan demanded over the common com. *"I was just about to secure us a ride off the planet, now there's nothing but chaos."*

His Evilness, Master of Chaos, Klick thought, amused. She wondered how much experience the grease bucket would try to weasel out of Rat for this one.

"There goes that little asher," Rat said. *"Headed for the comm station.* Without *my knife."* She settled into a better position, taking aim at Flea from atop the wall.

At the same moment, the doors to her opponents' staging area opened, and out stepped six Humans and Ooreiki who were most certainly not miners. They were wearing shielding and protective clothing and goggles. All were carrying gruesome-looking clubs.

"Uh, a little help?" Klick said, as they exited the huge door to spread out in a semi-circle around her.

"We've gotta be low-key about this," Rat said. *"Benva and I are counting twenty-one heads, plus the six in the ring with you."*

"I've got my eyes on thirty more," Sol'dan said. *"Though a few of them seem to have been stung by torraks."*

"That doesn't mean much to me," Klick noted.

"It's nothing we can't deal with," Rat told her. *"Any that get close to you, we'll just pick them off. Just make it look…I dunno…*believable…*that they're dropping 'cause you're spitting at them."*

"Can do," Klick said. She *really* wished the wet-eyed Ueshi greaser hadn't clipped her wings, but she could work around it. As the six fighters—Klick guessed they were members of the special-ops group calling themselves the Shard—started to carefully move around her, looking for an opening, Klick made a huge show of aiming her spitter at the closest one's mask…

"Ready?" Rat said. *"Go."*

Klick spat.

At about the same time her spit hit the polymer of his crowd-control shield, it was hollowed out by a plasma round, which, once it burned through the first barrier, was instantaneously followed up by a second shot.

It must have been convincing, because the ring of guys all looked over to their comrade as he slumped to the ground, and they looked back at her with wide-eyed terror.

"*Now face the wrath of Klick!*" Klick screamed at them, taking careful aim at another one.

"Ready?" Rat said. *"Go."*

Klick spat, and another plasma round ate away her glob of spit before it even had a chance to harden. "Klick the Magnificent, Slayer of Dhasha!" she howled.

All around her, hardened soldiers started to scream and run. She and Rat picked them off one by one as they bolted, much to the overwhelming enthusiasm of the miners. They let the sixth one pound at the walls, screaming for help, for several minutes before Klick casually walked up and offed him, to the insane delight of the gathered onlookers. Klick supposed that they weren't used to Marshi's own troops fighting in the pit, and the six of them falling had brought the fully-packed observation decks into a frenzy as they chanted, "Klick, Klick, Klick, Klick!" all around her.

Klick could get used to this. She bowed, accepting their reverence, turning circles in the center to gaze upon all her devotees.

"Careful," Rat said. *"We've got an incoming skimmer about a thousand feet up. Looks like it's going to fly directly overhead. Probably one of Marshi's curve-balls, so be ready."*

Klick, who had nowhere to go, hunched against the sand, looking up.

Thus, she had to do a double-take when the distant skimmer did a sudden roll, and its driver fell from the controls in a swan-dive for the ground.

No, Klick thought, *there's two of them...*

Even as the stalled skimmer slid to one side, barrelling towards the ground somewhere else in the city, the dive-bombing duo came into focus.

It was Flea...

...riding a Trith.

"What...the...?" Rat managed.

"Make way for Flea, Agent of Chaos, Slayer of Trith!" Flea screamed from above, his blue cloak billowing out behind him.

Klick was too stunned to scuttle to one side. The Trith's white-eyed body hit the ground less than a dig from where she stood, spraying her with cerulean gore as she stood there in flabbergastation.

Flea struck a heroic pose in front of her atop the Trith's deflated chest, his majestic blue cloak slowly coming to a rest around him. "For I am Flea, god to the grandfathers of gods, killer of those that cannot be killed!"

Too stunned to object, Klick poked the Trith. It was dead. *Very* dead. It looked like the fall had actually broken it into pieces.

"Is that what it looks like?" Rat asked quietly.

"Uh," Klick replied. "Pretty sure it is." It would be incredibly hard to fake the way the Trith's internal organs were seeping from a pressure-crack in its side, and the way its bright blue brain was leaking out its ears, care of its flattened skull.

All around them, there was stunned silence from the onlookers. Then Marshi piped up, "Fifty thousand credits and a pardon to anyone who can kill those two Baga in the ring."

• • •

Just as his Pepsi charm had shown him, Flea had arrived to see the Huouyt pacing the inside of the comm center, the equipment activated and humming, setting up some sort of blackmarket deal for his Trith.

The corpse itself was already loaded on the skimmer, leaving Flea no trouble whatsoever to land on the driver's dashboard, activate its buffers, and hit the throttle.

Then he was clinging on for dear life, careening out over the canyon and the miners' village, struggling to stay at the controls as the skimmer slung this way and that, threatening to dump him and his prize prematurely into the dirt.

It only took him a couple tics to reach the gladiatorial ring, at which point he put the skimmer into a spin and buzzed to grab the Trith and steer its fall as close to Klick as possible, for he was pretty sure he'd get more points from Rat the more dramatic his entry into the ring.

Off in the distance, the turrets stationed at the edge of town began a deadly, explosive rain of fire at

Flea's skimmer, the deadly barrage knocking it out of the sky to hit the recruitment center in a ball of blue fire, making Loog, who had been standing outside on the precipice overlooking the town, taking a piss, start and almost tumble down the cliff. Flea had just enough time to see the big Hebbut turn, his recruitment station exploding from the inside, when Flea fell inside the gladiatorial pit's huge walls had to brace himself for impact.

He hit the ground with enough force to partially deflate himself, which he managed to recover from before Klick saw it, straining and forcing his carapace back out into its proper shape while she was still staring at the dead Trith.

As soon as he was sure he hadn't broken legs, Flea struck a heroic pose atop the Trith's crunched torso, flipping his cloak out dramatically so that he was sure Klick was paying attention. At the top of his lungs, he shouted, "For I am Flea, god to the grandfathers of gods, killer of those that cannot be killed!"

Klick looked satisfyingly dumbstruck.

Before she could respond, however, Marshi piped up from one of the parapets, "Fifty thousand credits and a pardon to anyone who can kill those two Baga in the ring. And fifty thousand credits *more* to anyone who shoots him if he gets back in the air—wouldn't want that little sandling getting away."

Flea's mouth fell open. "But…" He looked around. Instead of the horror and awe he was expecting, the crowd was just staring at him blankly.

"They have no idea what a Trith is," Klick whispered. "Probably best to keep it that way."

Ridiculous! His greatest kill was not about to be *belittled* by a champion of pussies! Flea scampered off the Trith's body so that the crowd could have a better look. "Behold!" he shouted. "A Trith!"

Klick clapped one of her legs to her eyeballs in despair.

"*You want me to shoot him?*" Rat asked over the comm.

"Wait, *Rat's* here?" Flea demanded, turning to look for her.

"No, shhh!" Klick cried, reaching out for one of his arms.

Flea found Rat peering down the barrel of a Rodemax at him, using one of the balconies for support. "Rat!" he cried. He pointed. "*She's* the one you want."

"*I'm going to shoot him now.*"

Flea zigzagged and screamed, "Rat, Mistress of Pain, the universe's greatest assassin, is here on a quest to destroy your puny collection of Congie castoffs, just as I have obliterated your leader!" He made a disgusted gesture towards the dead Trith.

"*Klick*," Rat said carefully, "*get him to stop talking.*"

"There she is now!" he cried, jabbing his arm at Rat, "An assassin for Prince Mekkval himself! Look! Up there on the balcony! She carries a Rodemax! Do you know how *expensive* a Rodemax is?! Even her mere *boots* cost millions of credits!"

Rat took a potshot at him, then ducked away from the gun long enough to utterly obliterate one of Marshi's goons that had gotten a little too curious, dumping him over the edge of the balcony after pile-driving his face into a metal support post.

"Get her!" Marshi snapped, at the same time an enormous gray Jreet let out a *shee-whomph* war-cry from the battlements, and the wall collapsed as it rolled into the fray.

At the same time as *that*, Kroeg and her group of miners came barreling out of hiding, rushing Marshi's goons. Everywhere, men and women were screaming, fighting each other, running from the Jreet, getting thrown from the bleachers by Rat, or Benva, or Kroeg. Maybe it was the way Benva impaled one screaming Ooreiki on his tek and exploded another against a wall from the sheer force of his fist, but no one was paying attention to the two Baga sitting in the middle of the empty ring with a dead Trith.

The miners, likewise, were falling in behind Kroeg, dragging Marshi down from her booth before she could climb aboard her personal skimmer and escape. Some of the miners, thinking to get on Marshi's good side, were fighting back, and the brawl that ensued boiled over into the ring as Rat and a dozen others fell from the stands into the pit, kicking and punching.

Seeing the chaos he had wrought, Flea felt a little warm ball of joy begin to heat the center of his chest.

"Wipe that smirk off your face," Klick muttered. "You didn't have a character sheet, so it doesn't count."

Flea felt his mandibles fall open. "*No...*"

"I didn't see *anything*," Klick said, pointedly looking the other direction from the Trith. "You can't prove shit." Behind them, the Jreet screamed and slammed two Ooreiki with assault rifles against the stands, knocking out a section of the risers and tumbling the fight out into the town itself.

Flea put a foot on the Trith's face. "I have a dead *Trith*. That's *hundreds* of xp. Rat said so."

"Rat also said you needed to have your character sheet out for her to check off within thirty tics of the deed, or she'll have to count it all as heresay because you're a cheater." Klick smirked at him. "You don't have a character sheet." She made a show of checking her watch, which she didn't have because she couldn't read it. "And you've got...two thousand tics."

Two thousand tics!

In a panic, Flea launched himself into the air, knowing he needed to find a datapad and integrate the proper rudimentary Earth programming for a standard character sheet before he ran out of time.

Knowing his only shot at success was to get inside Marshi's home and locate one of her expensive gadgets, Flea launched from the sand of the gladiatorial pit, buzzing towards Marshi's mansion at a billion marches a second. He hit the roof hard, rolled down, caught himself on the eaves, and swung inside the window, barely pausing long enough to right himself after he tumbled onto the floor inside her study before hurtling across to the far wall, where Flea had seen a desk with a datapad through the open door as he'd been carried through the living-room earlier.

"Gotcha!" Flea cried, yanking the pad free and starting entering guesses into Marshi's unlock sequence, which turned out to be her name spelled backwards, which made sense because Ueshi were stupid. "Aha!" He quickly closed the emails from Representative Mekkval about a mission for the Shard and went straight to the integration section, where he found Earth after a frenzied search under *Exotics, New*. Synching with their integration system took more tics than he had to waste, and Flea found himself fidgeting as the little bar crawled across the screen, biting his fist and pacing.

Two thousand tics, Flea thought, horrified. *I only have two thousand tics to claim the Trith!*

Then the device had synched and Flea began poring through Earth's multitude of varied programs, though most of them seemed to revolve around 2-D visual sex, interactive holographic sex, or finding a compatible Human capable of sex. They cluttered the entire Earth-based interface, clogging the works, making it necessary to apply filters to even begin to sift through the trash for something usable.

Eventually, though, he hit the Mother Lode.

"Aha!" Flea screamed, finding a Standard Dungeons & Dragons Character Sheet Generator. He told the device to integrate it, then hastily filled out everything he could remember about his monk, who had spontaneously multi-classed into a sorcerer due to sudden and unexpected trauma that awakened the dragon within him, the rush of power saving himself and liberating an entire town in the process.

Yeah, that sounded good.

Outside, men and women were pummeling each other in the streets, and the windows of Marshi's mansion were being broken by stones and clubs as people climbed into the room with him to begin looting.

To stay out of the way, Flea crawled into a hollow created by an incinerator basket, a potted plant, a wall, and the desk. Then he continued to type out his latest experience, an epic quest the likes of which had never been seen, the completion of which would make him Flea the Divine, god to the grandfathers of gods. With every precious tic passing with unnerving speed, Flea sat as the looters wreaked chaos around him, agonizing over every word. *And then, after leading a great dragon army against the ensorcelled towers imprisoning the innocent citizens of Glaxxion…*

A big Hebbut carrying a gold-and-silver statue came to a startled halt above him, peering down into the crack between the desk and the wall where Flea had taken refuge to finish his character sheet. "Hey, look at this! It's Marshi's personal datapad! I bet there's all *sorts* of cool stuff on there!" The big greaser leaned down to take Flea's hard-won work from him.

Seeing that huge, ugly hand reaching for his character, Flea felt something feral uncoil within him. Without another thought, he launched at the Hebbut's face with a scream. "*I only have two thousand tics!*" he shrieked, riding it and punching it in the eyes. "*I don't have time for this!*" Then, as its other Hebbut friends stood around staring in horror, Flea launched at another one, thinking Hebbut were *really* stupid, so the others probably hadn't gotten the memo and he didn't want to be interrupted again.

The pounding of big bare Hebbut feet as they fled was music to his ears, and suddenly Flea was back to the solitude required to compose a masterpiece worthy of godhood.

And then, in a righteous blaze of glory, he cast his ensorcelled chariot aside and rode his enemy to the ground…

• • •

Rat was struggling to keep the enemies on the ground from overwhelming her—there were a lot *more* of Marshi's men than they had originally calculated, many of whom hadn't come out of the woodwork until Benva had knocked down one side of the gladiatorial ring. Klick had disappeared, assumedly to get out of harm's way, Sol'dan was unaccounted for, and Max was on the ground at Rat's feet, too big to do anything except get in the way for close-quarters combat.

That did not, however, stop the Huouyt-made Rodemax from giving a running commentary on her fighting technique.

"*You're tiring,*" Max noted. "*Working for Mekkval has made you fat.*"

"Oh shut up," Rat growled, twisting and planting her foot between a Hebbut's tusks. "I'm the same weight I was in bootcamp." She saw her opponent land splayed out in the sands of the ring before two others fell in to take his place.

"*Sloppy,*" Max commented. "*Had he been more alert, he could have taken you down with him.*"

"Not asking for a play-by-play!" Rat cried, throwing a bum-rushing Human over her shoulder, then dodging a swing from a much heavier Ooreiki and putting a plasma pistol round through the back of its head while it stumbled past.

"*I want to analyze the Trith's body,*" Max insisted for the sixtieth time. "*Don't let anyone take it until I've had a chance to analyze it.*"

"*We* are taking the body," Rat said, punching another opponent with her energized glove, knocking him backwards a few dozen rods, "back to Keval."

"*I despise sand,*" Max whined. "*Why did you have to drop me in the sand? There's* so *much potential for something abrasive to get where it shouldn't.*"

"It was either drop you or take a Hebbut's fist to the face," Rat shouted. "Stop complaining and figure out where Sol'dan is!"

"*Sol'dan refuses to speak with me directly,*" Max said. "*I told you this.*"

"Well. I'm. *Busy*!" Rat said, punctuating each major syllable with a kick or a punch or a knee to the face. "Tell him to get over it!"

"*Are you sure your Sol'dan isn't from the Na'shar family?*" Max went on casually. "*They were always elitist and arrogant corpse-defilers. Glad they gambled everything on Na'leen and fell like the highbrow snobs they are. All they had going for them was Ti'peth, anyway, and he's what destroyed them."*

Again with the complaining that Sol'dan refused to acknowledge the presence of her AI. Rat was getting really sick of it, but she didn't have time to think about it now. "Stop. Complaining. About. Sol'dan."

"He just doesn't strike me as a Ki'tashi," Max continued. *"Ki'tash are merchants and tradesmen. Sol'dan's a professional."*

Sol'dan and her gun had been feuding, each trying to turn her against the other in their moments of privacy, for several turns.

"Oh yeah?" Rat demanded, punching a Human in the throat, "Sol'dan thinks you're going to betray me one of these days I don't let you have the kill you want."

"The nerve." Max seemed amused more than anything.

"He's trying to get me to start leaving you behind on missions," Rat said.

"That would be a mistake."

"Yeah, well, so would pissing off Sol'dan."

"Where is he, by the way?" Max said coyly. *"I haven't heard anything from him since the torraks. Certainly would be a good time to use a distraction to his advantage..."*

Again with Max trying to make her second-guess her Second. "I told him to find us transportation," Rat said. "He's finding us transportation. Stop insinuating he's off doing something nefarious. It's pissing me off."

"Fine. I'll be blunt. I think your pet assassin is actually Ti'peth Na'shar, and I think he's going to mysteriously disappear for a few rotations because he's going to be busy bringing Trith genetic material to Va'ga to be processed and made into a plague to kill the rest of them."

Rat actually missed a kick.

As she fell awkwardly into the sand, Max continued, *"The Trith did, after all, destroy his family name."*

Scrambling to get back on her feet fast enough to avoid a Hebbut's club, Rat cried, "You're trying to tell me you think *Sol'dan* is the same piece of ash flaker that impersonated Zero's groundmate for fifty turns?"

"Wait and see. If he shows up a few rotations from now with a story about being left behind and having to use his wits to escape and connive and steal his way back to the Old Territory, when you and I both know he could be on the first flight out if he wanted to, I'd say it's safe for you to let me put a round between his eyes."

"That's not happening," Rat said, but she now had goosebumps all over her body. Sol'dan *had* been prone to random disappearances, often for rotations at a time. Was Max right and he was checking back in with Va'ga?

"He's probably also working with Forgotten on this one. Or at least exchanging memos."

Rat barely escaped the bear-hug of a burly Ooreiki, twisting to kick it in the oorei, instead. It went down like a sack of waste nutrient. "Max, remember what I said about pissing me off." It was unnerving her how easily the gun could get under her skin, making her question the loyalties of a friend and groundmate of almost twenty turns within just a couple tics of conversation.

A few digs away, a Hebbut was reaching down to lift Max out of the sand, and Max shocked it until it was smoking almost as a side-note. "*How else do you think that little pest managed to kill a Trith? Tell me again what he was carrying around his neck, that he no longer carries?*"

The little hairs on the back of Rat's neck were beginning to rise uncomfortably. Then she realized that Max, like all Huouyt who saw a weakness, delighted in making her uncomfortable, and she pushed the feeling aside. "Just drop it," she muttered, during a lull in the fighting. "Forgotten's got nothing to do with this."

"*I see a dead Trith approximately seven digs from where you're standing,*" Max said, "*Killed by vermin. And you seriously believe Forgotten had nothing to do with this?*"

Put that way, Rat felt stupid for not seeing it. "Okay, but why do you think Sol'dan—"

"Rat!" Flea screamed, buzzing up to her and smacking into her side with the speed of a runaway haauk. "Grease and ashes Rat I'm so glad I found you I almost ran out of time!" He held out what looked like a datapad, shoving it towards her hands. "You have to sign off on it! Hurry! Klick said I only had two thousand tics left and that was...*billions* of tics ago!"

Rat felt a spasm of anxiety as a cluster of combat-clad Hebbut came racing up to her, rifles up. "What, is Keval backing out of the op?"

The desperate Baga was utterly oblivious as she took aim at the cluster of Hebbut over his head and fired off three rounds, putting three more opponents in the growing pile in the sand around her as her high-grade plasma ate through the energy-resistant clothing they obviously had thought would protect them.

"What?" Flea said, frowning. "No, it's my *character sheet.* I need to claim my godhood before my time runs out!"

Rat missed another shot, and the charging Hebbut slammed into her from the side, driving her into the sand.

"*Rat,*" Flea whined, as she struggled to breathe as the beast crushed the air out of her ribs, "you need to *hurry...*"

"Remind me again why you associate yourself with these vermin?" Max asked.

"Flea...help," Rat gagged, as her insides tried to become her outsides.

"I would," Max said, *"but you left me to get sand into my crevices."*

"I mean, I killed a *Trith,*" Flea insisted. "Even if I'm late, I should get the credit for that."

"*Flea*!" Rat snapped.

"Yeah okay." Almost as an afterthought, Flea stuck the Hebbut holding her in the ear, making him scream and loosen his grip.

"But Klick doesn't have a character sheet," Flea continued, "so she doesn't get any XP for this, right?" Rat used Flea's distraction to elbow the Hebbut holding her in the face, then rammed her knee into his delicate stomach and lunged to her feet, blasting him in the head a few times with her plasma pistol, just to be safe.

"Not that Klick really did much of anything anyway," Flea went on, shoving his tablet at her again. "I mean, what, *six* guys? They'd only count as regular level six warriors anyway, right? I mean, they didn't even have basic comm equipmen—"

"Here it is!" Klick cried, scrambling across the sand, clumsily dragging a stolen datapad behind her. "I helped on this mission, so I should get the experience for the Trith!"

That immediately made Flea do a double-take. "Wait, *what*? No *way*," he whined, "the Trith was all *me*!"

Rat, meanwhile, was choking out a Human who had tried to come up behind her with a garrote.

"Look!" Klick cried, offering up her own datapad as Rat had to release her hold on the last Human to duck under the swing of another big Human that still had short hair from his stint with the Congies. "I even added 'godhood' to the character traits," Klick continued. "That means I can cast spells without prepping them first, right? I mean, like I just *think* them and they happen?"

"No fair!" Flea screamed, jabbing at his own datapad. "*I'm* the god here. *She* didn't do anything. You said *I* would get godhood if I—"

Rat twisted away from her fight to blast a hole through Flea's datapad. "The world explodes. Your character dies. Make a new character." Then she pistol-whipped an Ooreiki that had gotten too close, doing unfortunately little damage to its fleshy face.

Flea, having released it to hit the ground, rather than have the plasma eat his hand, stared down at his ruined datapad in horror. He fell to its side, reaching out in misery. "No…"

Klick, predictably, started laughing. "See?!" she demanded. "That's what you get for trying to cheat!"

In between taking down a rifle-carrying Ooreiki aiming at them from a parapet and kicking a Hebbut in the tusked face, Rat shot Klick's datapad, too. "Yours too," she said.

"Bahahahahaha!" Flea cried, pointing. "You suck!"

"You are both reincarnated as goblins," Rat said, headbutting an Ooreiki, whose soft heads were delightfully easy to injure if struck in the right location, "Your highest stat can be eleven. Ever."

The Bagans' mandibles fell open and they turned to face her in shock. "You can't do that!" Klick cried.

"Can and did," Rat said. Then she turned her back on the little furglings and went back to the fight.

Much too late, she realized that Max hadn't said anything snarky in a while…

• • •

"You know, for touching me, I could excite the water molecules within your cells and cause you to explode from the inside, but I'm finding this amusing, so I haven't yet."

Flea, who was grunting as he pulled the rifle backwards up the side wall of the gladiatorial ring, panted as he said, "So where should we stash him?"

Klick, who was shoving upwards from beneath the rifle, said, "How about we drop it off a cliff?"

"What part of 'exploding from the inside' and 'total, body-wide cell-death' did you not understand?"

"No, we don't want to damage it," Flea said.

"Indeed you don't," Max replied.

"We want to make her *quest* for it," Klick agreed. "How about we take it up the cliff? Make her climb up somewhere to get it?"

"That might be amusing—until she finds a skimmer and dispenses with the furglity."

"She'll never find it," Flea agreed, heaving the rifle another few digs up the wall. "She'd have to grow *wings*."

They shoved the Rodemax the rest of the way up over the parapet, then rested on the top of the wall as the gun clattered to the catwalk on the other side.

"I also have the ability to kill everything in a varying-radius sphere, out to three marches."

"You know," Klick said, panting, "we could just leave it here. She won't find it up here."

"Yeah she will," Flea said, wincing as Rat caught sight of him and gestured to her eyes, then to Flea, then to the ground, then made a slicing motion across her neck. "We'd better get moving." As Rat broke into a run on the gladiatorial sands inside the pit, he scampered down to pick up his end of the rifle. "Okay, let's fly out of here!"

"I didn't have time to fix my wings!" Klick cried. "I was working on my character sheet!"

Underneath them, Rat was shouting and climbing the rubble into the stands.

"She's gonna get here any second!" Klick cried. "Please, Flea! *Do* something!"

And Flea, suddenly flushed with the knowledge that Klick, virgin princess of a Bagan hivelord, was counting upon him to save the day, found himself strengthened by her desperation.

"Don't worry," he said. Straightening heroically, he flipped his cloak and said, "I can carry it by myself."

"She's coming!" Klick screamed, as Rat clambered up the crumbled wall after them. "Hurry!"

"Goodbye, Klick!" Flea cried. "May our paths someday cross again!" Then, grabbing the rifle by the barrel, he started buzzing as hard as he could, lifting it slowly off the ground with all the pressure he could put behind his wingbeats.

"Goodbye, Flea!" Klick cried, as he started to lift into the air. She came to stand below him, using one hand to shield the sun from her faceted red eyes. "I will never forget your heroism!"

That made Flea even more determined, his wings pounding even harder to stay airborne.

"Flea, dammit, no!" Rat snapped, as she came stumbling up, but was moments too late.

"*You know*," Max said, as Flea strained to carry them out over the alleys beyond the gladiatorial pit, "*This is an excellent angle to discover just how big a Baga's brain really is.*"

"Flea, come back!" Rat shouted from the parapet behind him. "You can have your Trith experience! You don't have to be a goblin!"

While it was tempting, Flea, sadly, had been deceived in the past. He kept going, struggling for every dig.

"Flea, I will *end you*!" Rat screamed at him. "Bring it *back*!" A chunk of debris went sailing past Flea's right wing. "Flea!"

"It astounds me that you survived as a species," the gun chuckled.

"There were a lot of us," Flea said. Another chunk of rock went whizzing by, this time bouncing off his carapace and making him swerve.

Flea managed to make it out of range, delighting in the total-city brawl that was unfolding in the streets and alleyways beneath him.

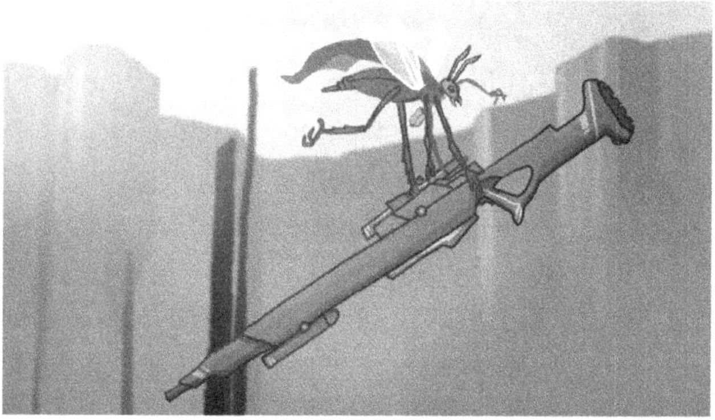

"Yes, well, as amusing as this is, this is exactly the kind of distraction that Rat's dear Sol'dan would have been looking for, and I take immense pleasure in thwarting his clumsy attempts at scheming. If you don't mind, turn me towards the Trith if you please? That is, unless you would prefer to be shocked into oblivion so that I can watch your disgusting body roast right before it explodes like an overstuffed balloon. I could do that, too."

Frowning, Flea turned towards the Trith, where a single Huouyt was crossing the sands towards the body.

"A little-known, but highly useful function of a Rodemax is a spot-vaporization, where I calculate physical coordinates on a three-dimensional basis based on your brainwaves, up to sixty rods away, and excite the molecules of the area to near-fission levels in a five-dig radius. It can only be used once every six hours, and only if my operator pushes the little black button inside the casing under the flap on the upper right of the scope. Press the button please?"

Struggling to stay airborne, Flea said, "I'm not sure Rat would—"

"You do *want to see what a spot-vaporization does, don't you?"*

Flea had to giggle inwardly. He pressed the button.

Out in the middle of the arena, the Trith's body became a circular ball of hellfire that blasted Flea backwards and flattened the arena walls in all directions, sending out a gust of dust and smoke that swallowed the other buildings in the area.

"Thank you, that will do nicely," the rifle said. *"Now stop touching me, vaghi. My operator will be looking for me."* And, at that, the rifle's matte metal form took on an electric current that locked every one of Flea's legs into total, uncontrollable spasm. He, along with the rifle, went plummeting to the ground as his wings lost what little lift they'd managed to gain, hitting the pile of rubble hard.

Flea bounced away from the rifle onto a heap of broken concrete overlooking a good portion of the town, jostled away by the fall. As he lay there, helpless, his head turned to see the pandemonium in the streets beyond, the rifle said, *"Ancestors' ghosts. It really* is *impossible to kill you miserable little vermin, isn't it?!"*

Though Flea himself couldn't move, Flea's translator worked by picking up brainwaves, so Flea said, "I wonder if Rat's okay. You exploded like half the town."

The rifle didn't seem too concerned. *"Her life-signs are stable and she is moving. I was actually hoping to kill that Huouyt, but I think it's still alive, as well."*

Flea grunted, already starting to get some feeling back in his feet. Staring at the sky as he was, however, he couldn't help but see the Congressional transport ship putting down in the spaceport outside town. "Hey, reinforcements!"

"I doubt it. Commander Halperi's probably here to instigate martial law."

Flea winced. "Rat's not on the books."

"This mission is highly classified," the gun agreed. *"I'm relatively certain Sol'dan already fled, and that Benva will end up eating a few Ooreiki before the night is over, just to keep up with blood loss. Even a furgling could see that the mission was doomed from the start."* Then there was a pause and, *"How did you kill that Trith?"*

"I spat on him," Flea said.

"Obviously," the gun snapped. *"But how did you get close enough to* do *that? Their very nature allows them to always see everyone coming."*

Down the mountain of rubble, Flea saw Klick and Rat arguing over who got to carry something dangling on a small thong…

He lunged upwards in reflex, then tumbled down the mountain of rubble as his feet refused to catch up with his brain. He landed in a dusty, dinged-up heap at Rat's feet.

Rat leveled a plasma pistol at Flea's face. "My knife and my gun. Where are they?" The way her face was utterly flat despite the fact her hair was gray and blown back with dust, her eyes the only clean parts of her face, Flea had the odd feeling she was about to pull the trigger.

"Gun," Flea said, twitching an arm to point towards the top of the pile, where the Rodemax was propped against a collapsed roof.

Rat didn't look. "And the knife?"

That was a little more difficult. "Uh," he said.

"So what's this do?" Klick demanded, nudging the Pepsi charm from where she sat on Rat's elbow. "Max said he thought it was some sort of weapon."

"It helps me with numbers," Flea said. "Press the bottom button."

"*Don't* press the button," Rat said, yanking it away before Klick could do so. "That's what the little asher wants." She jammed her plasma pistol between his eyes, squishing his head against the rubble. "I want my knife, Flea. That was a two *million* credit knife."

Uninvited, Flea's device said, "*Two million credits is approximately the price of a small resort condo on Kaleu, with around-the-clock access to a massage suite and bathing attendants for the life of the property.*"

Flea was flabbergasted, even a little horrified. "You mean I was carrying around a *condo*?"

"Yes Flea," Rat said evenly, peering down the barrel at him, "you were carrying around my condo."

"Wow, you must get paid a *lot* working for Mekkval," Flea blurted. "Like, *billions…*"

"*For once, I think your infantile grasping at anything past two digits finally hit the mark. Yes, Flea, it is probably billions.*"

"Wow," Klick said. "He's got his very own Max! I wanna try!" She skittered across Rat's arm and grabbed the necklace from her fist before Rat could fling her away. With the little blinking charm only ninths from her face, Klick said to it, "Benva says I have fifty billion in my account and I should spend more of it. What does that mean?"

"*That means you could buy a small planetoid, possibly even an uninhabitable, non-mineralized planet.*"

"I get it," Rat said, slowly lowering the gun with a look of divine comprehension. "You beat the Trith by doing something that *should* be impossible for a Baga. You were actually using *numbers*! Doing the impossible, so a Trith couldn't see it coming!"

Flea had to suppress his urge to laugh at the rudimentary lunacy of that idea and soberly said, "I *told* you guys I had a plan."

"I want it!" Klick cried, trying to scuttle away with his charm. "He knocked a *wall* over on me. I deserve it." Indeed, her normally black carapace was a dingy, dusty gray to match Rat's face and clothing.

"It's mine!" Flea shot from his prone position and tackled her, grabbing the cord with his fist.

"No, you have to roll for it!" Klick cried, kicking and punching at him. "*I* found it on the Huouyt body. *You* were incapacitated 'cause you were thieving from somebody else again. *I* get to keep it. *Raaaaaaaaat* doesn't he have to *rooooooolllll* for it?!"

"Your squeaky protestations are music to my ears, champion of pussies!" Flea cried, tugging it away from her head before she could put it around her neck. Holding her face at a distance with a foot, he slipped the charm back around his own shoulders triumphantly. A moment later, the line around his neck went taut as Rat grabbed the necklace and hauled upwards, leaving him dangling from her fist, choking.

"Well, this is convenient," Rat said, bringing him close to her face as he grabbed at the wire around his neck and struggled. "I'm not going to ask again, Flea. Where's my knife?"

Flea, because he was feeling the tendons of his head straining to disconnect from his body, desperately twisted his klett up to aim at her face.

Rat put the barrel of her gun to the bottom of his ass, never even flinching. Behind them, coming from the airport, Congressional megaphones were ordering all inhabitants out into the streets where they could be sorted and tagged as rebels—with the offer of free enlistment in the Ground Force for anyone wanting to avoid the mines—but Rat didn't look, just waited.

"Uh," Flea said, deciding to come clean, "I don't really have your—"

A moment later, a *second* Congressional ship, this one much sleeker, made of glossy black nannites instead of solid metal, settled down on the landing pad beside the first one, though it was immediately enveloped in smoke from the burning recruitment center.

Rat slowly lowered both Flea and the gun, staring at the ship. "That's a *Regency courier*." She said it with the same foreboding of someone watching a pissed-off Dhasha.

Then again, that was probably exactly what it contained.

Even Klick looked worried. Climbing onto Rat's shoulder to get a better view, she said, "We never told Mekkval we were gonna be on this op." She watched the ship's airlock open with trepidation. "What if Keval went behind his back?"

"Keval wouldn't go behind his back," Rat said, with the complete confidence of the totally naïve.

Flea used the distraction to wiggle free and climb onto Rat's other shoulder. With mutual foreboding, they watched the gangplank extend...

"*Joe*?!" Flea cried, stunned, as the Human Prime stepped down off the ship, closely followed by Jer'ait Ze'laa, in his full Peacemaker regalia, flanked by millions of what Flea recognized to be the Peacemaker's best men. All of them were armed with enough weaponry to take down a city

That made Flea frown. "Jer'ait would have had to get special permission from a Representative to use—" His carapace suddenly crawled. "Rat, is Benva around here somewhere?"

Rat was obviously thinking the same thing. "Oh burning ash—" She started running up the hill to grab her Rodemax, but not before the echoing *shee-whomph* of a Jreet battlecry tore through the streets, startling the small army of Congressional troops gathered near the crumbled gladiatorial arena.

It was answered from up near the burning recruitment center.

"Benva, *no*!" Rat snapped into her comm, snagging her rifle.

A third *shee-whomph* followed the second, and a cluster of Ooreiki in Congie black went flying as something huge and invisible barreled through them, towards the spaceport.

"*Benva*!" Rat screamed, at a run.

But the Peacemakers were hastily backing up in all directions as something huge and invisible shoved them aside to get closer to the town.

Flea and Klick, who had abandoned their mount for the relative stability of the mountain of rubble, watched with the curiosity and awe of two onlookers unable to tear their eyes from a freighter that was in the process of slowly pancaking itself into an asteroid. They climbed to the highest peak, to get a better look.

"Well," Klick said, as the two Jreet finally clashed amidst the recruitment center, shoving good portions of the burning building off the precipice and crushing parts of the tunnel-shaped barracks huts in their thrashings, "that's not good." Soldiers and Peacemakers alike were staying well out of the way, and now that the battle had started, Rat had ducked into an empty alleyway to avoid being seen.

"Yeah," Flea said, "Looks like they're gonna be at that awhile."

Klick gave him a sideways look. "You know what this means."

Flea returned her sideways look. "This is a ruvmestin planet."

Klick nodded. "Marshi owns the planet."

"And Marshi is busy with the Congies…" Flea continued.

"Which means!" Klick cried, raising up a hand, "Somewhere on this planet…"

"Is a dragon's hoarde!" Flea cried.

"We have to hurry!" Klick cried, rushing off the pile of debris with a speed that made pebbles scatter. "Before the invading army finds it!"

"I'll carry you!" Flea cried, buzzing up and grabbing her. "We have no time!" He took to the air, racing for the Ueshi's mansion. Congies were standing guard outside with laser weaponry, but he and Klick were able to enter through an upstairs window. They found the vault in a predictable place—not the downstairs study that the Congies were ransacking, but in an upstairs, 'unused' bedroom closet, hidden behind a mirror. Flea and Klick levered it aside in glee, only to be stymied by the huge number pad on the front interface.

"*The code is 8-21-94-17-3-20,*" Flea's device said, startling them. "*Or, to simplify things, 8, 2, 1, 9, 4, 1, 7, 3, 2, 0.*"

As Flea felt his eyes glaze over at the barrage of numbers and Klick gave him a similarly blank stare, the device continued, "*Let's start at the beginning. Remember how many legs, arms, and heads you would have if you suddenly sprouted a head out of your ass…?*"

• • •

The moment he heard the Jreet sound off a war cry from the middle of town, Joe knew he was burned. He didn't even bother trying to tell Daviin—who had spent the entire flight here complaining about how he was getting fat, and how the Regency was making him weak by preventing him from fighting, how not a single Jreet would challenge him because he was currently about as close to an honored legend as a Jreet could get—not to attack the other, unexpected Jreet in the city below. The moment that Daviin had heard its war-cry, which Joe recognized as coming from something *huge*, Joe had just gotten out of the Representative's way, because he knew Daviin would simply bowl him over if he didn't.

In retrospect, it was probably a wise move, considering the very first thing the two warring Jreet did was destroy every ship on the spacepad, then roll off the cliff in their contortions.

"I think technically I am supposed to make sure Daviin wins that match," Jer'ait said, as he and Joe leaned over the edge of the cliff to watch the two enormous, serpentine Jreet fight—one crimson and one gray, "but my excuse is that I couldn't possibly reach him in time."

Joe had already said burn it and was looking at their destination, which was more or less lying in ruin. "So what do you think happened here?" Joe asked, already feeling a headache building. He'd been minding his own business in a bar when he'd gotten a panicked call from Jer'ait saying Flea had been kidnapped, then over a rotation in transit listening to Daviin bitch while prepping to take down an entire assassin's ring purportedly run by a rogue Trith, only to arrive to...*this*. "The Trith saw us coming?" he asked. "Burned its town to hide evidence?"

"Perhaps," Jer'ait said. "But it could have something to do with Flea's arrival."

Joe knew better than anyone what kind of chaos the little Bagan asher could wreak, if he put his twisted little mind to it. Generally, though, one Baga wasn't enough to wreak havoc on a town. It usually took at least two...

"As far as I can tell," Jer'ait went on, "Flea was only here two days ahead of us. The Ooreiki spacers my men interrogated said they'd dropped him off for a reward, which suggests to me he wasn't in danger of being summarily killed." His blue-white, mirror-like eye showed indifference, but his violet one was filled with confusion. He gestured to the contingent of Congies, who were staying in the town, looking paranoid. "It's also clear that, whatever we traveled all the way here to prevent has already happened."

"I think I need a drink," Joe said, shoving Jane back into her holster.

"I'm going to go speak to the Congies, see if I can locate our missing Bagan friend," Jer'ait said. The Huouyt cocked his head. "You could come with me, instead."

Joe snorted. "You're the *Peacemaster*. Not sure what I've got to trump that." Besides, he'd heard there were Humans living on this planet, which had been more exciting than anything else, and his head was *pounding* at the thought of a good whiskey.

Jer'ait looked him over. "You should at least put on some Congie black if you're going to go carousing. This *is* a prison planet."

"I've got Jane," Joe said, patting his illicit weapon. "Anyone wants to mess with me, they'll have to go through her."

Jer'ait did not seem convinced. Joe didn't know what insulted him more; that Jer'ait was trying to manipulate him into skipping his drink—like *one drink* was going to hurt him—or that he didn't think he could handle himself in a town filled with Congies and criminals. "I'll see you in a few hours," Joe said. "Just come get me when you figure out what happened to the little leafling."

He recognized pity in the Peacemaster's violet eye before Jer'ait inclined his head. "As you wish." Immediately, Jer'ait gestured at his army of Peacemakers. "Scour the town!" he snapped. "Anyone not carrying an active Congie's chip goes into immediate lockdown!"

The two squads in Peacemaker gray spread out, making the Congies in the town back up nervously. It was easy to understand. Aside from two shuttle-length Jreet unexpectedly appearing in their midst, Jer'ait and Joe were surrounded by enough heavily-armed Peacemakers to take down Mekkval himself.

Which inevitably made Joe wonder—why *had* there been another Jreet prince in town?

As Jer'ait and his men moved forward into the town, Joe glanced over the edge to watch the two Jreet twisting in each others' coils below, their war-cries bouncing off the canyon walls as they tried to kill each other.

Fortunately, it was difficult for an ancient Jreet to kill another ancient Jreet. Over a lifetime of dueling, they developed a resistance to rravut, so unless one of them got an advantage and decided to break protocol and strangle the other, Joe could safely come back a few hours from now and they would still be at it.

Or Jer'ait could do it. After all, that *was* his job. Joe, who had no job because the Ground Force no longer officially acknowledged his existence, could do whatever the hell he pleased.

And right now, it pleased him to get a drink.

He was halfway to the town, headed toward what looked like a likely spot for a mess hall, when Jane said from his hip, "*Joe, you have a Rodemax aimed at your forehead. Initiating evasion and anti-personnel protocols now.*"

"Don't bother," Joe said, continuing to walk.

Jane hesitated. "Commander?"

"I'm not going to die," Joe said. "I've got a *destiny* to fulfill." He made a disgusted wave of his hand. Bitterly, he said, "Even if they shoot, they'll miss."

"Rodemaxes don't miss, Commander. We really should attack before—"

"Ignore it," Joe said. Like all of her kind, the Ueshi-made Nocurna had a grudge against the Huouyt and the Rodemax technology that they had stolen from the Ueshi, thousands of turns ago. To counter it, the Ueshi scientists who had survived the Huouyt massacre and theft of the Rodemax technology had made Nocurnas, instead. Jane was therefore smaller, more compact, and packing greater firepower—better in every way except raw AI processing power—and completely inoperable to a Huouyt.

They were also totally unable to concentrate when there was a Rodemax nearby. "*Commander, I really think—*"

Joe reached down and hit her *mute* button. If he was going to die, he was going to die. Much like the ancient Vikings, he'd learned there wasn't much point in fighting Fate, and the best way to face one's fears was with a good, stiff drink. Thus, when he found the town's source of liquid nourishment, he stepped inside and, finding no bartender available and the place deserted, stepped behind the counter and helped himself to the last dregs of the last bottle of Jim Beam. He had just poured the meager contents into a glass and was lifting it to his face when an Ooreiki in Congie black slapped it out of his hand, sending glass and whisky spraying across the counter in a wet tinkle.

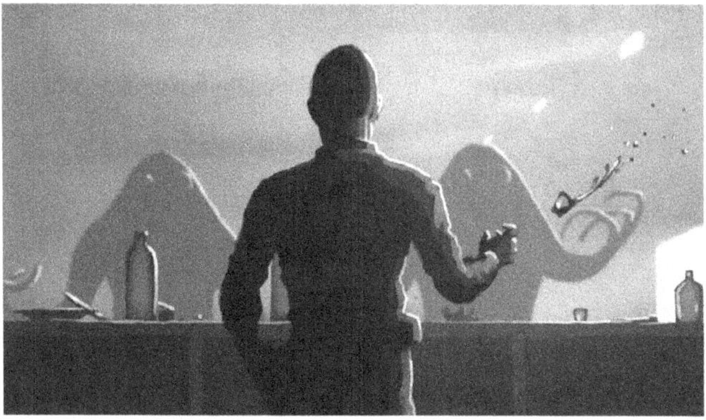

"You're on the job, asher," the Ooreiki grunted, sitting down at the bar with three of his buddies. "I'd like a Neoshin Sooter, and they've got their own orders. Make it good and we'll let you stay and bartend while we're working out this ashpile." To a fourth buddy entering with a stack of holoposters, he gestured behind the bar. "Put it over there, behind the counter, so those furglings have to look at his ugly face. Humans lose their little minds for that guy."

Joe couldn't stop staring at the amber fluid that was now leaking across the bar and dripping to the floor. He had this insane urge to go after it, to collect what he could with his *mouth* if he had to, but rage was beginning to make him see nothing but red. He looked up, slowly, and the Ooreiki posting the recruitment poster paused, glancing at Joe, then hesitantly down at the poster in his hand. "Uh," he said nervously, pointing to the image of Joe standing with his foot on the Dhasha's snout, a plasma rifle proudly held over one shoulder, "guys—"

Joe hurtled the table, going for the first one's throat.

• • •

"I'm pretty sure he's carrying a Nocurna disguised as a regular plasma pistol," Max said. *"If that's true, then she already told him we are watching him, and it's probably in our best interest to change locations immediately."*

But Rat was frowning at Joe. "He turned her off."

"It's obviously a ruse," Max said. *"He's waiting for you to let your guard down and will be circling around our flank, coming at us when we least expect it."*

Rat wasn't listening. She hadn't seen Joe on anything except the newsreels for almost twenty turns, and the change wasn't pretty. While she had seen some eye-opening things on camera—like Joe lashing out at a guy who got too close with a recorder—she'd had no idea the *depths* of the downward spiral he'd been on. He looked like the dead walking. His skin seemed pale, almost gray, and he must have stopped taking Congie *nuajan* nutrients regularly, because she could see a five-o-clock shadow on both his chin and his scalp.

He looked bad enough that Rat almost stowed Max away and went down to talk to him. *Almost.* Because, dammit, she was supposed to be *dead*, and he couldn't walk ten digs without running into a camera.

So it was with great sorrow that she watched her old friend walk aimlessly through the town, then duck into what could only be a makeshift prison bar.

"He's going to drop her decoy signal and be climbing out the back of the building, out of sight," Max insisted. *"We* need *to find a better positio—"*

Rat powered Max down. Then, watching the entrance to the ramshackle building for another minute, aching to go say something to him, she went to collect her team instead.

• • •

PART 5

THE FINAL CHOICE

(Or, if you're just trying to navigate this cluster and you got lost, RETURN TO PART 1: page 1, RETURN TO PART 2: page 41 or RETURN TO PART 3: page 205 or RETURN TO PART 4: page 243.)

"F*ive hundred and thirty-two,*" the device dutifully told him, as he stashed his final ingot up in an inaccessible crack in the cliff and launched back towards the town. "*Which is approximately enough ruvmestin to pay off all your debts, give or take nine credits.*"

Flea frowned. "*Nine*?" He had no idea how much he owed in total, but he was pretty sure it was several Kaleuian condos's-worth…which nine credits was *not*. Flea frowned and held the charm out where he could see it. "You planned this, didn't you?"

"*What gave it away?*"

Flea, who didn't mind being used as long as it was in good fun, shrugged. "Klick showing up."

"*Then let's dispense with the façade. You have one final choice to make, one that will determine whether you will become my agent or go back to being Flea without any knowledge of what transpired here.*"

"Hey, that's not fair!" Flea cried, indignant. "I already figured it out once after you gave me a brain wipe. I *deserve* to remember this."

"*Your choices are these,*" Forgotten said. "*If you continue to carry my talisman, I will immediately send you to help stop Joe from losing Prime Sentinel Raavor ga Aez's ceremonial ovi in a bar fight, then I will send you more missions as they come available. But, in working with me, you set yourself on a path that cannot be reversed. Three turns from now, on Earth, you will be given a choice with only two options. If you choose to live, you will regret it to the end of your days. If you choose to die, you will regret it even more.*"

Flea felt his carapace crawl. Three *turns*? To *live*?

Yet, if you drop my talisman right here, right now, you will immediately be safely whisked from Glaxxion and you will be able to return to life as it was before. You will die old and fat and happy in a hive of your own creation, and the outcome of that choice will mean nothing to you, but the fate of Congress will wither into a bitter, shriveled thing, filled with hatred and violence, until you hear of nothing but war on the waves, and most of the inhabitants of this dimension are afraid to sleep at night. But you *will be able to sleep, because the Baga will be relatively unaffected by this universal war, and in the end, your species will be one of the only ones to survive, since most other species can't survive an* ekhta." Forgotten allowed that to sink in for a moment, then said,

"Either way, you will not be able to tell Joe, Jer'ait, or Daviin what happened here today."

Flea grimaced at those options. "What's the third one?"

"The third one is that Klick followed you to your stash and is even now relieving you of your hoard."

Flea froze and looked over his shoulder.

"So," Forgotten said, "decide."

And, in a blinding flash, three choices flared into existence in the previous darkness of his mind…

END

ABOUT THE AUTHOR

Sara King usually sleeps more than this.
Because she's exhausted as hell, just do her a favor and sign up for her mailing list…

http://visitor.r20.constantcontact.com/d.jsp?llr=vwyl96lab&p=oi&m=1112323515093&sit=5y9cbnshb&f=ea280989-c632-448d-8419-12178cec9609

ABOUT THE ARTIST

Lance MacCarty is a freelance digital painter focusing on science fiction and fantasy art for publication and game development. He prefers to paint the fantastical, dark and light, ethereal and otherworldly. From covers to book art and concept design he has worked directly with authors and game designers to help see their creations realized. Lance resides in Oregon with his family where he enjoys the outdoors, painting, gaming, and geekery of all sorts. Visit www.lancemaccarty.com to find out more. (Oh, and if you're looking for that super-secret website link, it's http://lancemaccarty.com/agentofchaos)

www.ingramcontent.com/pod-product-compliance
Lightning Source LLC
Chambersburg PA
CBHW061538170626
46811CB00001B/19
* 9 7 8 1 9 4 2 9 2 9 1 0 9 *